Queen

DISCARD

of the

Assassins

AN ACADEMY OF ASSASSINS NOVEL

STACEY BRUTGER

Copyright © 2019 Stacey Brutger

Cover artist: Amanda Kelsey of Razzle Dazzle Design (www.razzdazzdesign.com)

Editor: Faith Freewoman (www.demonfordetails.com)
Proofreader: Missy Stewart of Ms. Correct All's Editing and Proofreading Services

ISBN-13: 978-1698275161

Other books by this author:

A Druid Quest Novel
Druid Surrender (Book 1)
Druid Temptation (Book 2)

An Academy of Assassins Novel
Academy of Assassins (Book 1)
Heart of the Assassins (Book 2)
Claimed by the Assassins (Book 3)
Queen of the Assassins (Book 4)

A Phantom Touched Novel
Tethered to the World (Book 1)

A Raven Investigations Novel
Electric Storm (Book 1)
Electric Moon (Book 2)
Electric Heat (Book 3)
Electric Legend (Book 4)
Electric Night (Book 5)
Electric Curse (Book 6)

A PeaceKeeper Novel
The Demon Within (Book 1)

Paranormal Romance:
BloodSworn
Coveted

Coming Soon:
Hunting Red
Exorcist
Forsaken
Shackled to the World (Book2)

Visit Stacey online to find out more at **www.StaceyBrutger.com**
And www.facebook.com/StaceyBrutgerAuthor/

I hope you love reading about the Assassins as much as I had writing about them. ♥ I hate saying good-bye to Morgan and the guys, but I'm thrilled they finally get their happy-ever-after.

A special thanks to
Faith, Missy and Lucy for helping me make this book shine.

And to my husband...thank you for believing in me!
And for listening to my harebrained plot ideas without telling me I'm crazy. lol

Chapter
One

Something's wrong.

Morgan sat frozen behind her desk as the link between her and the guys vanished.

Panic threatened to claw its way up her throat, but she forced it back for one simple reason—if something was truly wrong, it wouldn't affect them all at once.

No, they had gone off to plot against her.

Again.

They'd been doing it more and more often in the past week.

Morgan shoved away from the desk. Ignoring the rest of the people in the room, she calmly walked to the fireplace, pulled down the two short swords hanging there, and walked out of the room.

Better safe than sorry.

When no one in the office even bothered to question her, she knew her suspicions were correct.

The guys were up to something.

She wasn't sure if she was disappointed or excited about the upcoming confrontation.

It's been too long since she was alone with the guys, and her bones actually ached to be near them again. She didn't know if it was just normal yearning or the link binding them together urging her to complete the mating. It was like a constant itch under her skin, and the longer she went without touching them, the more it hurt.

It wasn't a case of blue balls—could women even get blue balls?

No, it was more like a piece of herself was missing without them, and the emptiness just kept expanding into a soul-sucking black hole when they weren't near. The only thing that relieved the aching emptiness was to have them close.

But even that wasn't enough anymore.

She needed their touch to keep her sane.

Two months had passed since the attack on the school, and though she'd gotten better at giving the guys their space, she still compulsively checked on them a couple of times a day, either in person or by touching the mating marks that adorned her body.

Instead of annoyance, the guys had seemed to enjoy the attention...until today.

She hated that they shut it down without a word of explanation, hated more that it left her anxious, which annoyed her even more. As a group, they had promised to keep the connection muted just enough to sense each other, but not enough to allow emotions to leak through and invade each other's privacy.

And it had been working...until today.

As she stalked through the building, the students pressed themselves against the walls to give her room, but none of them cowered in fear...it was pure awe. Though they saw her frequently, their reaction was always the same. She'd gone from an outcast to a leader, and the drastic change in the way they treated her still left her reeling.

To her surprise, the school was flooded with applications over the past month, hundreds of shifters and magic users wanting to train. Now that the school was no longer exclusive, a few students had left, which was fine—she much preferred loyalty over the old elitist snobbery.

Instead of going by the old rules, she created a council to review the applicants, a mix of assassins, witches, and a single wolf—people she trusted to have the school's best interests at heart. Applicants needed a majority vote of the council to be accepted into the Academy.

MacGregor and Mistress McKay accepted their invitations right away, and it tickled her to throw them together at every opportunity. She asked Ryder to pick a wolf he trusted. To her surprise, he didn't pick an alpha or anyone at the school, but an old, lone wolf who was more curmudgeonly and snarly than even MacGregor, and she smiled at the thought of them butting heads and swapping war stories.

Not wanting the responsibility of siting on the council herself, Morgan asked the Headmistress to choose a representative she trusted. And couldn't have been more stunned when she selected a faerie from Mount Olympus. Though having a faerie on the council left Morgan a bit uneasy, she was dumbfounded to find they'd received more than a few applications from the other realms for the new school year.

She opened the last spot up for elections, never expecting hundreds of different species to nominate their own candidates.

While the school continued to grow, she'd been training with Shade and Ward, learning to control her newly awakened powers, while Breanna was teaching her how to work with their new ghostly neighbors.

As Morgan worked her way farther into the bowels of the school, focused on the last place she sensed the guys, the walls became rough, the stone floors sloped, the lights only an afterthought. She began to recognize her surroundings…the parking garage.

Anger flared in her gut, the mild excitement of hunting them turning to disappointment.

They're leaving on another hunt without her.

While they didn't leave her often, her spirits plummeted at the idea of being left behind again.

Of being alone.

She rubbed her hands along her arms, but it did little to ease the ache. The only thing that helped was being near the guys. She treasured even their smallest touch, which had become all too infrequent recently, and her annoyance with their restraint was turning her into a raving bitch.

Male voices rumbled in the distance, and she slowed her pace, eager to learn their plan. She tried to focus her senses as she crept up on them, but even with her enhanced abilities she couldn't make out what they were saying. As she approached the last turn in the tunnel, a soft scuffle sounded from behind her and she whirled.

Only to be hit by what felt like a freight train.

She went flying backwards, landing with a hardy thump, the blades in her hands clattering to the ground and spinning off into the distance. Before she could crawl after them, a heavy weight slammed on top of her, knocking what little wind she had left out of her lungs.

A familiar, suffocating weight.

Loki gazed down at her, his bright red eyes brimming with triumph.

She fended off his questing tongue. Instead of rock, her fingertips met a soft, grey leathery skin. His wings were spread wide, the tips dusted a pale gold, the color similar to the tiny image of a burning phoenix blazed into his chest. When he was excited, the image darkened to a deep red and shimmered like flames.

The once small palm-sized gargoyle dog was nearly as big as a small car now. He reminded her of a baby dragon, except his jaw was squarer and he had a hide instead of scales and horns.

As he continued to look down at her, mischief sparked in his eyes. He seemed to grin, his tongue lolling out, clearly proud that he managed to take her by surprise and tackle her, and she grimaced as a string of drool slowly inched ever closer to her face. "Don't you dare!" But it was already too late.

Despite lifting her arms to protect herself, Morgan couldn't escape as the lumbering beast leaned forward and proceeded to wash every inch of her face and neck. A sharp whistle interrupted her bath, and Loki jerked his head up, instantly alert.

Morgan tipped her head back to see the guys all staring down at her in various shades of amusement.

"That was completely uncalled for." She glared at them, knowing they'd set her up. Instead of coming to her rescue, they crossed their arms, gave her a smile or rolled their eyes.

"You're the one who trained him to hunt us." Draven leaned against the wall with a smirk playing on his lips. "It's not our fault he considers you fair game."

Morgan grunted rather than admit Draven was right.

In the past two months, Loki had grown into a massive beast—nearly two hundred pounds of love. She'd been training him to fight, taking him to watch Ryder teach the shifters, and then she and the gargoyle Mal would take turns in mock battle with him. Mal would attack Loki from the sky, while she fought him from the ground. Loki's wings were strong enough now that he could glide through the air like a bird, and Morgan knew it was only a matter of time before he actually took flight.

Loki was smart.

And lethal.

And she couldn't resist teaching him to stalk the guys like prey, her own demented way to keep an eye on them.

While it was funny as hell to see them taken down by the beast when they least expected it—being on the receiving end wasn't nearly as much fun. She shoved at Loki, but the beast only settled more firmly onto her torso and legs. "Up."

But instead of obeying, Loki laid his massive head on her chest and looked up at her adoringly. Her heart melted, and she scratched him behind the ears before glancing at the guys. "A little help would be appreciated."

The guys came closer but made no move to obey, and she narrowed her eyes in warning. "I already know you're leaving. I give you my word I won't follow."

She pouted, aching to have them all to herself for just a few more minutes.

She missed hunting with them.

Fuck, she just flat-out missed them, period.

Stupid adulting.

Organizing the school took all their attention. When they had a few minutes to spare, most of the time the guys fell directly into the bed, completely exhausted, only seeing her in passing.

It wasn't enough.

Her heart ached at the sight of them—watching them go was going to hurt.

Kincade crouched next to her with a small smile, then reached into his back pocket and removed an envelope.

She recognized it immediately…it was how MacGregor assigned his hunts.

And her name was on the front.

A smile of pure delight broke over her face, and she lunged for it…only to be stopped dead by Loki. That didn't mean she didn't try to squirm out from under his bulk and dive for it again. "Give it to me."

Kincade slowly shook his head and rose, backing up to stand next to the others. "We have our orders."

That's when she noticed the van was packed and ready to go.

She peered up at Kincade, the hope welling in her chest almost painful. "A hunt?"

He only shrugged and wiggled the envelope. "We don't know. We were ordered to report here and wait for you."

Before she could grab for the envelope again, he shoved it in his back pocket, then headed toward the van and climbed inside.

Bastard!

Even though she didn't say it out loud, she knew she must have broadcasted her emotions through the connection when they chuckled.

"Wait! Where are you going?" She tried to shove Loki off her again, but he only sighed and nestled down more firmly on top of her.

Atlas strode near her head, then bent to look down at her. "We were each given an assignment. Kincade got an envelope and a map. Ascher was ordered to ready the van. Ryder's assignment was to gather supplies, while Draven was to get the beast to distract you."

She smiled up at his serious expression, unable to stop herself from stroking the strands of hair that dangled down to brush against her face. "And what was your job?"

"My job is to kidnap you." His sexy smile was enough to rob her of breath.

Chapter Two

"**Y**ou're brooding." Ryder leaned into her personal space, his body all loose-limbed and lethal. They were in the back seat of the van, which gave them a small bit of privacy. Even though he hadn't touched her, she felt surrounded by him. The palm of her hand where she bore his mark tingled with the temptation to reach over and run her palms up along his thigh—anything to relieve the ache building at his nearness.

She turned away from studying his reflection in the window and gave him a small smile. "Maybe a little."

His heat warmed her, but a small thread of uncertainty lingered underneath her happiness.

In the two months since the attack, not once had any of the guys taken her up on her offer to bring their relationship to the next level. She spent time with each of them, together and separately. While affectionate, they kept things respectful.

Fuckers.

Could a girl die of sexual frustration?

She slept in their rooms every night, rotating among them, adoring the way they held her close. Often, when she was with Ryder, Draven would sneak into the room, the big wolf not seeming to mind the intrusion. It was the only thing that relieved the way her skin felt too tight, the slight fever that seemed to rage under her skin and build higher every hour without them.

When she was alone with one of them, she would go as far as to touch them, but when things became more intimate than a kiss, they would wrap her in their arms and go to sleep.

She was going fucking insane being handled with kid gloves.

"The school—"

"Is in good hands." Ryder bent, affectionately rubbing his cheek against the top of her head. While he might like her scent, he enjoyed putting his own on her a lot more…his stamp of ownership. When she leaned into him, he blew out a heavy breath, then pulled her close until she melted against him, and she couldn't stop her hum of contentment. His voice vibrated in his chest when he spoke, "MacGregor, Mistress McKay, and the Headmistress have taken over the running of the school. Harper will look after your duties. Mal, Aila, Loki, Breanna and the guys are going to watch over your young charge. Darinius will be safe."

Since the return of Alia, his long-lost love, Mal spent most of his daylight hours awake, and more human than she'd ever seen him. He actually smiled and laughed…usually only when Aila or Loki were near, but it was a start. Morgan suspected she amused him more than anything, but she shrugged it off since a lot of people seemed to have the same reaction around her.

"But—"

"The new building you had constructed for the shifters is fully functional. The new students are mostly getting along. Even the Primordial Realm is quiet while everyone's busy putting their lives back together." Ryder rested his chin on her shoulder, rubbing his face alongside hers to whisper in her ear, "What's really bothering you?"

How could she tell him that, despite being surrounded by people all the time, she was lonely? While she missed the hunting, what she actually missed was feeling like part of the team.

Missed being alone with the guys.

Each of them was so busy, they didn't even have time to catch their breath most days…so why did it feel like they were missing out on their life together?

"It's not important." She cuddled against Ryder, allowing her melancholy to slip away. She refused to allow her mood to ruin their precious time together. She tipped her head back and smiled up at him, batting her lashes. "So when do I get my assignment?"

Kincade's eyes crinkled in the rearview mirror when he smiled. While the other guys gave them privacy, falling asleep within ten minutes after they left, Kincade had tipped the mirror down so he could keep an eye on her. He raised a brow at her question, as if assessing her, then reached down and pulled out her envelope.

Even with his eyes closed, Ascher took the envelope and passed it back to her without a word.

She turned the envelope over in her hand, the paper still warm from Kincade.

Now the assignment was in front of her, she was nervous.

Shaking her head at her fanciful thoughts, she straightened, then ripped it open to see MacGregor's scrawled handwriting. Nostalgia hit hard, and she couldn't believe how much had changed in the past six months.

"What does it say?" Draven asked.

When she glanced up, it was to find everyone watching her. "We've received a request to investigate an abandoned coven. A year ago, the residents simply disappeared, so the Academy shut it down to investigate later. With the recent influx of paranormals, the witches have decided to reopen it."

Ascher watched her through narrowed eyes. "What's the assignment?"

Morgan hesitated a moment, then decided to go with the truth. "Actually, I think MacGregor is matchmaking." She folded the letter, completely amused by the old coot's antics. "He knows I've missed being alone with you guys. The assignment is to check out the property of the defunct coven and verify if the place can be

QUEEN OF THE ASSASSINS

salvaged or if it needs to be torn down. Six weeks ago a team of hunters were sent to check it out...and never returned."

Ryder squeezed her arm, and she tipped her head back to peer up at him. A small smile curved his lips and lit his eyes, and her breath caught at the sheer masculine beauty of him. Because his wolf was content, Ryder was more confident in his role as leader of the wolves and a member of her personal guard.

His hair was tied back, the brownish-blond strands subdued...the way he usually wore it when he came off his shift. Her stomach tripped when she realized he was in such a rush he hadn't paused to change or eat on his way to visit her. He must have been missing her as much as she missed him.

As if noticing the direction of her thoughts, he tightened his lips to smother his smile and untied the string holding back his hair. "Better?"

She cocked her head, then turned in his arms and thrust her fingers into his hair. "Much."

But, as usual, he gently tucked her against him instead of kissing her, and she huffed in frustration. His erection strained the front of his pants, so it wasn't like he found her unattractive. She discreetly sniffed herself but detected no odor.

She just didn't get it.

If anyone would tell her the truth, it would be him. She edged closer and blinked up at him, trying to look innocent. "Ryder—"

"Switch!" Instead of waiting for a response, Draven climbed over the back of his seat, squeezing himself in between them.

And damn if that rat bastard Ryder didn't look relieved to escape her clutches.

She narrowed her eyes at the guys, suddenly wondering how often they passed her off to avoid getting too intimate. Instead of waiting for the vehicle to pull over, the wolf crawled over the back seat, and she barely resisted the urge to smack his ass.

Morgan stifled the urge to growl when he took his seat and refused to face her again. She was reaching forward to stick her hands in his hair when Draven caught her wrist and wove their fingers together.

The guys were up to something, and she was determined to worm it out of them, one way or another.

And she had the perfect idea to shatter their control.

After a week alone with her in the middle of nowhere, they'd be begging for her affections, and she smiled in wicked anticipation.

Ryder was breathing heavily when he crawled into the front seat, his chest aching from maintaining the distance between him and Morgan that the guys insisted on keeping. He stared down at his hands blindly, then slowly uncurled his fingers. His claws had gouged into his palms, the wounds weeping blood. He kept his eyes lowered so the guys wouldn't see how close he was to losing control over his wolf.

It wanted out, demanding they claim their mate. It was all he could do to curb the impulse, but the longer he went without marking her, the harder it was to pretend he was unaffected. He was an alpha, and his wolf recognized her as his mate even though she wasn't a shifter. He wouldn't be satisfied until she bore their mark.

He tried keeping his distance, but that only drove his wolf crazy, the beast clawing up Ryder's insides to get near her. Holding her in his arms was both heaven and hell, and he already missed having her weight pressed against him where she belonged.

But when Morgan tried to work her wiles on him, his wolf snarled and demanded to be set free.

Mine!

Draven saw his panic and took action, but it was only delaying the inevitable.

All the guys were at the end of their rope. The longer they kept their distance, the more their control frayed and tempers shortened. When she wasn't near one of them, every one of them was ready to rip out the throat of anyone who got too close. They had to do something before they accidently killed someone.

MacGregor was the one who suggested a hunt.

Time alone with the woman they loved more than life.

The guys immediately agreed—anything to have her all to themselves.

He knew they each had plans to seduce her. His wolf practically begged for a chance to be alone with her…and that's what terrified him.

He would never forgive himself if he couldn't control his beast and frightened her, or worse…accidently harmed her in his haste to claim her. She smelled of pack. She was the only home he had ever known. Without her, nothing else mattered.

When he risked looking back at Morgan, the anxiety in him calmed, his beast snarling at the very idea that he would dare harm her. Draven sent him all the reassurance he could, a silent promise that they'd find a way to keep her safe. If Ryder thought she'd let him get away with keeping his distance, he would've tried it even if it drove him insane, but Morgan was too stubborn.

She would never let him go, and he was infinitely grateful when she strode into his life and turned his whole existence on end.

Heat burned his cheeks when he realized he'd have to explain the mating habits of wolves to her. But between him and Draven, they'd find a way to make it work.

Chapter
Three

$\mathcal{T}$he rest of the ride passed swiftly, the steady hum of the engine lulling Morgan to sleep. She woke when the van thumped and groaned along a path so rutted it was more of a trail than an actual road. Draven slowly loosened his hold so she could sit up from where she'd been sprawled across his chest. A quick glance showed the rest of the guys were already awake, staring out the window.

All she saw were trees.

They crowded the road like monsters, their branches clawing at the sides of the van, almost like they were trying to warn them against going farther. Sunlight dappled through the trees, giving everything a golden, otherworldly glow.

It made her skin crawl.

She had enough visiting of other worlds.

Enough of nearly dying.

She shook off her thoughts, cataloging what she could see.

The angle of the sun indicated they'd been on the road most of the day. Even with the windows closed, she could smell the sea air, reminding her of the coven where MacGregor raised her, and she was surprised to feel nostalgic about the place she'd always believed she hated.

When Kincade drove around the last bend in the road, they

were greeted by a large, three-story mansion. The trees were overgrown, the garden invaded by weeds. Ivy had crawled up the sides of the house, either wanting to tear the mansion down or trying to take it over. In less than a year of neglect the aggressive vegetation made the land look like it had gone wild for decades.

To her surprise, the actual house itself appeared to be in good repair, just rundown.

"Magic," Kincade muttered as he parked the car, and she realized she'd spoken her thoughts out loud.

The guys surveyed the property for anything that might pose a threat. Only when it looked clear did they open the doors and allow her to exit the vehicle. As they gathered in front of the house, Morgan tipped back her head to study the dingy gray exterior.

Though worn down, the coven was a majestic building that could've been pulled out of antebellum time. Large columns held up the second-floor porch, and the roof was pitched and angled, coming to the point in the center, a small window visible under the decorative eaves.

Magic lingered within the walls, and Morgan held out her hands, feeling the wards tingle against her fingertips. The mansion wasn't sentient like the Academy, but there was a sense of urgency surrounding the building in the way it reached out to her and urged her inside the protective walls and away from danger.

Since she wasn't a coven member, she'd expected the magic to push her away, not welcome her home.

The silver necklace she wore warmed, then began to stretch and pull, the metal twisting and spinning until a skull and crossbones dangled from the chain. Liquid silver gleamed up at her, the ghoulish smile of the skull making her stomach pitch.

Morgan dropped her arms, calling up her blades as she whirled. The metal of her rings and cuffs melted, the cool liquid warming as it snaked down her hand until two black knives took shape in her palms. Whispers claimed the black blades were the only weapons that could kill any creature, and so far they were right.

The guys saw her reaction and immediately leapt into action, gathering in a protective circle around her, weapons at the ready. Ryder seemed to bulk up, a snarl curling his lips as he faced the forest, his fangs lengthening, his claws extending. Steam rose from Ascher, smoke rising from the dead leaves beneath his feet as they threatened to catch fire. Kincade planted himself firmly in front of her, his skin turning gray as his gargoyle awoke.

Ryder and Atlas crowded closer to her, their scents of warm brownies and cinnamon wrapping around her as they took up a vigilant stance to cover her back. While she was conscious of their movements, she kept her focus outward, throwing open her senses.

She wasn't sure how she'd missed the eerie silence when they exited the vehicle. Even the wind through the trees seemed hushed, carrying an ominous feeling that something was coming. It rustled through the leaves and along the overgrown weeds, sweeping toward her, like it was hunting.

It was all she could do not to let her instinctive need to fight take over.

When no danger jumped out at them, Draven broke the silence. "What do you sense?"

Ryder huffed, and she could practically feel him roll his eyes. "Don't you feel it? Listen."

It didn't take long for the others to notice it.

"No insects," Atlas murmured.

"No animals of any type," Ascher corrected.

Morgan took a step back to the house, and the guys mirrored her. "There's a wrongness in the woods." A smell she couldn't quiet grasp reached her, neither beast nor magic, but a combination of both. It had turned sour…tainted. "Something's been hunting in those woods for a while."

The guys stopped when she reached the top of the steps. Kincade turned his head to speak to her, but kept his attention trained on the woods. "It's probably what killed the hunters and possibly the original coven. Can you open the doors?"

He meant break the wards.

Get inside and away from whatever was stalking them.

She tightened her grip on the weapons for a second, still not fully confident in her ability to use her magic despite the long hours of practice. She no longer worried her magic would consume the men. They were a team, a part of her, and her magic would never allow harm to come to them. What worried her was the vast amount of power that begged to be used whenever she called upon it. If she used too much, she was likely to freakin' blow up the house instead of opening the door.

But the guys trusted her to do her job.

While she might be an elite hunter, she also occupied the witch's position on the team, which meant anything magic-related was her problem to handle. Open portals, banishing demons, and figure out how to get past something as simple as a fucking ward any first-year student should be able to handle.

"You can do this." Atlas backed closer, purposely brushing his arm against hers in a rare show of comfort.

Her skin tingled at the contact, and her anxieties eased. Since he was the only one on the team with any magical ability, albeit small, he took it upon himself to train her an hour a day, practiced using magic and weapons together in combat.

It was different from the intense training Ward and Shade offered. Ward was all about control and spells, while Shade was more instinctual, no spells, but pure brute force to guide the magic. It was exhausting, but it was working. The magic no longer threatened to consume her, no longer escaped her control to wreak havoc around her.

It waited patiently—or impatiently, most of the time—for her to call on it, a warm presence that would do anything to ensure the survival of her and the men.

"Just like we practiced," Atlas murmured.

Atlas was more subtle in his teachings, showing her how to read spells others cast, how to twist them and make them her own by making the magic bow to her needs.

Very reluctantly, she released the blades, watching them swirl back up her hands and wrists and turn back into benign jewelry. Magic crackled around her in protest, still sensing the danger. She turned toward the door, then placed her palm flat against the surface.

The painted wood was flaked, prickling against her skin. As she pushed her senses deeper, the ancient magic rooted in the building awakened and reared its massive head. The wards bowed under the influx of her power, like her magic was knocking on the door, and the wards crawled down her arms to inspect her.

Her fingernails each carried a tiny universe trapped in what looked like fingernail polish. They began to swirl as the magic snapped along her flesh. It reached past her wrists but seemed content with what it found. Not a second later, it retreated and the doors cracked open, the wood creaking from neglect.

Ryder and Atlas used her distraction to slip into the building first. She huffed in annoyance and scrambled to catch up. The interior was a large room, similar to the coven where she was raised. While comforting, there were enough differences so as not to give rise to the bad memories she'd buried years ago.

Atlas went right, Ryder went left, quickly clearing the main room, searching for any signs of threat. "Clear!"

As the rest of the guys entered, they began to spread out and take point. As soon as they all crossed the threshold, the house slammed the door behind them with a resounding bang, the locks clicking ominously. The guys halted, while Kincade remained at her side. "Anything?"

Morgan closed her eyes, allowing her senses to stretch out. The magic in the house crackled at their presence, as if waking from a long slumber. "The wards and magic are still intact. Whatever is outside hasn't breached these walls. The wards are weak, but stable for now."

He gave a sharp nod, taking charge. "We'll split up in twos and clear the house. Ryder and Draven clear the third floor. Ascher and I will take the second floor. Atlas you're with Morgan." He gave the elf a lingering look, a warning that Morgan better not come back with even a hangnail or he was going to take it out of his hide.

Instead of protesting, Atlas nodded in complete agreement.

As the guys headed for the stairs, she wanted to snort at their overprotectiveness. Though her skills as a hunter rivaled or even exceeded theirs, she kept her lips firmly sealed. She wasn't going to question how they did things, not when they were finally including her.

She trailed after Atlas, double-checking while he systematically opened doors, thoroughly sweeping the rooms for any type of threats, magical or otherwise.

As they moved through the house, she noticed even the layout was similar to the coven where she grew up. The furniture was different, the setup slightly altered, but she found comfort in the familiarity. While the magic kept the house protected, dust had begun to collect everywhere. Some of the books were damaged, the carpets worn, the few paintings on the walls dingy and dull.

The place almost looked…rifled through. She frowned. "Could someone enter this place without breaking the wards?"

Atlas glanced at her as they moved to the next room, his attention sharpening. "It could've been the other hunters or even rodents."

She hesitated, then shook her head. "Hunters would never loot the place. They'd know better than to disrespect a coven that was meant to keep them safe." They were taught better than that. "And if they dared, they would've taken the spell books, not the knickknacks and trinkets."

She and Atlas cleared the kitchen last. The cupboard doors were open and bare, while the dining room chairs were knocked over, like someone cleared out of the place in a rush. Even the air in the house tasted stale.

No one had lived here for a long time.

So why couldn't she get over the feeling that they weren't alone?

Atlas relaxed when they left the kitchen, and she nodded to the door partially hidden under the stairs. "Basement."

She ignored the way her skin crawled at the thought of investigating the lower floor. The witches in the coven where Morgan was raised loved to keep creatures caged in the basement, working to steal the very life force from other supernaturals just to gain more power, and she shivered as she remembered the bite of cold metal when she woke up in one of those cages. She managed to escape, set free a few of the prisoners in the process, but the witches soon found more subjects and filled the cages up again.

"You don't have to go." Atlas waited patiently while she stood frozen in front of the door, and she shook off her memories.

"No, I need to do this." She couldn't afford the weakness. She reached out and wrenched open the door, half expecting the stench of death to reach for her…only to relax when fresh air seemed to swirl around her instead. A florescent green light brightened the darkness at the base of the stairs. More than a little curious, she headed down the steps, Atlas a comforting presence at her back.

The farther they traveled into the darkness, the brighter the room became. When they reached the bottom, her breath caught at the beauty.

The whole area was a secret oasis.

A large pool took up the majority of the room, covering nearly the entire length of the house. Plants had taken root and grew around the perimeter of the room, creating the hauntingly beautiful glow. Vines and leaves covered the walls, breaking through the windows, allowing a cool breeze to swirl around them. The water in the pool seemed to glow, and she couldn't resist crouching to trail her fingers over the surface.

"It's warm," she blurted out, startled by the information.

"Spells." Atlas finished sweeping the room before coming back to stand protectively next to her, unable to stay away. When she leaned against him without hesitation, so trusting, his heart skipped a beat despite his control.

She'd affected him this way since the first day he met her.

He should've become used to her nearness by now, but every touch was like the first.

Not wanting the moment to end, he crouched next to her and nodded to some of the workbenches around the edges of the room. "It's a grotto. The plants were for medicine and spells. Elves and other creatures often use places like this to relax and mediate."

He didn't mention that elves frequently enjoyed their lovers in places like this for hours on end. The thought of having her alone, his to touch and pleasure, was almost more than he could process. Against his will, his cock hardened, and the darkness that resided in him demanded they stake their claim, mark her as their own, so she'd never be able to escape.

Instead of giving in to the craving, he remained perfectly still, regulating his breathing, struggling not to shatter.

He would not be controlled by lust.

He needed to wait until the right moment, a time when they'd have more than a few stolen moments.

Days, even weeks, would never be enough time, but he'd settle for a few hours.

To start.

To keep himself from putting his thoughts into action, he gently ran a finger along one of the vines, speaking in his native language, the musical syllables rolling off his tongue. Warmth glowed in his chest when she leaned closer to him, as if she couldn't resist the pull.

Magic rose from his blood, and the plants began to stretch and grow. Small buds bloomed and then unfolded and opened into vivid blue flowers that reminded him of her eyes when she looked at him with hunger—like she was now.

He plucked one, then swept into a deep, courtly bow to show her how honored he was to be one of her chosen mates, offering the flower much like he wanted to offer his heart. A small tremor shook his fingers, and it was all he could do not to pull back and hide the way she affected him.

But this was too important.

His future depended on what she said next.

"Will you do me the honor of joining me for a swim after we dine?"

Morgan was stunned by both the romantic gesture and the use of his magic, too awed to do anything but gape at him when she realized he was actually asking her for a real fucking date. Her heartbeat raced, and she was suddenly nervous in the face of his absolute calm.

There was an intensity in his expression—intensity he normally kept hidden—that sent heat shooting through her veins, making her skin tingle from scalp to toes. She wanted more of that...more of him. He saw behind the walls she built—to the monster who lingered beneath her skin, the one she kept chained—and he didn't flinch, the warmth in his emerald green eyes never wavering.

She almost gave in to the urge to cheer when she realized he was no longer running.

A fucking date.

Finally!

She couldn't stop the smile that spread across her face as she accepted the flower. She lifted the bloom to her nose, the sweet fragrance reminding her of the wildflowers that grew in the jungle. She lingered over the scent, trying to resist leaning over and demanding he kiss her senseless.

It would only take one kiss for her to become lost.

But oh, how she wanted to get lost in his arms.

She had a feeling she would never be the same afterward.

"A date?" She peered up at him, half expecting him to take back the invitation, her hope almost painful, and he nodded once in affirmative.

"Yes."

She gulped, then slowly got to her feet, not giving him a chance to retract his offer. When he remained kneeling, something about seeing him at her feet, the worshipful look in his eyes, made her mouth go dry, almost like he was waiting for her to command him.

Something dark and seductive unfurled in her at the idea of being in charge, making him obey her every desire. She took a step back, barely resisting the urge to push him down and start their date right the fuck now.

Chapter Four

$\mathcal{B}$y the time Morgan and Atlas headed back upstairs, the rest of the group was waiting for them.

"The upper levels are clear." Kincade turned toward Atlas.

"Ground floor and basement are clear."

Draven glanced up from his phone with a frown. "There's no reception. I'm going to see if I can get the generators working."

As he headed toward the door, Morgan automatically followed. When the others only stared, she shrugged. "No one should leave the coven alone, not until we can figure out what happened here and what was waiting in those woods for us. I also want to check the wards."

Kincade grunted in agreement, then began directing the others. "Unload the van and let's get this place cleaned. I want it secured before night falls."

Draven opened the door for her with a flourish, then smiled and wiggled his eyebrows at her. "Can't resist my charms, huh?"

Morgan sputtered on her laugh, then, unable to resist, she brushed her lips against his cheek as she headed out the door. "It's not your charm that I find irresistible."

He stopped as if she'd hit him with a two-by four, then almost tripped over his own feet as he scrambled to catch up to her. He stared at her, his mischievous expression gone, leaving behind the bare bones of the man she loved. He touched his cheek where her lips had touched, then reached over and grabbed her hand, threading their fingers together.

The darkness he carried within him retreated a bit more.

She loved the way he looked at her, like she alone was the center of his world.

As they walked through the overgrown garden and weeds, the wild beauty of the place stole her breath. It was like time had forgotten it. No demands from the school. No one ordering her to practice. The stress of the last few months melted away until she could breathe again.

"You like it here." Draven's eyes caressed her, a small smile playing about his lips.

She was startled to realize he was correct. "The place is beautiful—there's a certain wild charm to it." She gave him a shy smile. "I think it has something to do with the people in it."

He brushed his thumb over the back of her hand, squeezing her fingers. Then he let her go and opened the door to the shed. Darkness seeped out of the opening, a musty odor seeming to reach for them, and she stumbled back, slamming into Draven.

He grabbed her close, slipping his arms around her waist to catch her, then froze as if afraid to move and scare her away. He stared down at her, his throat moving as he swallowed hard. He was so confident around other women, she found it charming that he turned into a teenage boy with his first girl when he was around her.

Shed forgotten, she turned in his arms, skimming her hands up his chest, thrilled at the moan that escaped him. Slipping her fingers along the nape of his neck, she used her nails to scratch along his scalp, almost smiling when he shivered.

Draven tried to count to ten but only made it to three before he forgot everything but her. The plans the guys had so carefully constructed during the previous week turned to ash. The only thing he could think was how much he wanted to seduce her and make her fall hopelessly in love with him. He tightened his hold around her, possessive now she was in his arms, and he'd swear he smelled the salty air of home when she was near. It was all he could do not to shove her up against the shed and beg for a kiss.

"Are you just going to stare at me or kiss me?" She batted her stunning blue eyes up at him, and Draven knew he was lost.

He wanted to taste her more than he wanted his next breath.

But he knew if he started, he wouldn't stop, and he wanted better for her than a quick fuck against the garage like a heathen. He wanted to show her she was different from the other girls, show her that only she mattered.

Ignoring the ache in his cock, he desperately grabbed for his last coherent thought before she slipped her fingers into his hair, but it was a failing battle, like trying to catch fairies.

Something about this place relaxed her. She was like the rest of them…they never had a real home to call their own, but he saw her yearning for more. Despite the danger that had run off the previous coven members, Morgan was drawn to this place.

And he wanted to give her all the things she never had when she was growing up.

"Draven…"

At her husky tone, he swallowed hard, knowing he couldn't resist giving her whatever she wanted. He cupped her face, mesmerized by her beauty, not sure how he was lucky enough to find someone who matched him so perfectly. He carefully brushed his lips against her forehead, everything inside him yearning for more.

"Later." He stepped away, nearly shaking with need as he turned her down, looking anywhere else, knowing one look from her would lure him back into her arms. He wanted the chance to romance her, but he didn't have the first clue how to make a woman who was immune to his charms fall madly in love with him. His balls ached so bad it hurt to walk. "If I kiss you now, I'll never get the generator up and running. When I kiss you, I want everything to be perfect."

He took a chance and peered down at her.

She gazed up at him, her slow smile stealing his breath, and nearly making him spill himself in his pants like an untried youth. "Everything we need to make it perfect is standing right here."

Spit dried out of his mouth, the blood left his head, and Draven could only stare down at her in awe. He was one lucky son-of-a-bitch—no other woman suited him so perfectly, like she'd been made specifically for him, and he couldn't help but thank his lucky stars. Every minute of his hellish life had been worth it, because it brought her to him.

Fuck it!

Unable to resist her a second longer, craving just one taste, he bent his head.

"Hello!" A female voice yodeled from the trees, and Morgan snarled in frustration, wanting to rip the bitch apart for interrupting them.

They couldn't have waited five fucking minutes?!

She could practically taste Draven on her lips…until some bitch interrupted them.

Draven turned, shielding her with his body to give her time to pull herself together. Tucking away her desire, Morgan turned to see three people had walked onto the coven property, and it bothered her that she hadn't noticed them standing there sooner.

Her suspicions doubled when she realized the wards hadn't warned her of their arrival either. Draven didn't smile in welcome or try to charm them while he inspected the intruders.

He never took her safety for granted.

"Who are you, and what do you want?" It was all she could do not to call her blades.

The woman in the group lifted her hands in surrender and smiled. "Peace. My name is Leanne. We were sent to keep an eye on the place. They warned us of your arrival, and I wanted to welcome you."

Draven took the lead, asking them questions while they wandered closer, and it was all Morgan could do to resist hauling him back and shoving him toward the safety of the house. The overwhelming stink of perfume assaulted her nose, instantly deadening her scents, and she struggled not to flinch and back away.

While the woman said all the right things, Morgan narrowed her eyes on the group, scanning them quickly. Magic tingled against her skin, but she couldn't tell if the strange woman was a witch or if the prickling sensation signaled the presence of a massive spell of some kind.

The two men were clearly warriors. While they were physically fit, it was the way they held themselves, the way they were continually scanning the area, constantly on guard, that gave away their training.

And for some reason she couldn't get over the feeling that she and Draven were the prey.

The woman was good-looking, but not stunning, her straight dark hair expertly groomed. Her smile was friendly, her posture open and welcoming, but there was something about her aura that screamed danger.

Morgan tried to pin down what made her uneasy but couldn't pick any one thing.

Until she looked into the other women's eyes.

Instead of pleasure, the green eyes glittered with pure malice.

"I would like to invite you over to our house to discuss the coven." The woman glanced around the glen, as if she suspected they were being watched. "How about tomorrow night?"

Morgan wanted to say no but held her tongue.

They needed the information the woman offered if they wanted to learn what the fuck was going on here.

Draven glanced at her, raising a single brow in question, and against her better judgement she confirmed a meeting tomorrow with a nod. If these people were a threat, she would rather face them directly. Once the details were figured out, she watched them walk away, noticing Draven never once took his gaze off them either.

"What did you sense?"

His brows furrowed. "MacGregor didn't send them. He would've warned us."

Morgan grunted her agreement. "They obviously have some connection to the coven."

Draven nudged her back toward the house, the mood between them shattered. "And why didn't they report back to the Academy? Why stay behind?"

As they walked up the steps to the mansion, she couldn't resist glancing back over her shoulder to where the visitors had disappeared. "Or maybe the better question is how did they survive when apparently no one else did?"

When they entered the coven, Draven gave a sharp whistle. In a matter of seconds, all the guys came running. It didn't take long to update them about the new development.

Kincade took his time processing the information. "We need to decide if the mystery of the coven is worth investigating or if we should leave now and have the place torn down and the area scrubbed clean."

Morgan wasn't ready to give up her free time with the guys, no matter what the danger. But there was more involved than that. Every instinct said abandoning the mansion would be a mistake. "I don't think leaving will solve anything. I think it'll make everything worse."

"Explain." Atlas casually leaned against the wall as he studied her, his expression intent.

Morgan reached out and touched the wall behind her. Magic answered sluggishly. It was healthy and whole, just weak. "Whatever happened, the coven is miraculously still standing. I worry that if we decommission the coven and take down the wards, whatever attacked it will be set free to roam the world."

Ryder prowled over to the window and glared out at the exact spot where their visitors had stood, as if he could still sense them. "I don't like that they were able to cross the outer wards."

Then he sneezed, as if he could smell the overabundance of perfume that lingered in the air.

Ascher waited a beat, his blue eyes heating, the smell of charcoal and fire sharpening. "You're assuming they crossed the wards. If they're really part of the original coven, they could still be living on the grounds. They could be telling the truth. It could be a spell gone awry. They could need our help."

Morgan grimaced—Ascher could be right. It would certainly explain the taste of magic that clung to their visitors, but that didn't mean she had to like it.

"We won't know more until we meet with them." Kincade glanced at all the men. "Just to be safe, no one is to go out alone. Draven and Ryder, finish the generator. The rest of us will get to work making this place habitable."

While Draven and Ryder headed out, the rest of the guys seemed to be waiting for something.

Then realization dawned…they were waiting for her.

They wanted her to choose a partner. "Actually, I'm going to go around the house and reinforce the wards. Just to be safe."

Kincade crossed his arms and Ascher scowled, while Atlas remained neutral. It was Kincade who always challenged her, always pushed her, and she smiled to ease his worry, valiantly trying to ignore the urge to push his buttons. It was becoming one of her favorite pastimes. "Very little magic is needed to reinforce the wards." Then her smiled widened, and she blinked up at him innocently. "I promise not to blow up the house."

Ascher snorted and Kincade rolled his eyes, both of them grumbling as they turned away. Atlas gazed at her, his cinnamon scent soothing as he slowly pushed away from the wall and sauntered toward her. He stopped inches from her, so close to touching she instinctively swayed toward him. When he gazed down at her, her breath caught at the emotions in his forest green eyes, the shards of umber splintering the color while her beloved dark elf peered down at her.

"Don't leave the building."

Morgan rolled her eyes, but he kept talking before she could interrupt.

"Don't exhaust yourself."

Her skin tingled at his husky tone, and her annoyance with him evaporated, the suggestive words making her body warm, and she suddenly couldn't wait for their after-dinner date.

After giving her another look that made her blush to her toes, he turned on his heel and left the room without another word. Morgan sputtered at his retreating back but it was too late. He was already gone.

Devious bastard.

He was getting her worked up in anticipation of their date…all without once touching her.

She would be seriously annoyed with him if she didn't want him so badly.

For the next hour or so she wandered around the mansion, shoring up the wards, the walls eagerly soaking up her magic as if starved. She felt the place become stronger, a small hum of magic whispering to her, so similar to the Academy that she smiled at the touch of home.

The spots of mold on the walls vanished, as if soaked up by the magic. Dust swirled around and disappeared out under the doors and between the window cracks. The water damage faded, the wood groaning as it straightened, the stains on the wallpaper seeming to flake off. Books fluttered, the bindings tightening, the pages crinkling as they straightened.

She fed the house more power, allowing it to choose how to put things to rights. Without the guys near, heat began to tingle against her skin, making her body ache. Her insides felt sensitive and raw from channeling so much power, her eyes tender from the headache building as a result of the strain.

"I'm going to run to town for supplies."

Morgan yipped and whirled when Ascher spoke, her magic sparking around them like a camera flash. Only when she got herself under control did she glare at him for sneaking up on her. "Don't do that!"

She rubbed at the beautiful, almost dainty, obsidian filigree marks that swirled up from the tips of her fingers and twisted halfway up her right arm, but it did nothing to soothe the tingling that seemed to activate with his nearness.

She suspected only his touch would help, but she would rather eat a warty, slimy gremlin in all its stinky glory than mention it. If anything happened between her and her guys, she wanted it to be their choice, and not because they were forced to act because of the mating marks.

The longer she spent time with the guys, the more she let down her guard. It had taken months, but she no longer viewed them as a threat…which meant they took pleasure in seeing who was best at creeping up from behind and scaring the crap out of her.

Assholes.

Ignoring her outburst, he gave her a charming smile. "I came to ask if you would like to join me?"

It seemed forever since they had any time alone together. They met years ago, each saving the other many times when danger threatened, and she missed working as a team, when it was just the two of them. Joy shimmered to life at the thought of spending time alone with him, and she couldn't stop her grin. "I would love that."

Tiny wisps of steam rose from his chest and shoulders, revealing his pleasure, and she was glad he no longer tried to hide himself from her. His blonde hair was messy and so sexy her fingers ached to touch him, and when he turned to open the door for her, her eyes automatically dropped to check out his ass. All the guys were fit, trained to be deadly assassins, their devotion to their job shown in how they honed and maintained bodies to survive—they were works of art that she never got tired of watching. Without anyone to judge, she allowed herself the freedom to openly admire the guys, permitting herself to finally relax and be herself around them.

If they weren't going to make their first move, she had every intention of making her interest known.

No more misunderstanding.

No more avoiding the issue.

Starting tonight on her very first date.

After this week, come hell or high water, they were going to be a mated team no one would be able to divide.

**Chapter
Five**

$\mathcal{A}$s soon as the doors to the vehicle closed, the locks clicked, trapping Morgan inside with him. Ascher shivered as the intoxicating scent of warm wildflowers enveloped him, almost like she was snuggled in his arms.

Home.

She was home to him. He had thought his life was over when he was enslaved, but he'd go through it all again just to be with her. She might not realize it, but she had each of the guys wrapped around her little fingers.

And fuck if he didn't love it.

His beast gave a contented rumble, no longer fighting to be free, both sides of him whole—because of her. He didn't mind sharing her with the others on the team. He would take whatever help he could get to keep her safe. What made it work was the rest of the guys worshipped her just as much as he did.

Each of the guys had their own demons, but those didn't matter to her. Despite all their faults, she chose them—how could they not fall in love with her? He turned over the engine and put the van into gear.

About a mile down the road, she thrust her hand across the console separating them, and his whole being clenched with dread. No matter how much he tried to control it, heat began to rise under his skin. Though he knew he could touch her without harming her, he still wasn't used to the luxury.

It would kill him if he hurt her in any way.

When she wiggled her fingers in demand, he almost smiled.

"Morgan—"

"You have a choice of driving slowly and holding my hand or you can pull over, let me crawl into your lap and kiss you the way I've wanted to since before this trip started." The heated look in her eyes had his cock surging to full mass so quickly he went light-headed. He couldn't take his eyes off her mouth, and he licked his dry lips, imagining the taste of her on them.

The van hit a rough spot, sending it swerving off the gravel road, and he slammed on the brakes while he wrestled it back onto the single lane. As the van rocked to a stop, his heart threatened to beat out of his chest, and he raked his fingers through his hair. "Shit! You can't say stuff like that. You have no idea what goes through a guy's head when—"

Then he nearly swallowed his tongue when she unbuckled her seatbelt, gave him a wicked grin and began to crawl over the console separating them.

"Great choice," she practically purred, her voice husky, her blue eyes darkening with lust.

He opened his mouth to ask her what she thought she was doing, but he couldn't seem to remember how to form words.

Then, when her body slid into his lap, he didn't fucking care, and it was all he could do to keep his hands from settling on the curves he'd been daydreaming about for years. The minx squirmed until she settled against his erection.

"There." She tipped her head back and smiled up at him. "Isn't this better?"

Fuck, yeah.

His hellhound groaned with pleasure at her nearness, desperate for the taste of her, and he struggled to remember why he'd been keeping his distance. He didn't give a fuck if she accidently blew him up with her powers…it would be worth it.

When she leaned closer, he dipped his head to meet her lips, only to jerk back at the last second, pressing himself back into his seat. "Morgan, do you have any idea what you're doing?"

She lifted a cocky brow at him. "I'm not a virgin, if that's what you're worried about."

A snarl tore from him at the idea that someone else had touched her, caressed her curves and kissed her body, and he struggled to stifle the desperate urge of his beast to hunt down the prick. It took all his concentration to pull back, and he shook his head to clear it. "Not what I meant. I want this to be special, not rushed in the back of a van."

"Ascher."

His mouth snapped shut at her soft tone.

She was no longer laughing.

No longer smiling.

And she was no longer the warrior he first met. Instead, her face was gentle as she gazed at him.

"I love you. Being with you *is* special. It doesn't matter where…just that we're together."

His heart stopped beating. There was no air in the van. Smoke began to rise from his skin, but he couldn't move because everything he ever wanted rested within his grasp…if only he was brave enough to accept it.

"I'm not afraid of you or your hellhound, because I know you would never hurt me." She grabbed the front of his shirt and pulled him forward until they were only separated by inches. "Now kiss me and show me you feel the same way."

Morgan waited, unable to breathe after she made her demand.

He loved her, she was sure of it.

She wasn't sure how she'd missed the signs for so many

years…the way he protected her, the way he watched her when he thought she wasn't looking…but she was done hiding.

When he got into the van and smiled at her, his face so open and relaxed, her heart melted. When she demanded that he hold her hand, his smile had vanished, and so did her confidence…for a half second. Then she saw the fear churning in the blue depths of his eyes. She would not let him fear touching her, not when they both craved it so much.

When he nearly lost control of the van, she barely contained her laugh, delighted with her ability to fluster him. As the van skidded to a stop, she took advantage of his shock and climbed into his lap. If he didn't want her, he could fucking tell her to her face.

Ascher groaned, closing the distance between them, kissing her like he needed her more than air. His kiss was all heat and passion, drowning them both in hunger that had been denied too long. His hands came to rest on her waist, the heat of them soaking into her skin, making her crave more.

Now that she had a taste of him, she wanted all of him.

She broke the kiss and leaned over to grab the lever of the seat, not even trying to stifle her groan when his erection rubbed her in just the right way. Then he was kissing her neck, and she shivered, her every nerve ending lighting up, demanding more.

When she finally found the lever she wanted, she yanked on it hard, then squeaked when the seat dropped straight back and she ended up plastered against his chest. He went into protective mode, his arms automatically wrapping around her.

Her breath caught at being wrapped up in the warmth of his arms, and she couldn't resist snuggling against his chest and rubbing her face against the side of his neck. When laughter rumbled in his chest, she jerked back, until a foot separated them, and glared. "What's so funny?"

"You are absolutely perfect." He dragged his hand up her back, as if he couldn't bear to put any more distance between them, and carefully tucked her hair behind her ears. "I love everything about you—the way you fight for those you care about, the way you struggle to show people how you feel." He slipped his fingers into her hair at the back of her scalp, refusing to let her duck away from his gaze. "I especially love that you didn't give up on me. The hunger in your eyes when you look at me. Your clumsy but enthusiastic attempts to seduce me."

Her cheeks burned at the intensity on his face. His expression conveyed so much laughter and love, her heart clenched, and she swallowed the lump in her throat. "You love me."

"Of course." He rolled his eyes. As if he ever had any other choice. "I've loved you since the first time I set eyes on you." He rubbed his thumb along her jaw, his eyes steady on hers. "How could I not? You saved me and gave me hope when I had none. You showed me a future I never dreamed possible for myself…then you granted me my deepest wish I didn't even dare hope for…by claiming me as your own."

Morgan snorted on her laughter at his outrageous statement, but her stomach dipped and whirled wildly at his earnest expression. "I think you got it wrong…we saved each other."

Before the last word was out of her mouth, he lunged forward, his kiss demanding, taking everything, stealing her heart again. She placed both hands on his chest and shoved him back until he landed heavily against the prone seat with a grunt. Then she straightened until she was straddling his lap, fighting against the urge to squirm against the erection nestled so intimately against her.

Giving him a seductive smile, she reached down and pulled her shirt and camisole up and over her head, baring herself to him. Lust darkened his face, his hunger so deep he looked savage and wild, like when she first met him, when she wasn't sure whether he was going to attack or run.

Steam rose from his skin, his shirt turning into tatters before it disintegrated. Her eyes dropped to the shimmering lines of the mating mark covering his shoulder, the black lines highlighted by a dusky red that resembled live coals, as if he was heated from within.

And she wanted to get burned.

She had to forcefully tear her eyes away from the glorious muscles on display or risk drooling. She gave him a crooked smile, unable to stop a small laugh. "Do clothes normally fall off you when you see a pair of breasts?"

"Only yours." A roguish smile lit his eyes and curved his lips, not the least bit embarrassed as he ran his fingers along the skin above her waistband, as if marveling at the smoothness, his touch not leaving even the smallest mark. "My hellhound has only ever been interested in you. I think he's trying to entice you."

Morgan grinned, charmed that his clothes would fall off around her.

And fascinated.

Curiosity got the better of her and she reached back to touch his thigh—and touched bare skin.

As in—he was completely naked.

He took advantage of her distraction by leaning forward and taking the tip of her breast into his mouth. She immediately clutched him to her, a groan torn from her. When he cupped her other breast, paying specific attention to her nipple, the outside world disappeared. He was slow and methodical, using his tongue and teeth, the heat making her squirm until she found herself rocking against him.

When he pulled back, she nearly whimpered.

A gleam of masculine pride crossed his face, his hand dropping to stroke her leg from knee to hip. "Do you trust me?"

Morgan scowled down at him, then rolled her eyes. "Would I be naked with you otherwise?"

Eyes sparkling, he grinned with a pleased growl. "I hope these aren't your favorite pants." He didn't say any more, simply ran a single finger down the seams of her pants...burning away the leather. He couldn't seem to stop touching her, marveling at being able to do whatever he wanted without fear of harming her. Heat kissed her skin, but instead of pain, it awakened all her nerve endings until she had to bite back a moan at even the slightest brush of his fingertips.

And he didn't stop until her clothes were lying around them in tatters.

Instead of feeling embarrassed at being naked in front of him, she basked in the lustful appreciation in his eyes—a look he reserved just for her. Then he kissed her, no longer holding back, and she went up in flames.

He ran his hands over her body, the heat in them making her shiver, leaving her skin sensitive to his touch, and she wanted more. Unable to hold back any longer, she tore her mouth away from his and nipped along his neck, enjoying the growl that rumbled through him, making the tips of her breasts harden even more.

His fingers sank into her hair, and she desperately wanted to break his control. She tried to move down, desperate to explore him further, but the limited space in the vehicle blocked her attempt. With each wiggle, she groaned at the feel of the hard length of him right where she needed him. His hands immediately clamped down on her hips, stilling her movements.

"Baby, if you do that again, I'm not sure I'll be able to hold myself back from taking you hard and fast." His voice was pure grit and need.

Her breath stalled in her throat, lust pouring through her at his warning, and she leaned back, peering down at him. "I don't recall saying anything about wanting it slow."

With a feral growl that showed his teeth were a little sharper than human, he easily lifted her, pausing when he was poised at her entrance, love and possessiveness darkening his eyes. "Are you sure? Once we do this, there is no going back. The missing piece of the mating bond will lock into place. You will never get rid of me."

It was both a warning and a threat.

Morgan leaned forward, her lips stopping just short of touching his. "I think you got that backwards. If we do this, *you'll* be stuck with *me*." A sliver of vulnerability shot through her, and she searched his eyes. "Last chance to change your mind."

It would tear her apart to let him go, but more than anything else she wanted him to be happy.

His mouth smashed against hers at the same moment he slammed her down over his cock, capturing her gasp of surprised pleasure. While his tongue and teeth devoured her, he held her hips still to give her time to adjust to him. When he pulled back, his eyes were glowing blue and harder than any diamond. *"Mine."*

Unable to resist the compulsion to mark him, she bent and bit his shoulder where it met his neck. A guttural groan escaped him, a shudder tearing through him, and then he began to move, holding her above him, giving him the power to control the depth and speed of his penetration, and hitting a spot inside that sent her soaring higher and higher with every thrust.

Her body heated, her skin tingled, until she could no longer tell herself apart from him. Then he jackknifed up into sitting position, leaving her straddling him, sending his cock deeper than ever before. He wrapped his arms around her tight, and she couldn't stop the way her hips moved over him. She tipped her chin up as stars scattered across her vision, but his own gaze held her captive, and she couldn't look away.

"Mine," he growled again, as if incapable of saying anything else. Then he leaned forward and sank his teeth in the same spot on her shoulder where she bit him. Heat spread under her skin, almost as if the bite had connected them. Instead of pain, the warmth seared along her insides, triggering her release.

She heard him grunt, his thrusts becoming erratic, as if trying to get deeper inside her, before she felt him swell and find his own release.

She opened her mouth to scream as a second orgasm tore through her, but the pleasure stole her breath. It was all she could do to stay conscious as she floated down to earth wrapped in his arms. He was breathing heavily against her, and she gently ran her hand down his ribs, barely stifling a groan as he twitched inside her at the touch.

He gently lifted his mouth from the crook of her neck, sending another wave of pleasure coursing through her, and she couldn't stop her hips from rocking against him again. A growl tore from him, not in the least bit human.

"Do that again, and we won't make it to town." He couldn't seem to look away from the mark he left on her shoulder.

Morgan ducked down until she saw his eyes. Instead of a proud swagger she expected, she saw uncertainty and vulnerability. "What's wrong?"

"I bit you."

She couldn't stop a wry smile. "To be fair, I bit you first."

He only shook his head, clearly still troubled, and she shoved his shoulders until he was lying flat against the seat again. "Look at me." His attention snapped to her. "Do I look injured?"

His eyebrows pulled down, and he slowly examined her. Her body warmed under his attention, craving his touch again, and it was all she could do not to squirm in his lap and demand they start again.

"No." His eyes lifted, landing somewhere near her jawline.

She lifted her brows at him. "Now tell me what upset you."

It wasn't a request.

"My hellhound has laid claim to you." He couldn't seem to look her in the eye.

She couldn't stand it. She grabbed his jaw and forced him to look at her, not understanding why it was such a big deal. "So what?"

His eyes snapped to hers, anger hardening his face. "I lost control! I could've hurt you! If you were human, my bite would've killed you." He ran his fingers through his hair, his gaze once more dropping away, as if he couldn't bear to look at her.

She hated that he was hiding—it wasn't how she wanted to start their life together. She leaned forward until her face was mere inches away from his. "But I'm not human, never have been. Your bite only gave me pleasure." She waited a beat. "Do you regret claiming me?"

"What?" His eyes snapped up to hers. "No! Of course not."

"Then what's the problem?" She was beginning to lose her patience.

"When two hellhounds mate, their spirits are joined, and they become stronger. Most hellhounds don't have the ability to cast fire until they're mated. I've never bitten anyone before." His soul looked shattered. "What if you gain some of my abilities? You're already struggling to control your own powers. What if this pushes you past your limits?" He sat again, crushing her to his chest, as if he thought something would try to take her away from him. "I couldn't bear to lose you, not because of something I did."

Morgan tightened her hold around him, then gently pushed him away. "Look at me." She waited until she had his complete attention. "Am I going to turn into a hellhound?"

He scowled and rolled his eyes at the absurdity. "Of course not."

"Then we're good. If the impulse to mark me was anything like what I felt, I don't think you could've prevented it even if you tried." Morgan refrained from mentioning the burn from his bite was still spreading underneath her skin like she'd been injected with something.

Telling him would only make him worry.

Heat gathered under the mating marks, the sensation feeling like they were searing together, pushing the marks deeper, before the lines gradually cooled and eased the ache that had been plaguing her for the past few weeks.

"Whatever comes, we'll deal with it together."

He blew out a heavy breath, a small smile curving his lips. "Together."

She cocked a brow at him, then swept her gaze down his naked torso. "I hope you have a spare set of clothes for us. Otherwise, be prepared to cause quite a stir when we arrive in town naked."

Ascher was unable to resist watching Morgan while she dressed, worshiping her curves with his eyes as she wiggled into her pants. His mouth went dry as the urge to taste every inch of her, the impulse nearly bringing him to his knees. It took all his control to turn away, and he struggled to pull his own pants up over his erection.

Thank the gods they hadn't unpacked the van completely when they first arrived. The last thing he wanted was to parade back buck naked in front of the guys. He wanted to keep what happened between him and Morgan private.

After a few seconds, he couldn't help but turn back, unable to keep his eyes off her.

She was toned and curvy in all the right places, and his hellhound rumbled with pleasure at seeing their marks on her body. As she pulled on her shirt, throwing him a smile over her shoulder, he realized he'd never tire of watching the graceful way she moved. It was all he could do to curb the impulse to walk over to her, pin her against the van and take her again. Unfortunately, the sun was close to setting. If they didn't get to town soon, the stores would be closed.

He refused to let her go hungry simply because he couldn't control his lust. As they climbed back into the vehicle, he started the van, then hesitantly reached across the console and held his hand out toward her, needing the comfort of her touch.

She cast him a brilliant smile, then wove her fingers with his, his heart skipping a beat at her touch. She always had that effect on him, even after all these years, and he doubted it would ever change.

He'd never intended to finish the full hellhound mating ceremony, unwilling to risk her life simply to gain more power. He'd been content to bind his life to hers, knowing he would never become a hellbeast with the ability to cast fire in his human form. He didn't need it—she made him complete.

Apparently fate had other ideas.

He just hoped she didn't suffer any side effects. He'd need to talk to the guys, have them keep an eye on her to make sure.

As they pulled into town, he watched her from the corner of his eyes, looking for any symptoms. Though she might have the ability to withstand the heat from his beast, being able to control hellfire was something else, usually reserved only for the creatures descended directly from hell.

While she might have walked through hell, she'd survived with her soul intact.

He had every intention of keeping it that way.

Chapter Six

*T*he bell above the door to the grocery store chimed as they entered. There were four old men sitting in a row at the counter drinking coffee, all of them quieting when Morgan and Ascher entered. Three of the old men sat on the customer side, while one sat behind the counter. Weathered old eyes scanned them. Two of them seemed intrigued by seeing new people, while the other two dismissed them as unimportant.

Ascher edged closer, weaving their fingers together before gently tugging her away. He picked up a basket by the door, handed her one as well, then began to browse the shelves, grabbing the groceries they needed to fill the gaps in supplies they already brought with them. By the time they were done, they ended up carrying two baskets each.

"You must be planning to stay for a while." The grisly old man behind the register with tired blue eyes stood, his expression both friendly and curious. "Are you renting a cottage or staying with family?"

It was a not-so-subtle quest for information.

Ascher remained tight-lipped, but Morgan had no such hesitation, finding something about the old man charming. "We're staying at the old Tremaine place."

The old man stopped scanning items, his face drooping and turning grave. "Sweetie, that's not a place you want to stay. Those woods are haunted. Dozens of people have gone missing just in the past year."

"If you want a place to stay, my grandson has a nice cabin on Torbin Lake," the man sitting next to them at the counter offered before taking a sip of his coffee. It was so strong and black she could smell it despite the distance. "I can get you a deal."

Ascher stiffened behind her, going on alert at the mention of the woods being haunted, but he remained mute, letting her take the lead. But she could tell that it cost him when a little curl of smoke began to rise from his shoes.

Morgan gave the old man a polite smile. "That's so nice of you, but I promised my grandfather we would look in on the place and decide if it's something we want to keep in the family or sell."

The next man down the line leaned forward to study them. His hair was darker than the rest, meaning it wasn't solid gray. He was lean, almost emaciated, his clothes practically swimming on him, his eyes haunted, and he pointed to a bulletin board at the end of the store. "You might want to take a look at that before you head back."

Even from the distance, she saw the board was covered with missing person flyers. As she got closer, she realized there were close to a hundred sheets of paper tacked to the board, most of them pinned one on top of the other as they ran out of room. While some of them were older, the majority of them were posted in the past year.

Campers.

Hikers.

Students.

And there were almost triple the number of missing animals.

"Ascher—"

"I see it." They all went missing in the woods surrounding the coven. He began to snap pictures with his phone. "We need to get back to the others."

She nodded and headed back to the counter, where the rest of their items were tallied and bagged. She pulled out her wallet and paid with a credit card issued by the Academy. While Ascher began to carry out their supplies, she turned back toward the gentlemen. "What's causing them to go missing?"

The guys exchanged a look, and the one closest to her shrugged. He was old, his hair thin, his shoulders bowed by time. He was still in pretty good shape, but the beginnings of a belly stretched the front of his plaid shirt. "Since no bodies were ever found, the police think they wanted to disappear, but those who've lived here longer know the truth."

He waited, as if watching for her reaction, and she found herself leaning toward him. "Which is what?"

"Monsters." The old man at the end of the counter spoke for the first time. "Not that you'll get any of the police to admit to it. They say bears, wolves and cougars, but there ain't none of them critters in these areas any longer. There ain't no animals a'tall."

The man next to him nodded and took a gulp of his coffee. "The hunting has gone to shit—pardon my language—the past few months. All the animals have either been slaughtered or run off scared."

The man behind the counter handed her the last bag but didn't release his hold. "We don't mean to be scaring you, miss, but you beware. Those woods ain't safe. The police mean well, but they're not equipped to deal with things that go bump in the night." He shook his head at the foolishness.

While the younger generation might call them delusional, they'd lived too long, seen too much unexplained stuff to dismiss it so casually. Most people would just ignore the unexplained for the most logical reasons, but some people were too aware, too observant to believe the excuses of others.

She lifted down the bag and nodded to him. "Thank you for the warning. We'll be careful."

The three guys next to her went back to their coffee, one shaking his head, while the other two muttered to themselves about the foolishness of youth. "My grandfather taught me to protect myself in situations *exactly* like this."

She leaned forward and smiled at them, letting the bloodlust darken her eyes. "The men who are with me are trained to hunt things normal people aren't capable of believing are real, much less knowing how to kill them."

All the guys swiveled in her direction, doubt and curiosity in their expressions.

"Other hunters have said the same and failed," the man in the middle muttered, and she understood the haunted look.

"I'm sorry for your loss." And she was more determined than ever to put a stop to the killing. She couldn't get over the feeling it was all connected to the coven, which meant it was their fault. And their job to clean up the mess.

The old man waved a hand to shoo her away. "Pssssh." Then he glanced at her, his expression fierce. "Just make sure you don't end up like them."

She wanted to reassure them, but Ascher stood in the doorway and shook his head, obviously reading her mind. He was right, of course. Humans were too vulnerable and soft to deal with the supernatural world. It's why the Academy and the assassins were created...to protect them.

She leaned forward and impulsively kissed each of the guys on the cheek. "We'll be careful."

By the time they loaded up the supplies in the vehicle and headed home, the sun had finally dipped below the horizon. Thanks to her re-setting the wards before she left, she felt them brush lightly against her skin when they crossed the boundaries to the property. Though not one hundred percent yet, they were stronger, and hummed in welcome, as if pleased to have her back.

They were twenty minutes from home, the gravel road rutted, when something ran in front of the van. Ascher slammed on the brakes, sending the rear end kicking out, but he easily kept control of the vehicle.

"What was that?" It looked like a large bear, but it almost appeared to be standing on two legs. She'd swear she saw antlers and glowing yellow eyes, but the creature vanished too quickly for her to get a good look. She tried to peer into the darkness, but despite her enhanced senses, she saw nothing but shadows. A heavy smell of decay lingered in the air—much like a skunk scent that had gone bad—and there was no escaping it. Ascher didn't wait to investigate, slamming his foot on the gas, and the vehicle lurched forward.

"Hang on!" Ascher barked.

Not a second later something slammed into the side of the van so hard that it rocked sideways on two wheels. The side panel caved with a boom, and she saw two large hands and the side of a face imprinted into the metal. Claws easily tore into the metal with a screech of protest that hurt her ears.

The smell of death seemed to reach inside the van like they were buried alive in a mass grave that had turned into putrid soup.

Whatever was out there wasn't a normal supernatural.

Whatever it had once been, it had been now tainted and twisted beyond recognition.

Ascher struggled to keep the van on the road, nearly clipping a tree as they skidded sideways. "Morgan—"

"Keep going!" They couldn't risk stopping, not unless they wanted to be dinner. The hellhound grunted, clearly pissed about not having the option to go out there and take down whatever was messing with them, but everything inside her screamed danger.

Instead of sitting passively by, Morgan rolled down the window.

"What are you doing?" Ascher growled, grabbing the back of her waistband, ready to yank her back to keep her safe.

Magic surged from her bones even before she had a chance to

call it, swirling inside her like a galaxy coming to life. The marks carved into her back tingled, as if waking from a long sleep. Power began to heat along her veins, her body sloshing with so much magic it began to snap and crackle down her arms.

"Putting a stop to this." She watched as the creature picked himself off the ground, shaking his massive head to clear it, as if a one-ton vehicle hadn't just smacked into him. Then he charged after them.

"Protect," she whispered to her magic, then thrust her hand out the window. Thanks to hours of practice every day for the past few weeks, her skills were vastly improved. She only needed to use sigils for the more complicated spells.

Without further prompting, her palm cooled until it burned, then a stream of bright light burst out of her. It slammed into the beast so hard, he flew ass over teakettle. But instead of bursting into tiny pieces, the creature roared with rage, then calmly reached down and stabbed his fingers into the road, leaving behind deep furrows.

Then he planted his other three limbs into the ground, pulling himself to a stop. He lowered his head, bared his fangs, his yellow eyes a feral gleam as he locked his gaze on her, promising retribution. Lumps of dirt kicked up behind him as he took off, muscles flexing at his powerful movements.

"Shit." What could take a blast of pure magic and not be even be fazed by it?

"Hang on!" Ascher's shout had her whirling in her seat.

Only to see a second creature standing directly in the middle of the narrow road. The beast crouched low, as if bracing himself.

"Don't stop." Morgan braced herself for impact as Ascher tightened his grip on the wheel and stomped on the gas until the engine screamed.

If they stopped, they were dead.

Ten feet.

Five feet.

At the last second, the creature leapt straight up in the air, disappearing above the van.

Metal screeched as the creature punched through the roof, barely catching himself before tumbling off the rear. Then claws thumped heavily into the metal as the creature dragged himself across the roof toward them.

"Get down!"

"I got this." Morgan ignored Ascher's order, placing both palms on the roof of the van and letting loose her magic with one thought in mind—to destroy.

Static filled the air until the van crackled with energy. The roof began to glow a fierce red before turning white. Little bits of liquid metal began to slowly rain down into the van. The sizzle of burned flesh saturated the air, a howl of agony echoing loudly in the tiny space. She yanked her hands away, drawing the power back into herself until it felt like acid coursing through her veins, the pain nearly dropping her to her knees as her magic fought her to finish the job.

Giant paws the size of a grizzly began to punch through the roof, the van caving under the weight of the creature. "Brake!"

Ascher didn't hesitate, slamming on the brakes so hard the back end fishtailed. The furry monster tumbled down the front of the vehicle, cracking the windshield and denting the hood before disappearing briefly and rolling down the road.

Without missing a beat, Ascher slammed on the gas. The vehicle lurched forward and plowed into the creature. Metal and bones crunched, the van tipped, and the tires struggled to climb over the lump of flesh on the road. The engine screamed as the back tires hit seconds later.

Ascher stopped the vehicle, threw it into reverse and drove over the creature again, making the van feel like some demented carnival ride. The remaining headlight showed only a lump of flesh and fur remained on the road, the gravel stained red with blood and gore where the creature's insides were strewn down the road.

The silence in the van was deafening, the only sounds from the night were the pinging of the engine and a screechy whine of a damaged belt. "What the fuck *was* that thing?"

A shattering of glass answered her, and she jerked around to see Ascher battling a creature that was trying to pull him out the window. The thing was freaking massive, its face misshapen, a mishmash of human and wolf, but it got all smooshed up wrong. His skull gleamed through his fur, where patches seemed to have rotted away to reveal the evil lurking beneath. His teeth were at awkward angles like porcupine quills, but it was the stench of death and decay filling the cab that made her gag and her eyes water.

Ascher used his feet as leverage, bracing them against the door, and managed to pull away from the creature, but the beast would not be denied. He roared in fury, then latched his teeth around Ascher's arm with a possessive growl.

Morgan leaned forward, only to have Ascher thrust his arm out, shoving her back. "No. Stay back!"

She narrowed her eyes and gritted her teeth. "Then burn the fucker."

Without waiting for him to respond, she threw her leg over the console separating them, and jammed her foot down on the accelerator. The van leapt forward obediently while Ascher grunted and grappled with his opponent, his hesitation betraying him when his eyes dropped to where she was pressed up against him, afraid he would burn her.

The fucking idiot. "Do it!"

Jaw clenched, he gave a nod, and the charred scent of rotting flesh saturated the cab. The beast howled, releasing its hold on Ascher. She yanked on the wheel, steering them toward the ditch, the van dipping precariously as it went up the embankment, and they careened toward a large tree.

The scent of blood and rot made her want to gag. It was all she could do not to cringe away from the stench. "Hang on!"

As the tree loomed nearer, she yanked on the wheel again, and the front fender crunched, the screech of metal rending the air as the tree scraped along the side of the vehicle. The side mirror exploded in a shower of glass and plastic.

Then the beast was peeled off and rolled between the tree and the van, his body pancaked and smearing along the side of the van. The vehicle lurched as they mowed down shrubs and smaller trees, bucking again as they were flung back up onto the road. From the way the vehicle lurched wildly, she knew they'd broken something underneath.

Ascher turned, taking back control of the van, not letting up on the gas as he looked in the rearview mirror.

"You've got to be kidding me!"

Morgan whirled, half expecting to find more of them after them…only to find the road completely empty.

The two bodies had vanished.

**Chapter
Seven**

While the guys looked over the vehicle, Morgan sat on the steps and watched the shadows, expecting more monsters to attack. She'd swear they were being watched, but she didn't sense any malicious intent. No matter how much she searched, she couldn't find anything.

Frustration getting the better of her, she flipped her blade end over end, wanting to charge into the trees and hunt down the creatures that had tried to kill them.

Yet everything remained silent and still, which only put her more on edge.

Ascher walked around like he wasn't injured, showing the others photos of the missing people from the grocery store bulletin board in town. Each of the guys became progressively grimmer as the minutes ticked past. Kincade looked up from the pictures to stare at her, concern darkening his eyes.

"Atlas—take Ascher upstairs and tend to his wounds." Kincade didn't once look away from her. "Draven and Ryder—make sure the grounds are secure."

Kincade turned back toward the van and began to collect the scattered supplies…those that weren't destroyed or melted by globs of metal. "Morgan—why don't you help me carry in the supplies and prepare supper."

She caught the tip of her blade, her lips tightening against the urge to tell him no. She wanted to hunt down what was hunting them, not stand aside like the little woman who wasn't allowed to do anything more than cook and clean. "And the creatures?"

Kincade turned and cocked his head as he studied her. "You're a good hunter, but you're reckless. You act impulsively if any of us are in danger." He grabbed some of the bags, then deposited them on the steps next to her before going to retrieve more. "This wasn't a random attack. They were waiting for you to leave the property. And don't forget, whatever is out there already took out two squads of hunters and a coven of witches."

Morgan pursed her lips, unable to refute his point. "But we're hunters. We've trained for this."

"Not at night. Not without a proper plan and more information." He hefted out the last of the bags, turning to walk toward her. "The majority of people on those missing posters vanished after dark. We'll do some research and head out in the morning when we know what we're hunting."

She sighed, hating it when he sounded so reasonable. When no one else protested their duties, she blew out a heavy breath, knowing he was right. To go out hunting in the middle of the night in an unfamiliar territory was just asking for trouble. The pictures of hundreds of missing people were proof that they were up against something well-organized enough to avoid being caught.

The wards around the house would protect them until they could come up with a plan of attack. Pushing off the ground, she swiped the dirt off her ass, allowing her blade to melt back into a cuff around her wrist, and accepted the bags Kincade held out for her.

"Thank you," he murmured, and she knew it was for more than carrying the bags.

As she tromped back inside the house, she stopped short to see the interior had been transformed. Lights filled the place, the dust gone. The storm damage was nearly nonexistent, which made it more obvious the house had been ransacked, stripped of any gold or shiny objects, which was strange, since the place should've been warded against such a thing. "You guys were busy while we were gone."

"Your magic did much of the heavy lifting. The rest…" Kincade shrugged, giving her a cocky grin. "We wanted to surprise you." Kincade nudged her away from the door, kicking it shut behind him. "The rooms upstairs have been cleaned as well, and your bags are in your room."

She hesitated at the bottom of the steps, fighting the need to check on Ascher, allowing herself to gently probe the connection between them. His annoyance over the injury quickly turned to warmth as he sensed her, and thoughts of them together flooded her mind.

Blushing, she pulled away, knowing if she went upstairs, they wouldn't be leaving the bedroom anytime soon. Forcing her feet away from the near compulsion to do just that, she followed Kincade into the kitchen, tucking her naughty thoughts away.

She set her bags down next to his and began unpacking, only to stop dead when she saw him take out a towel and tie it around his waist. She studied him as he puttered around the kitchen, bemused that he seemed completely at ease.

"You cook?" For some reason she couldn't picture him as a master chief.

Instead of answering, he took out another towel, snapped it open, then walked over to stand behind her. He slipped his arms around her waist, his chest snuggled up to her back, and she shivered when his breath whispered along her neck. She froze as he wrapped the towel around her hips and tied the ends in the front, his strong arms completely enveloping her.

The scent of freshly turned earth and hot stone made her want to linger and bask in his warmth. He rested his hands on her hips, forcing her forward until she was pressed up against the counter, him remaining tight against her back.

"My mother taught me to cook when I was young." He began gathering supplies, keeping her between him and the counter the whole time, and she watched in awe as he put together a meal fit to feed a king…and enough for an army.

"You miss her," she observed.

"Of course." Kincade gave her a small smile, his jaw brushing along her cheek in the best fucking cuddle ever. "Her laughter filled the house, making everyone smile whenever she was near. She fought as hard as she played, and my father worshiped every strand of hair on her head, every breath she took."

He patiently showed her what to do, but she watched in fascination the way his muscles flexed as he stirred the ingredients.

"She never let anyone in the house go to bed mad, even forced us to sit together in silence until sunrise if we refused to make up, and she could fix everything." He moved away and absently began to mix things in the pan, lost to the memories. "She would've hated what I've become."

Morgan stepped into his path when he went to reach for a spoon, and she quickly cupped his face until he was seeing her and not the past. "She'd be damn proud of you."

"Not until you." His face softened as he gazed down at her, the loneliness haunting him fading. "I might've been the best warrior, but my life revolved around nothing but wreaking vengeance on the creatures who took everything from me." He reached up and pushed a strand of hair behind her ear. "Little did I know it would lead me to you. All my training, the pain and loneliness, have been worth it."

Her face warmed under his attention, and when she would've leaned into him, he pulled away and began shoving pots and pans on top of the stove and into the ovens. Hiding her disappointment, she cleaned up the clutter, saddened the evening was over—until she noticed him taking down a large bowl and beginning to put together something else.

"What are you doing?" She wandered closer, unable to stay away from the way he was opening up to her about his past…opening up to her about everything he'd kept hidden and apart from her before now.

"It's a surprise." He nudged her aside, not letting her go far when he grabbed her hips and lifted her up on the counter. Instead of walking away, he placed the bowl in her lap, forcing her legs apart. "Stir."

She fumbled with the spoon he handed her, wishing it was him instead of cold steel between her legs. As he began to measure ingredients, delicious aromas filled the room. She watched, mesmerized by his smooth, practiced moves as the mixture in the bowl turned into some sort of chocolate concoction that made her mouth water.

When Kincade turned away, she lifted her spoon and licked the back of it, closing her eyes when dark rich chocolate exploded on her tongue. As she opened her eyes to dip the spoon again, she froze when she saw Kincade watching her lips in fascination, a hungry look in his light green eyes.

Her hand clamped around the spoon as the dainty, molten silver filigree marks began to tingle almost painfully. The sensation followed the marks and swirled up from the edges of her fingertips and twisted halfway up her right arm.

The sensations demanded she lay claim to him, and it was all she could do to keep her hands to herself.

When he kept staring at her mouth, she wiped the back of her hand across her lips and smirked when he followed the movement like a predator about to pounce. She lifted the spoon out to him in a silent taunt and blinked up at him using her very best innocent expression. "Want some?"

He prowled toward her, then lunged to close the distance between them, ignoring the spoon completely. His hands slipped around her neck, preventing her from getting away, but his worries were groundless—she had no intention of going anywhere. Then he pressed his lips against hers, demanding a taste, demanding she respond, and she was helpless to resist.

All the bottled-up yearning building over the recent months came rushing back, and she dropped the spoon to pull him closer, only to curse when the bowl dug into her stomach, keeping them apart.

He pulled away, giving her a crooked smile, and she nearly growled in frustration. But instead of retreating, he stuck his finger into the chocolate concoction, then held it up between them with a challenging arch of his brow.

Butterflies exploded in her stomach, taking flight as she slowly leaned forward, never removing her gaze from his as she closed her mouth over his finger. She watched his pupils dilate when she grabbed his wrist and ran her tongue up the outside of his finger. His breathing hitched, his eyes dropped, and his chest stopped moving when she sealed her mouth over his finger, running her tongue around the digit until every speck of chocolate was gone.

His breath exploded out of him, and he leaned forward as if in a trance, his eyes locked on her lips.

"Oh, no you don't." She leaned back and placed her hand on his chest, pushing at him to maintain the distance between them. His expression froze, like a wolf eagerly waiting for a command. Only when she was certain he would obey did she dip her finger in the bowl. When she lifted it up between them, she peered up at him from under her lashes.

Kincade watched her blue eyes turn sultry, and his muscles locked tight while she slowly lifted her finger to her mouth. Then the tease slowly traced her lips, leaving a small smear of chocolate behind.

A tortured groan escaped him, and he quickly caught her wrist, his fingers encircling the delicate bone. Before he could take back control of the situation, she leaned closer, and he watched, mesmerized, as she slipped that teasing finger into her mouth, her lips closing around the digit.

Fuck if his cock didn't jump to attention, imagining her mouth doing the same to it.

Every nibble, every lick sent him closer and closer to the edge of oblivion. With great reluctance, he pulled her arm away and withdrew her finger barely in time to avoid embarrassing himself. He'd wanted her for too damn long to endure her teasing.

When she pouted up at him, he swallowed hard, struggling against the urge to rip off her clothes and take her like some beast. This wasn't the way it was supposed to happen. He wanted to wine and dine her. Give her the romance she deserved.

Then she innocently dipped her finger back into the chocolate cream, lifted her hand to her mouth, but ended up drizzling it over the tops of her breasts where her shirt dipped low.

"Oops!"

And his control snapped.

He grabbed the bowl and shoved it aside, wedging himself between her spread thighs, the heat of her scorching as he dragged her even closer. He bent low, his lips hovering over her waiting mouth, loving the way her breath caught in anticipation.

Then he ducked, licking and nibbling at the chocolate across her breasts. When she arched into him and groaned, he tightened his grip on her hips, and he knew there was no way he was going to be able to let her go without claiming her, his good intentions be damned.

He lifted his head, growling when she looked at him with such emotion his heart hiccupped against his ribs in the face of the truth. "You love me."

Instead of denying it, she gave him a sultry smile...that completely belied the snark in her next words. "Of course I do, you idiot."

He blinked at her confession, awe making his green eyes

shimmer with emotion. "I—"

Then she reached down and pulled off her shirt, leaving her in nothing but a skimpy camisole that made his mouth go dry. The ability to speak vanished, which only seemed to make her grin widen.

"Now, where were we?" She lifted her legs, sliding them around his hips, locking him in place as if she thought he would try to escape.

As if he could leave behind his own heart.

Kincade tipped his head back, trying to remember the carefully constructed seduction he had planned. If he wasn't careful, she would make him lose control, and he was determined to last more than ten seconds. He reached out, coiling her hair around his fingers, tugging her head back, forcing her to meet his gaze. She seemed to melt into his hold, and it was all he could do not to strip her then and there.

"Impatient little minx."

She snorted and rolled her eyes. "If you call waiting months being impatient."

"We were trying to be considerate," he said through gritted teeth. One second he wanted to kiss her senseless, the next he barely resisted the urge to spank her. "We saw all the demands placed on you and didn't want to add to them."

She grabbed the front of his shirt, dragging him closer, the playfulness in her eyes suddenly making him leery, but he was helpless to resist her.

"So you guys decided to whisk me away to have your way with me?"

The seductive purr made his head spin, all his blood heading south, and he wasn't sure if she would smile at him or drag out her blades and chop him into tiny pieces—and he loved that about her.

He cleared his throat, his voice a husky whisper. "Or maybe we saw that you needed to get away. If anything happened between you and any of us…" He couldn't stop the way his eyes dragged over her exposed flesh, practically able to taste her. "…we would consider ourselves lucky bastards."

Her fingers tightened possessively on him, and he watched a blade slowly formed in her palm. While most would've flinched, Kincade stood his ground. Seeing her with a blade only made her so much fucking hotter.

With a quick slash, she sliced his shirt right down the middle, and a growl rumbled up in his throat at the feel of the warm metal. A trail of heat ran down his chest where the blade rested against him, the pressure not hard enough to break skin, and his cock throbbed, eager for her to strip him. "Like I said—impatient little minx."

His good intentions, his determination to take it slow and easy, went up in smoke. He didn't give her a chance to reply but slammed his mouth over hers. He thrust his tongue into her mouth, the taste of her and chocolate making his balls ache. He couldn't prevent his hips from shifting against hers in the need to get closer.

The scent of her arousal called to his beast, and the primal need to stake his claim roared through him. He tore his mouth away and leaned back only long enough to rip her camisole over her head.

At the sight of her perfect breasts, he barely paid attention to her tugging off his shirt, and he gave in to the craving to take what he wanted.

One moment Morgan was teasing Kincade, then something in him snapped. Her blade vanished so she could grab onto him as he ravished her. A tidal wave of lust crashed over her with his kiss, dragging her under, and she had no wish to escape. His lips were drugging, his mouth dragging along her neck before nipping at her collarbone. He gave a tortured groan and feasted on her breasts.

A moan escaped her throat and her body melted, but it wasn't enough.

She needed more.

She needed him.

She tugged at the towel around his waist, taking savage pleasure in watching it drift to the ground. Her gaze was drawn to the swirling pattern of the mating marks that covered his entire shoulder, the lines spilling down his arm to his elbow. Instead of dainty lines, the dips and swirls of molten silver were bolder, more masculine, and her fingers tingled with the need to touch him.

She reached for his jeans and encountered a blade tucked against his side. She pulled it out, tossing it onto the cupboard beside her.

Only to find a second and third one in quick secession.

Kincade leaned back with a crooked smile. "There's no such thing as too much protection."

She snorted at his corny joke, reaching for his jeans, determined to get him naked this time, when he quickly caught her hand. When her gaze shot to his, his flirty smile was gone. "Speaking of protection…"

Morgan cocked her head, something about his stillness making her pause. "Do you not want a family?"

His light green eyes darkened, turning his expression vulnerable. The corners of his eyes crinkled as his lips flattened. He opened his mouth to speak, then closed it abruptly, and she cupped his face, hating the lost expression he wore.

"I've never had a family, not really." Morgan lifted her hand, revealing a tiny hieroglyph etched into the base of her palm. "Harper showed me a spell to prevent pregnancy, but I would like to have a big family one day."

Suddenly feeling uncertain, she looked anywhere but at him, laughing nervously. It was the house—the way the guys were acting—cooking and cleaning, making the place a home. It was giving her crazy thoughts. "Never mind. I'd probably be horrible at it anyway—"

"Oh, beautiful."

Tears flooded her eyes at the ragged tone of his voice, his unbreakable hold turning gentle as he cupped her chin and lifted her head.

"Whenever you're ready…wherever…it would be my greatest honor." He cuddled her closer, wrapping his arms tightly around her, burying his face against her neck, his body trembling. "I never dreamed of having a family of my own. I gave up that hope a long time ago because I never imagined finding anyone like you, never imagined you would want me."

His hands tightened, and he pulled back, his expression fierce. "Whether the child is mine or not, I will always treat her as my very own, and protect her with my life."

Morgan blinked away the tears that burned at the backs of her eyes and smiled up at him. "You're that sure it will be a girl?"

He stared at her for a single heartbeat, then cracked a smile that filled his entire face, happiness shining from deep within. "Yes, she will be a girl, a miniature of you—black hair and bright blue Irish eyes, full of mischief."

Morgan winced, and she shook her head. "I wouldn't wish that on anyone."

Kincade pushed her back, toppling her over until she was lying down with him hovering over her. His smile faded, his eyes churning with hunger as he reverently touched her face. "I can't wait."

Then he proceeded to kiss her until she forgot her own name. Less than a heartbeat later, they were naked. He worshiped every inch of her body with his hands and mouth until she thought she'd die of frustration.

She slipped her fingers into his dark brown, shoulder-length hair, then yanked his head back until she was sure she had his attention. "You either finish what you started, or it will be *my* turn to torture *you*."

He swallowed hard at her threat, his cock hardening even more at the thought of the pleasure of her torture, then threaded his fingers into her hair, his face hovering over hers. "Next time. If you touch me now, I won't last even a second."

Morgan shivered at the rough, growly tone of his voice. She couldn't stop the way she arched up against him, desperate to get closer. When his fingers trailed up the inside of her legs, her thighs trembled, and his smile turned devilish.

"So eager," he whispered against her lips, then he kissed her just as his fingers found her core. The gentle touch stole her breath, and a whimper caught in her throat as she arched up, demanding more. His muscular chest begged for her to explore him, and she was helpless to resist tracing the lines of his mating mark, her fingers warming at the touch. The stubble on his jaw made him look hard and dangerous.

Everything about him was sculpted perfection that captivated her from the first moment she saw him. She would never get tired of looking at him.

When he made to kiss his way down her body, she jackknifed into sitting position, wrapping her legs tightly around him, and bit his bottom lip in warning, loving the groan that rumbled in his chest. His erection rubbed at her deliciously, making thinking difficult. "You've had your chance, Cade. My turn."

Before she could put her plan into action, he twisted them, lifting her clear off the counter, his hands supporting her ass, his easy strength making her breath catch. "But where's the fun in that?"

Instead of waiting for her reply, he lifted her higher, the friction of his chest against her breasts making her squirm. His cock rubbed against her core, and she forgot what she was even going to say, too lost in the drag and pull of his hips as he brushed against her. With a throaty groan, she gripped his hair to keep herself grounded, loving that he kept it long just for her.

He ducked his head, capturing her gaze, the love in his eyes making her forget everything but him. Only then did he slide home.

"Open your eyes."

She snapped her eyes open at the husky command, not completely sure when they'd fallen shut.

Then he began moving, supporting her easily, each thrust sending her need higher and higher, hitting a spot that made her world dissolve. He quickly followed her a second later, his skin hardened like steel beneath her as he lost control. She shifted at the feel of warm stone stretching her, squirming as he continued to rock gently against her, the polished stone sending her over the edge again.

She sagged against his broad shoulders, knowing he would never let her fall, trying to remember how to breathe. She was afraid to move, afraid to trigger another orgasm and black out completely. Stone heated, melting her muscles, and she savored his warm earth scent.

The mating marks tingled and burned, sinking into her flesh, searing into her bones until something seemed to click into place. Instead of pain, the constant ache she felt when near Kincade vanished, and the relief made her go boneless. She hugged him closer.

She knew the instant he came back to the real world—his skin softened and he turned human. His hands slid up her back slowly, rubbing against her soothingly.

"Look, I'm sorry—"

"Don't you dare say it." She lifted her head, slapping her hand over his mouth, then smiled when he kissed the center of her palm. She couldn't resist leaning forward and kissing the back of her hand where his mouth rested, too smart to release him until she had her say. "Now listen here…you don't have to hide from me. When I say I love you, I mean *all* of you."

The shadows in his eyes cleared, his mouth curling against her palm as he smiled, his reply muffled against her hand. He grabbed her wrist, rubbing his thumb back and forth across her pulse, and she reluctantly lifted her hand.

"Do I get to talk now?" His eyes crinkled with amusement, and he rested his forehead against hers, his hand cupping her ass to hold her against him.

"Sure," she heaved a sigh. "If you must."

He snorted a laugh, then smacked her ass sharply, startling a yelp out of her before lowering her to the ground. "Go get ready for supper before the others come down, and I'll finish putting the table together."

At the mention of the rest of the guys, knowing she only had a few minutes, she scrambled for her clothes and scowled at him. "You distracted me on purpose."

Like he wanted her to get caught with his scent on her.

His grin was smug as he tugged up his pants and fastened them. "Any time. Anywhere."

Heat bloomed in her cheeks as she hastily yanked her shirt over her head and hustled toward the door. It wasn't that she was ashamed of what happened. The others knew what they were doing. But it was one thing for them to know and another for them to see.

She scrambled for the stairs, only to stumble to a stop at the top when she saw a trail of flower petals strewn across the hallway. She followed the path to find a stunning suite waiting. The place was immaculate, the wood floors gleaming, the bed so large she could sprawl across it spread-eagled and be nowhere near the edge. Flowers covered every surface, making it smell like a hothouse. As she looked around the room, she spotted touches from each of them, and butterflies took flight in her stomach at knowing they spent so much time and care in making her comfort a priority.

A pair of sexy boots rested on the floor, while a stunning black dress lay across the bed.

Unable to help herself, she reverently touched the silky skirt, shivering when the cool fabric slid through her fingers.

Never in a million years would she have chosen it for herself. She didn't know how to be girly and dress up.

A knock sounded behind her, and she whirled to find Draven waiting for her. But instead of his normal fighting clothes, he wore black pants and a white button-down shirt that was open at the collar to reveal a tempting expanse at his chest. His hair was swept back and done up with some goop. Then he spun for her perusal. "Do you like it?"

His words were teasing, but she saw the nerves in his eyes, and she answered honestly. "You take my breath away."

He flashed her a smile, seeming to know that she wasn't talking about his clothes. He gave her a courtly bow, watching her from under his lashes, and despite having just had sex, she felt her body soften and crave his nearness. Lured forward by the temptation to touch him, she'd just taken a step closer when he straightened and wagged a finger at her.

"If you look at me like that, we'll never make it to supper and Kincade would have my ass." Draven ran a distracted hand down his chest, and she followed the movement, loving the way his eyes flashed in warning. "I know you're probably thinking why let the fox into the hen house, but—"

"Not if I'm the fox." She prowled toward him, and he swallowed hard, his eyes widening comically as he held up his hands like a maiden trying to ward off an amorous suitor. Something about being here, or maybe finally being alone with the guys, triggered the mating marks, and the urge to claim them became increasingly urgent.

"Wait!" His voice squeaked adorably. "Into the shower. They sent me to be your handmaiden and help you dress, since none of them have any fashion sense."

"Maybe." Morgan cocked her head, then slowly shook it and pouted. "Or maybe they sent you because only you would have the self-control to not take me up on my blatant seduction."

He blinked at her owlishly, a blush sweeping up his neck and across his cheeks. He opened his mouth, then closed it, which she found totally endearing.

Deciding to give him a break, knowing the others were waiting for them, she turned and gathered the supplies resting on the bed. She paused before entering the bathroom, loving that she could unbalance him, and looked at him over her shoulder. "I can't wait to see how much you can take before I break that control."

She shut the door, hearing him mutter a curse from the other room. "Sweet Jesus, she's going to kill me."

Chapter Eight

$\mathcal{A}$s Morgan entered the kitchen, chairs scraped as the guys shot to their feet. She shifted uncomfortably under their wide-eyed scrutiny, hiding her clenched fists in her skirt as they gaped at her.

The dress clung to her curves, the slinky fabric crossing over her breasts like a wrap, dipping low to reveal her cleavage. The material hugged her waist before flaring out at her hips. The black sleeves were just a drape of fabric that fell into a light ruffle, brushing her arms as she moved.

The back of the dress reached below her knees, but the front crossed mid-thigh, leaving her legs on display. The boots were a black leather that ended just below the knees.

Unsurprisingly, Draven left her with no underwear, so only a thin layer of fabric concealed her from their hungry gazes.

How was it possible to feel insecure and sexy at the same time?

Ryder was the first to recover, shaking his head as if to wake himself. Then he strode to the end of the table and pulled out the empty chair.

Morgan smiled gratefully and took her seat. He gently pushed the chair forward by practically picking the thing up off the floor. Then he leaned close, whispering in her ear, his voice gruff, "You look beautiful."

She glanced up at him over her shoulder, pleasure warming her cheeks as she smiled at him. "You look very dapper yourself."

And he did.

While he still wore jeans, they were black. His shirt was new, the material still creased, the cotton molding to his muscular torso and slim waist. The outfit made the highlights in his brown hair all the more mouthwatering, and she itched to touch him.

As if he read her mind, he ducked his head and moved toward his seat, but not before she saw the naked hunger in his eyes. As the rest of the guys resumed their seats, she gawked at each of them in turn.

Atlas's almost silver hair was tied back, drawing attention to his pointed ears. Since the sun had set, his pale skin now had a lavender tint, but it was the slivers of dark burnt umber in his emerald green eyes that made her body hum with yearning.

The normally cold eyes held so much emotion that she had to tear her own eyes away or risk drowning in them.

The rest of his outfit…wasn't in the least bit human. The black silks were embroidered with silver flowers in a fleur-de-lis design, the details so intricate and delicate she'd swear they moved as she watched. There didn't appear to be any seams, almost as if the outfit had been woven onto him.

She was distracted when Kincade began to put food on her plate, and she finally managed to look away from the spell Atlas had cast over her.

Kincade gave her a gentle smile. "We wanted to do something special for our first night here as a family."

"Thank you." She glanced at each of them, knowing that they would never understand how much this meant to her.

The guys relaxed, as if they'd expected her to run away from them.

Foolish boys.

Conversation and good-natured ribbing began to flow around the table while the food was passed among them. Kincade looked like the lord of the manor, his gray shirtsleeves rolled up to his elbows, revealing strong forearms with a dusting of hair and just a hint of his mating marks. He wore creased dress pants and shoes that actually shone.

Ascher wasn't wearing anything near as fancy. His dark jeans were pressed, his white button-down shirt had a comfortable look that made her want to snuggle up against him.

He clenched his hand, then shook it out, pulling his arm under the table when he saw her looking.

Her brows knitted and concern flooded her.

"You're not healed." It wasn't a question.

Conversation around the table trailed off, everyone's attention zipped between the two of them.

"It's healing, but slowly." Ascher shrugged, completely unfazed. "Sometimes injuries inflicted by supernatural creatures take longer to heal."

Morgan didn't like it.

She reached for the connection between them, then sucked in a sharp breath when it felt like his veins were on fire. A second later he kicked her out. She half rose out of her seat, reaching for him. "Ascher—"

"You worry too much. The injury will be gone by morning." Of course he felt her probe. He gave her a small smile meant to soothe her, but he obviously felt her worry. "I promise. Please, let's enjoy tonight."

Only very reluctantly did she resume her seat, determined to corner him after the meal and get the truth out of him one way or another.

The silence lasted only a second when a loud crash sounded from upstairs, followed quickly by a deep, creepy chuckle, and the thud of footsteps thundering across the floor above them. The guys shot to their feet, immediately slipping into warrior mode.

Unsurprisingly, each of them pulled out weapons from somewhere on their person. Morgan was a step behind them as they rushed out of the kitchen, her own weapons appearing in her hands without thought. Kincade took the lead, silently directing the guys to split up into groups of two.

Ryder and Draven headed up the stairs and branched right, while Kincade and Atlas headed left, leaving her and Ascher to guard the stairs.

But the instant the others disappeared a crash sounded from the library. Ascher waved her back and entered cautiously on his own. She glared at his broad back, annoyed at being left behind.

But as soon as she took a step to follow him, the creak of the door under the stairs caught her attention. She whirled, expecting to find one of those monsters lurking behind her despite the wards being silent...but found nothing but air.

She cast a silent look in Ascher's direction, knowing she should call him, but hated the idea of dragging him into another fight while he was still injured. If anything in the house meant them harm, the wards would've alerted her to them long before now.

She crept down the stairs, her eyes adjusting to the florescent light, leaving most of the vegetation in shadows.

What caught her attention was a shiny coin in the middle of the walkway. The silver gleamed in the darkness, almost like it was spelled to draw her attention. She shook off its hold, magic fizzing against her skin as she stepped over it and continued to survey the room.

A small shape stepped out of the shadows across the pool from her, a man no more than eighteen inches tall. He had a full trimmed beard and a vivid green top hat that covered his shockingly red hair. He wore a tiny green vest and jacket, his buckled shoes shining even in the gloom.

"Ye not be after me money, then." He waddled more than walked as he sauntered closer. "Why invade me home if not for me treasure?"

A freakin' leprechaun.

She shook off her amazement and pursed her lips. "It's not

your home." She cocked her head as she studied him, his youthful, expressive face giving nothing away. "But you're trapped here just the same, would be my guess. You took refuge in the only safe place in the area, and the wards are keeping you protected from the monsters at the door."

His face twisted with fear and anger, his arms swinging as he strutted back and forth. "Those monstrous beasts be damned. They canna be stopped. They eat everything and anything they come across. Ye can escape, ye and yer men."

Morgan released her blades and shook her head. "We can't. The wards are weakening. If they fail and the creatures get out…we can't allow that to happen."

The little man shook his head, pity shadowing his face. "Nothing ye can do can stop the wendigo. When they turn, the monsters be insatiable. Ye'll only get yerself kilt."

Wendigo.

As much as she scrambled for information about them, she couldn't place the name as anything but an ancient myth.

"I thought they were extinct."

He shrugged. "They are'na from my world."

Morgan crouched and picked the coin off the ground. The leprechaun froze, his eyes gleaming, and he licked his lips. Maybe he really cared for their safety, but she suspected he equally wanted to keep them away from whatever treasure he had stashed away.

And she realized he must be the one who'd ransacked the house.

That he was able to pass the wards and enter the house meant he didn't intend harm.

She had to trust that.

"Ye hafta catch me ta get yer three wishes."

His voice was both lyrical and snarky.

Like he wanted her to hunt him.

"I don't need your wishes." Then muttered to herself, "I have more than enough trouble with my own magic. No need to borrow more."

She flipped the coin between her fingers, watching him follow the movement, his eyes avid, full of hunger and greed. It was a leprechaun's nature to collect shiny objects—the bigger their treasure, the stronger their magic.

She'd guess he chose to come to this world when the portal ripped open, so he could avoid having the magic sucked out of him and turning him into a more primitive version of himself. Not that she could blame him.

He was just unlucky enough to have landed here.

"Let's make a deal."

Instead of refusing, his green eyes sharpened with interest until they almost seemed to glow. Leprechauns were always on the lookout for deals, a way to charm more treasure out of the unsuspecting. Crinkles fanned out from his eyes as he narrowed them on her.

"What do ye have in mind, lassie?"

She flipped the coin again, watching it flash across the pool standing between them. Without missing a beat, the little man caught it handily, clutching it in his fist. He brought it up to his mouth, biting it as if to assure himself of its authenticity. Only when he was sure did he grunt in satisfaction, and the coin disappeared into his pockets so fast she wasn't sure where it went.

"This was a test." She was sure of it. She heard the guys above them, stomping and yelling. It wouldn't be long before they found her. She could already feel them probing the connection between them, the mating marks warming under their attention. She sent them a wave of reassurance that she was all right, and they reluctantly retreated.

She had a feeling they only allowed it because Atlas was creeping ever closer to her location, watching over her. His spicy cinnamon scent wrapped around her, offering her comfort without even trying, letting her know he wouldn't let anything happen to her.

"Aye." The leprechaun's eyes were both pleased and calculating. "Me name is Séamus."

"The deal—you can stay here, keep your treasure, and we'll protect you. In turn, I want your help with the wendigo."

A scowl scrunched up his face.

"I'm not asking you to fight, but you've been here long enough that you know their routine, and where they go to ground. Share that information with us, promise you won't harm my men, and you have a deal."

He rubbed his chin as he paced, casting her looks every now and then, clearly searching for loopholes or tricks.

"Her word is her bond. She's not one to lie, even to save face." Atlas walked out of the shadows, stopping at her side, never taking his eyes off his opponent. It didn't matter that the creature was less than two feet tall—he took any threat to her seriously.

Atlas carefully inched toward Morgan, his fingers itching to reach for his blades, but no matter how fast he moved, he would never be able to beat the leprechaun. His heartbeat thundered in his ears, and he forced his breathing to remain steady. If Morgan thought for one second he was in danger, she'd do whatever it took to protect him.

His every instinct said to throw her over his shoulder and run, but the second he blinked, the leprechaun could literally vanish. It was part of his natural, inherent magic.

The reason no one hunted leprechauns anymore wasn't because they were believed to be only a myth—the carnivorous little bastards would hunt down anyone who tried to steal their hoard and take great pleasure in consuming their flesh.

While they normally were herbivores, leprechauns were vindictive little pricks. If their treasure was at risk, they'd make an exception for those who tried to steal from them and consider it a delicacy.

"Morgan." He gently cupped her elbow and lifted her to her feet, stepping protectively in front of her. "The others are looking for you. You need to go upstairs."

Morgan looked between him and the leprechaun, her body tensing. "What's wrong?"

The little fucker gave a menacing chuckle. "Methinks he's a wee bit worried about me slaughtering ye in yer sleep. He thinks he'll be fast enough to catch me."

Which only set off another wave of maniacal laughter. The leprechaun jumped, his feet moving like he was running on nothing but air, before he landed in the same spot.

Atlas slipped his hand around Morgan's waist, pulling her back against his chest, surprised when she relaxed against him willingly. Despite the danger, the smell of sunshine rose from her skin, a bright beacon in the madness.

He refused to allow anything to take her away from him.

Refused to sink back down and lose himself in the darkness again.

"None of us are interested in your treasure," Morgan spoke, and Atlas tightened his hold, not wanting her anywhere near the damn creature.

The leprechaun snorted, as if he found her comment absurd. "Everyone wants me money."

"We're her men." Atlas tensed, poised for the creature to attack. "She's the only treasure we need. Take her from us, and we'll never stop hunting you."

The little man glared at him, not liking the threat, but Atlas meant every word, and the leprechaun knew it.

Nothing would happen to her on his watch.

Morgan softened against him, and it was all he could do to keep his focus on the leprechaun and not the warm woman he'd spent the past few months dreaming about every night.

"Do we have a deal?" Morgan repeated.

Atlas gritted his teeth, not trusting the slippery little bastard.

"Aye, ye have me word," the little man spoke grudgingly.

"Then we'll meet in the morning to discuss what has taken over the woods in this area." Morgan smiled, distracting him, and Atlas made a mistake—he glanced away from the leprechaun for just a second.

It was enough.

The little bastard vanished.

Almost faster than he could track, the vegetation around the room swayed, and a second later, Morgan was ripped out of his arms. Maniacal laughter echoed around the room as he watched in horror while Morgan fell backwards, landing with a splash into the pool, her head disappearing beneath the surface.

He had a choice to go after the little fucker or rescue Morgan.

It wasn't a choice.

Without hesitation, he dove into the pool after her.

Chapter Nine

$\mathcal{M}$organ twisted as she hit the water to avoid an epic belly flop and most likely ended up resembling a cat desperately trying to avoid a dunking in the bathtub. The water barely rippled as she went under, and only one thing came to mind…that little asshole was freaking fast!

He took her out at the knees.

She was just lucky he hadn't been armed.

She suspected he dunked her in retaliation for touching his treasure.

She could only imagine what he would've done if she'd kept it.

As she fought her way back to the surface, she froze in awe as she saw Atlas arch his body over the water and arrow through the surface to get to her. No movements were wasted, his face a mask of determination to save her.

Only she didn't need saving…she just needed him.

When he reached for her, she wrapped her arms around his neck and reached up to kiss him. For a stunned second he didn't move, and they sank deeper into the water.

Then he was kissing her back and air became unimportant.

Any control he might've had vanished. She loved she had the power to do that to him, and an insatiable hunger for more ignited low in her belly. He dragged her closer, and she automatically wrapped her legs around his waist, trusting him to keep them afloat.

He seemed to know just when her lungs began to protest the lack of oxygen, and shot them topside. As they broke the surface, she cursed the need for air, still able to taste him on her lips.

A single kiss wasn't nearly enough.

He swam them toward the edge of the pool, his arm securely around her, refusing to release her. But instead of lifting her out, he pressed her back against the edge of the pool, the chill of the smooth tiles prickled against her spine.

"Watch," he murmured in her ear, and she gulped at the husky tone.

Then he reached over her shoulder, pressing his hand flat on the surface of the floor. Magic floated in the air, and she watched as vines around the room began to stretch and bloom. Flowers as big as her fists uncurled, the bioluminescent blues, greens and reds were like a hidden world inviting her to explore, the glow turning the darkness into their own private grotto.

"It's beautiful!" she whispered, unable to tear her eyes away from the wonder. "But how?"

Atlas lifted an imperial brow. "All fae have magic of one sort or another. I can do more than just sense magic. Mine is working with plants and such. It's weak, so I'm only able to do small parlor tricks. Not really a helpful talent for a warrior."

"You're the one who put the flowers in my room." She wanted to smack herself, annoyed that she didn't make the connection sooner.

He gave a wry, self-deprecating smile, as if embarrassed by the uselessness of his gift. She cupped his face until he focused his green eyes on her, the dark umber splintering through the rich green, making her breath catch. "I fought battles to protect humans from monsters who wanted to devour them, protected the Academy from creatures of the damned who wanted to destroy it, even went to hell to try and save you. I've never done anything but fight.

"I've been beaten, stabbed, nearly drowned, and practically tortured to death. I've battled gods and almost been eaten by a fucking dragon. Never once in my life has anyone ever given me flowers." And she couldn't stop the way her insides melted. She skimmed her hands along his jaw, threading her fingers into his hair at the nape of his neck. "Do you think it's too late for me to learn how to be normal?"

"Yes." He pressed her up against the side of the pool, the heat of him nearly scalding her as he slowly lowered his head, blunting the sting of his reply. "Normal is boring, and you'll never be boring…but maybe we can begin a new life together."

He braced his hands on either side of her, blocking her in completely. Instead of being intimidated, she basked in the luxury of being alone with him. Unable to be so close and not touch him, she trailed her fingers up his wet shirt, marveling at the muscles beneath.

"You are more than a soldier," he murmured. "You deserve to be romanced." He brushed his lips lightly against hers, drawing back when she tried to follow. "You deserve more than flowers and chocolates."

This time he nipped at her bottom lip hard enough to startle a moan out of her, while his hands slid up to hold her head steady. "You deserve to be worshipped."

Any uncertainty left over from the past few months vanished.

They loved her.

Needing to be closer, Morgan wrapped her legs around him, her skirt hiking up to her waist, then nearly moaned again when his erection pressed against her core, sending a delicious shiver along her nerve endings.

"You'll have to be patient with us." Atlas drew back, resting his forehead against hers. "None of us have ever been in love. We're inept and clumsy, but you're everything to us. We can learn how to be more than soldiers…together."

"I want that more than anything." Morgan slid her hands up his chest. His wet shirt revealed more of him than it concealed, his defined muscles made her itch to explore every inch of him, but she held back, suddenly nervous.

The guys were everything to her. She didn't want to fuck this up. "Just don't give up on me."

"Never." It was a vow, his green and umber eyes darkening with promise.

Wanting more, she tugged at his shirt, and he took the hint. Grabbing the back of it, he dragged the material over his head, leaving his torso bare except for the bold Celtic knot tattooed across his upper chest. The design was a deep forest green that reminded her of his eyes, the edges shot through with a dark, liquid gold that almost seemed to be moving, similar to the mark she bore on the inside of her arm. The lines on her mark were daintier, but the colors no less vivid.

The compulsion to get closer to him burned brighter, and she wasn't able to resist feathering her fingers across his mark, watching, entranced when his eyes closed, almost able to feel his devastating yearning through their connection. Her own mark tingled in response, sending pleasure ghosting along her skin.

The dark umber in his eyes brightened and magic thickened the air. A vine slithered across the floor, wrapping around her wrists, then snaked around her waist. Her eyes widened, and she gave an experimental tug, but they held her secure.

She turned toward Atlas, but before she had a chance to question him, she was lifted clear out of the water. She gasped in surprise, twisting her hands to grab the vines, worried about toppling to the floor. She swayed, but the cords held her firmly. Vines wrapped around her middle, holding her tight, easily supporting her weight. They shifted every time she did, the cords so comfortable she felt weightless.

A petal floated past her, then another, before they began to rain down on her in shades of pink and red.

The air around her became balmy, the lights dimming to create a fairytale wonder, and she became lost in awe at the secret world he created for her. Her heart warmed at the romantic gesture, charmed he'd go to so much trouble to show her how much he cared.

He'd kept his emotions bottled tight, never letting her get too close.

At first she thought he kept his distance because she wasn't good enough.

Now she knew it was because he loved her.

Fae didn't fall in love, and they sure as hell didn't admit to having emotions. They considered it a weakness. That Atlas would do this for her, that he would bare his soul to her at the cost of his precious heritage…it meant everything.

She swallowed hard, turning to look for him, suddenly anxious and feeling more than a little vulnerable.

Only to see him pull himself out of the water in a move so effortless her breath caught. Water sluiced off him, leaving his clothes plastered to him and left nothing to her imagination. Every muscle was outlined. And when she looked lower, her mouth dried to see the outline of his magnificent erection.

To stop herself from reaching toward him, she kept her hands tangled in the vines.

She would not beg.

But she might have whimpered.

He walked toward her with a determined look, very much the dark prince ready to lay claim to his prize. Reaching behind him, he pulled out a wicked-looking blade, and her heart slammed against her ribs, but it had nothing to do with fear. As soon as he came within touching distance, she reached for him, then scowled when she remained firmly caught.

She tugged on the vines, using her advanced strength. One of the cords around her ankle snapped, but she wasn't free for more than a second when another vine wrapped snugly around her.

Morgan growled in frustration at being unable to touch him. It was like an itch she couldn't scratch.

She needed to be near him.

"Cut me down." It was a demand.

A self-satisfied smile curled the corners of his lips, his voice husky when he spoke. "No."

Then he came to a stop next to her, using his blade to quickly remove every stich of her clothes in under a minute, the tatters fluttering to the ground.

She tsked in annoyance...*what was it with men destroying her clothing?!*

Her magic rose in response to his nearness, and panic had her struggling against the vines as she desperately tried to pull it back. "You need to step away."

But instead of listening, Atlas raised a cocky brow at her. "Your magic won't harm me."

"You don't know that," she snapped, fear tightening around her throat and threatened to choke the air from her lungs.

"But I do." As he ran his fingers along the outside of her thigh, barely brushing her skin, but it had the power to steal her thoughts. "Your magic is instinctual." Then he leaned closer, his breath ghosting along her neck before he whispered in her ear. "And what you want most in this moment is me."

Smug asshole.

"You wish." Morgan snorted, closing her eyes to help her resist temptation. But if she was honest with herself, he was right. The yearning to touch him was a physical ache.

As if in agreement with her, her magic broke loose from her control and swirled in the air. She snapped her eyes open to see it settle around Atlas with a crackle. Atlas stood still under the caress as it curled along his body, tugging at his clothing. He was panting by the time the magic faded, the hunger in his eyes making him look almost feral.

She relaxed against the vines when he appeared to be

unharmed, comforted by the slight sway.

But she spoke too soon.

She watched in bemusement when a second later his fae clothing began to disintegrate, the strings unraveling to pool in a pile at his feet, leaving him bare to her gaze.

His pale skin took on the lavender tint that she loved, his body smooth, like sculpted stone, and her fingers twitched to explore him. The small movement gave her away, sending her swaying while he stood perfectly still, allowing her to look her fill, no doubt being able to tell what it did to her by the way her pulse sped up.

Atlas latched onto her ankle, steadying her, his fingers skating up the outside of her leg, brushing the undersides of her knees in a way that made her squirm. As he explored her body, he made note of what made her twitch or moan, ever patient, never rushing, until her skin became so sensitive that even the brush of air as he circled her made her tremble.

She struggled against the vines, the need to touch him a bottomless ache that burned, but he stubbornly ignored her demands for release. "You're going to pay for this."

He arched a brow at her, his lustful expression sharpening. "I certainly hope so."

Then he was standing between her legs, slipping his fingers into her hair and pulling her head back until she was looking up at him. Instead of ravishing her as she hoped, he brushed his lips against hers so lightly, the taste of him slipped away before she could savor it.

She tried to chase his lips, but his grip on her hair remained firm, the tug almost painful.

He caressed her face with his lips, as if he was memorizing her features, his sole focus on her pleasure, worshiping her in a way that made her tremble, leaving her unsure where he would touch her next.

Then he made a mistake.

He got too close.

Quick as a snake, she turned her head and struck, capturing his mouth in a demanding kiss. He stiffened like he was going to retreat, then reached out and grabbed the vines holding her wrists and pulled her closer.

The kiss turned hard, his tongue demanding everything from her. A tremor ran through him, and excitement surged at the thought of him losing control.

"Pleeeaaseee," a breathy moan escaped her.

He pulled back with a snarl, his chest heaving as he glared down at her. "Do you want me to start over?"

Morgan didn't think she succeeded in covering her whimper, and she narrowed her eyes on him, determined to get what she wanted. Magic seeped out of her, catching along the vines, and she watched, fascinated, while he got tangled up in them before he could retreat.

Vines slid up his leg, along his arms. He tugged on the vegetation as it continued to ensnare him, but he didn't fight the way she expected, only raising a brow at her in challenge.

Her magic loosened the vines' hold, allowing her enough room to finally reach out, and she greedily touched his chest. Just when she thought she had him captured, he leaned forward, his face stopping inches from her. "Male elves are taught how to pleasure their partner for hours. Do you really think I will give up my control so easily?"

He slowly shook his head, a wicked smile curling his lips. "Would you really deny me the privilege of showing you pleasure?"

She shivered at his husky tone, but something about the wording didn't sit well with her. "Male elves? What about female?"

In complete seriousness, he answered, "They train their bodies to withstand pleasure and make the experience last, so when both partners find their release, they experience *la petite mort*—a pleasure so great it is said they experience a taste of heaven."

She gulped at his confession, her breathing a little erratic, and it took all her concentration to form words. "That sounds more like torture than lovemaking."

"True, but the best kind of torture." The tone of his voice was pure honey. "The anticipation is half the fun." He leaned closer, licking the side of her neck, and she shivered, her skin so sensitive she squirmed.

"Or it will be the death of me," she muttered, her voice hoarse.

She didn't want his trained seduction. She wanted the man who threatened to ravish her against her bedroom wall. Determined to get her hands on that man, she rested her hand on his chest, right over the mating symbol. The connection between them snapped open, and if she'd been standing, she would've collapsed to the floor. An avalanche of lust practically buried her, devastating her mind and leaving her panting for air as every inch of her body tingled.

Just one touch would send her over the edge.

She knew he felt her emotions when he sucked in a sharp breath, trembling under her palm like she was stroking his cock instead of just touching his chest.

Then he locked his knees and snarled at her. "Cheat."

She gave a negligent shrug. Instead of being intimidated, desire pooled inside her, ratcheting her need up higher. The vines around her tightened, leaves feathering against her sensitive skin, and she moaned his name as her senses overloaded, "Atlas."

Nothing existed but them.

"Again." Atlas pressed his forehead against hers, his fangs peeking out between his lips.

Her eyes fluttered open, and she looked up at him in confusion, the haze of lust consuming her. "What?"

"Say it again." He nipped painfully at her lips, his control hanging by a thread, the dark umber in his eyes almost completely taking over. "Say my name again."

Morgan cupped his face, her heart hiccupping at the way he leaned into her caress, the plea in his eyes a demand she couldn't resist. "I love you, Atlas."

He sucked in a startled breath and didn't move, didn't breathe, his face so heartrendingly lost, she repeated it again and again.

When he opened his eyes, the cool, levelheaded man she expected was completely gone. What remained was all emotions, a man determined to claim his mate. With a snarl, he tangled his fingers in her hair and held her still while he entered her in one smooth thrust.

She clung to him, the vines leaving her helpless to do anything but feel. Instead of ravishing her, he did something even more devastating…he made love to her slowly and thoroughly. He kept his thrusts short and shallow, his hands and mouth worshiping her body as if he couldn't get enough of her, his focus wholly on driving her completely out of her fucking mind with lust.

When she was about to lose her shit and demand more, he released the vines from around her ankles and wrapped her legs around his hips.

And made a vital mistake.

The move allowed her a tiny bit of control—it allowed her to set the pace—and her smile turned devilish.

Turnabout was fair play.

When she tightened her legs around him, the length of him slammed into her, earning a muttered curse from him and a groan from her. Unable to stop himself, he flexed his hips with a growl, driving himself deeper. The swing did most of the work, holding her steady so they could focus on each other.

Pleasure immediately spilled through her as his hands kneaded her breasts, his mouth scattered kisses and bites along her neck.

Each time she tightened her legs, it sent him deeper and deeper, until her whole world centered him.

He growled, thrusting harder and faster, his hold turning deliciously rough, and pleasure began to spiral through her. Her lips tingled, her limbs shook, and she clawed at the vines, unable to let go without him.

"Atlas..." It was a breathless whimper, both a demand and a plea.

She couldn't catch her breath while she waited, suspended.

He lifted his head, his green and umber eyes glowing. Love shone from them so brightly her breath caught. He reached between them, touching her in a way that stole the last of the air out of her lungs. "Now."

The combination of his touch, his command, and his hard thrusts sent her over the edge. Jerking one of her hands free, and she dug her nails into his spine, shivering when he groaned. In retaliation, he leaned down and nipped the top of her breast hard enough to set her off again.

He groaned as he came a second later, and leaned heavily against her, panting against her shoulder like he didn't have the strength to stand.

After a minute he straightened, his arms sliding under her as the vines gently released their hold. He scowled at the red marks the vines left behind, gently carrying her to the edge of the pool, then walked them into the waist-high water.

She floated on her back as he began to bathe her, paying careful attention to the marks left on her skin. She was too contented to argue that she could take care of herself.

It actually felt nice to be pampered.

Until she noticed that he didn't look at her once.

The pleasant haze began to fade, and she quickly grabbed his hand to stop him.

"What's wrong?"

When he refused to look at her, she stood up, the water barely covering her breasts. Not giving a fuck about modesty, she planted herself in front of him and lifted her chin.

"Do you regret what happened?" Morgan wasn't certain she was strong enough to hear his answer if he said yes, and her stomach rolled threateningly.

"What?" His head snapped up, his eyes wide. "No, never," his tone was vehement.

Tension left her spine and she gave a sigh of relief. She cocked her head, tapping her lips as she studied him. "You enjoyed it as much as I did, so it can't be that."

His mouth tightened, his refusal to speak getting the best of her, and she smacked his arm hard enough that he lost his balance and got a good dunking.

He came up sputtering, his usual glare back in place as he slicked back his silver hair. "What was that for?"

"Ruining my postcoital glow," she snapped.

He opened his mouth, then clicked it shut.

Part of him looked almost ready to run, and she narrowed her eyes in warning. "Don't even think it," she warned. "You're not leaving until I know what's wrong."

His shoulders sagged, and he turned partially away, running a hand along the top of his head. "We barely lasted an hour."

Morgan snorted, then nearly swallowed her tongue when he glared at her. "You're serious?!" she sputtered. She felt like smacking her own forehead. "Of course you are," she murmured.

She leaned back into the water, floating on her back as she tried to keep a straight face. "Did you know having sex is not the same as making love?" She continued before he could speak, gazing up at the ceiling. "What you described was sex. What we did was make love."

When he remained silent, she tipped her head back, looking at him upside down. He was staring like he'd never seen her before, and she gave him a lazy grin. "But if you're worried about staying power, there is always practice makes perfect."

She gave a squeal when he lunged for her, wrapping his arms around her as they slid under the water. When she dragged herself to the surface, he was still wrapped around her and staring down at her with a beautiful smile, his eyes bright. "Practice, huh?"

"Mmm-hmm." She peered up at him from under her lashes, then rested her head against his chest. "But later. Morning is going to come early, and we have monsters to catch."

Chapter
Ten

$\mathcal{A}$tlas insisted he finish washing her, a contented smile playing about his lips the whole time. Then he carried her out of the pool, saying something in a musical language she could almost understand, and she watched in awe while his clothes mended themselves.

He dried her with his shirt, the silken material caressing her skin, greedily soaking up the water. Then he offered it to her, gallantly slipping it over her head. The fabric floated around her, then lengthened and tightened until she was wearing a full-length, billowing nightgown that hugged her curves and showed off her cleavage.

She touched the nightgown in awe. "Faerie blessed?

Faerie blessed clothing was sewn together with magic to transform the garment into whatever the user needed. Not only did it cost a fortune, the clothing was granted to only a few souls who were deemed worthy. As Atlas pull on his pants, she almost lost her train of thought when his ass flexed.

She bit her lip, deciding against asking what he'd done to earn the clothing. She had a feeling it was something that cost him more than sweat and blood. Atlas didn't do anything by half measures.

He turned toward her, his pants hanging deliciously low on his hips. Instead of offering his arm, he caught her behind her knees and swept her up against him, resting his cheek on the top of her head as he carried her toward the steps. She snuggled close, tracing the edges of the mating mark partially hidden under her head. The mark on her arm connecting her to Atlas no longer ached, the fire had etched the symbol into her bones then vanished, and her entire being relaxed.

He came to a stop outside her door, tightening his hold, as if reluctant to let her go. Then he sighed, allowing her to slide slowly down his front until she could stand on her own. He kissed her forehead, then stepped back, removing the temptation to crawl back up his body.

He walked down the hall, and she twisted to keep him in view, unable to resist watching the way his back muscles flexed. He halted in the shadows, waiting for her to enter her bedroom, unwilling to lose sight of her until she was safely ensconced inside.

Blowing him a kiss, Morgan opened the door, then closed it behind her. As she walked by the window, she scanned the grounds, swearing she could feel eyes on her. She stepped to the side, careful to keep to the shadows, and waited.

When five minutes passed and nothing jumped out at her, she shook her head at her over-active imagination. She turned toward the bed, more than ready to get some rest, and froze when she saw both Draven and Ryder waiting for her. The men were stretched out on the bed...or more like camped out on the opposite sides, leaving a space in the middle for her.

She didn't get the impression that they wanted to avoid touching each other, more like they were saving her the most comfortable spot.

It was also a threat.

If anyone came for her, they would have to go through them first.

The mating mark on her hand tying her to Ryder itched with the need to touch him, a compulsion pushing her to complete the claiming. She thought being with the other guys would've helped, but it only seemed to intensify her condition.

She tore her attention away from his sexy body, wanting their time together to be natural, not rushed by the mating marks.

Only to have her attention drawn to Draven as if pulled by an invisible cord. Seeing him was like a blow to the gut, triggering heat in the mark at her side, quickly spreading lust through her system that she'd just barely managed to tramp down a second ago.

Draven blinked sleepily, as if sensing she was near, then held up the blankets in invitation to snuggle down with them. The movement woke Ryder. He rolled to his side, then pushed a third pillow to the center of the bed, as if to make an even more comfortable nest for her to sleep.

Morgan hesitated for a second, gawking at the beautiful picture they made. Neither wore a shirt, their shorts riding low on their hips. While Draven's chest was slim and smooth, every muscle etched in relief that her lips tingled to trace, Ryder was broad-shouldered with a dusting of hair across his chest. It trailed down his eight-pack abs, doing little to hide the delicious muscles that begged to be touched.

They waited patiently for her, all sleepy and rumpled, and her insides turned to goo. She rubbed at the ache along her skin, knowing from experience the only thing that would ease the building heat was their touch. Hiking up her nightgown, she crawled into bed between them. Instead of pressuring her for something more, Ryder rolled to his side and wrapped her into his arms, cuddling her back to his front.

Draven didn't hesitate to twist and snuggle closer, draping himself over her. She should've felt smothered and anxious being pinned down by their arms, but the scent of warm, gooey brownies and a wild forest instantly relaxed her, the nearly insatiable lust faded, and she melted in their arms.

While the guys' hold remained firm, they sighed in

contentment and fell asleep within seconds.

Morgan fought her drowsiness, wanting to savor this moment. Despite being surrounded by danger, she'd never felt so safe or loved.

Ryder woke trapped between heaven and hell, holding an angel in his arms. Morgan's curves were plastered against him, the comforting smell of home bringing his wolf close to the surface. Her nightgown rode up during the night, leaving his hand resting on her bare hip, and once his brain processed the thought, he couldn't prevent the way his fingers tightened possessively.

Morgan groaned, shifting closer in her sleep, her ass rubbing against his cock.

But his cock was so greedy it didn't care that she was sleeping and went to full staff so fast he had to stifle his groan, all the blood flooding to parts south until his dick throbbed painfully. He froze, afraid to move, not wanting her to pull away.

It took all his concentration to keep his wolf in check and not take her right then. It would be so easy, and she smelled so tempting.

He shook his head, trying to clear it of the wolf's influence.

She deserved better than to be pounced on even before she was even halfway awake. He wanted to make it special for her, something she'd never forget. After all the commotion during the past few weeks, she deserved more from them.

From him.

And he was determined to give it to her.

He almost had himself convinced he had the restraint to pull away when Draven shifted in his sleep. When the siren reached for Morgan, his wolf surged forward, taking control completely, and all human thoughts vanished except one.

Mine.

With a vicious growl he dragged her closer, his claws lengthened, his fangs cutting into his lips. His brain kept yelling at him to pull back, but his wolf refused to listen.

Fear curdled in his gut when Morgan stiffened. Shame heated his face at the thought of her witnessing his beastly actions, and she lay frozen in fear, completely at his mercy. His stomach lurched and twisted until he thought he'd be sick. The feeling was so strong it gave his beast pause, and Ryder had no idea how to fix this clusterfuck without ruining things between them.

Morgan woke to a ferocious snarl, convinced the wendigo had managed to break through the wards. It took her brain a few seconds to realize everything was all right when she was jerked roughly against Ryder's hard chest, his claws dancing dangerously over her skin as he tightened his grip possessively.

Draven's eyes immediately snapped open, and he took in the situation at a glance. Instead of fear, he slowly pulled back his hands and untangled their legs. Despite the danger from Ryder's wolf, she immediately missed Draven's warmth.

He stood and stretched, scrubbing his fingers through his hair, his yawn so wide his jaw cracked. "First dibs on the shower."

He gave her a reassuring smile, gathered his things, and vanished. While he acted like she was perfectly safe with Ryder, she noted that he didn't go far, leaving the bathroom door open a crack.

But Morgan didn't have any doubts.

Beast or man, Ryder would never hurt her.

When she tried to roll and face him, his arms tightened around her, squeezing the air out of her lungs. "Ryder—"

"I'm sorry." He buried his face against her neck, shuddering, his hold turning gentle. "I would never have let my beast hurt you."

The desperation in his voice almost broke her heart. She reached up and wrapped her hands around his forearm where it rested across her chest. "The only one with any doubts is you."

She half-turned to look at him over her shoulder, the back of her throat burning when she saw him hesitate to meet her eyes. "Maybe you don't know it, but your beast and I are friends. Of course he wouldn't hurt me."

She'd swear she actually heard his wolf chuff in agreement.

She reached up behind her, slipping her hand around the back of his neck, allowing her fingers to thread into his hair, pleased when a rumble of pleasure vibrated in his chest. "Now you have a decision to make."

The sound stopped abruptly, and he stilled, everything about him going on alert. He swallowed hard, as if what she said next meant everything to him. "What?"

"You have to decide if you trust me."

He looked appalled, opening his mouth to reply, when she covered his mouth with her hand. "Don't just answer. Think about it. Your answer matters."

She couldn't resist brushing her fingers along the morning scruff on his face. "If you trust me—" She ignored the way he nodded, his voice muffled behind her palm. His hand came up to wrap around her wrist, but not to force her hand away, more like he needed to touch her to steady himself. "Then you don't get to shut me out. You don't get to hide behind your fear."

She lowered her hand, but he didn't loosen his hold, and she shifted to lean back against him so he wouldn't have to look at her when he answered. "Are you afraid of me?"

He snorted at the absurdity and shook his head. "Of course not."

"Even though I have the power to destroy you with just a thought?" she persisted.

"You would never hurt me." His expression became pained when he understood her point. "But that's different."

"But it isn't...not really." She lifted his hand and kissed the back of it. "Neither you nor your wolf would ever hurt me. If you can't trust yourself, then trust me."

He looked tortured. She played with his fingers to give him time to think, marveling at the textures and calluses that littered his hand.

"You don't pull any punches," he grumbled.

It was her turn to shrug, and she glanced at him over her shoulder. "I don't love just a small part of you and ignore everything else. I fell in love with everything—wolf and man. You're mine, and if you'll trust me with your beast, I'll be yours...forever, if you want it."

"I want it." He didn't even hesitate. He kissed the top of her head. "I love you."

His lips trailed down to brush against her ear, then nibbled along her neck, the sharp nip of his fangs making her moan. "I trust you," his voice was hoarse, barely audible as he whispered in her ear.

She wiggled to get closer, and felt his erection nudge her ass.

They both froze.

She reacted first, reaching behind her to cup him through his shorts. His breath whooshed out, his hips bucking against her hand, his moan turning into a growl. In response, his callused hand settled on her bare hip, skimming upward, reawakening every nerve ending along the way. Her nightgown seemed to shimmer until she was wearing a tiny baby doll top that left nothing to the imagination, tiny strings the only thing holding it closed.

He reached beneath the gown, cupping her breasts in his big, strong hands, and it was her turn to moan and squirm. Her grip involuntarily tightened around his length, and she scowled at the material separating them.

Before she could open her mouth and order him to strip, her magic rose with a hum, and she suddenly found her hand on warm flesh. The man was so huge, she couldn't wrap her hand all the way around his cock, his skin so smooth she marveled at the texture. She couldn't stop herself from stroking him, her grip firm, loving the low growl he gave against her back.

She twisted, eagerly seeking his lips with hers. His kiss was without restraint, animalistic in the way he tried to devour her. While he continued to knead her breasts with one hand, he trailed the fingers of his other hand down her stomach.

Before she had a chance to catch her breath, his fingers dipped between her legs and boldly stroked her. A pleased rumble tingled along her back when he found her slick and waiting for him.

But it wasn't enough.

He grabbed her leg, pulling it back so it rested over his thigh, giving him room to shove his knee forward, opening her up for him to do anything he wanted to her. He didn't waste any time, his fingers spearing her deep, setting up a rhythm that made her forget how to breathe.

She ran her fingers up along the length of him, using her fingernails to gently tease him. He paused for a second, shivering at the threatening caress, then bucked against her. The length of him settled between her legs so near her core she could feel the heat of him, and she arched against him, wanting more.

Wanting all of him.

When she angled him toward her entrance, he grabbed her hand, pulling it in front of them, then threaded their fingers together and wrapped her up in a giant bear hug. She tore her mouth away from his, panting with need, looking up at his glowing brown eyes in question.

"Trust me?"

She didn't even think twice. "Of course."

"My beast wants to lay claim to you this way." He nipped at her shoulder, lust darkening his features when she shuddered, and she arched her neck in the need for more. "But in order for me to control myself, you can't move." His lips whispered down her neck, biting and sucking as he made his way back up. "If you move, my wolf will become more dominant, more aggressive. I need—"

"I trust you." She turned, catching his lips in a quick, hard kiss that was over too fast for her taste. His need to dominate was instinctual, something he couldn't control, not without denying part of his soul.

She couldn't do that to him.

She refused to deny him anything he needed.

She barely finished speaking before his arms tightened around her like bands and he surged into her with one powerful thrust. There was a pinch of pain at the intrusion, then he held still, allowing her to adjust to him. She could tell waiting cost him by the slight tremor that ran through him.

Instead of feeling trapped, or a body used to slake his lust, she knew from his reaction that he'd never been with anyone else in this way.

She was special to him.

His mate.

Warmth spread through her at the thought, and she shifted her hips, needing him to move. He immediately tightened his grip, his hold almost bruising. He wasn't kidding when he said he needed to dominate. She doubted he could control it. He was trusting her to keep herself safe from harm by following his instructions.

She made herself go completely still, and his hold softened, turning almost loving…and yet he still didn't move. Frustration began to build, the feel of him stretching her a delicious ache that was driving her insane, when a devious idea made her want to laugh.

She tightened her internal muscles around him, nearly groaning when she felt his cock jump, hitting her just right and sending a spark of pleasure shooting through her limbs. His fangs immediately came to rest along her shoulder, biting down hard enough to be a threat, and her muscles tightened around him involuntarily, unable to control the demand for more pleasure.

He surged forward with a snarl, sending another wave of pleasure streaking along her limbs, and a low, tortured groan bubbled out of her. The sound seemed to shatter his control and he pounded into her. He reached down to where they were joined, touching her lightly, as if warning her not to move, testing her resolve, daring her to disobey.

When her hips shifted of their own accord he would stop, then slowly start all over, until all she knew was him and where they were connected. Being unable to move should've been frustrating as fuck. Instead, the lack of control allowed her to let go and simply feel.

In less time than she thought possible, her orgasm ripped through her so strongly her vision dimmed. She was vaguely aware of his roar, felt him swell inside her, pressing in just the right spot to trigger a second orgasm.

She lost her breath for more than a few seconds. His brutal hold loosened, his hands running soothingly along her body, rousing her from where she hovered between awareness and sleep. When she shifted, closing her legs, a groan from sore muscles caught her unaware. When she would've rolled away, Ryder grunted and clutched her close—this time more in desperation than to establish dominance. The drag of his cock felt heavenly inside her, and she groaned when another orgasm threatened.

"Don't move." He ran his hands along her arms in soothing strokes, but the strain and slight panic in his voice had her stiffening.

"What's wrong?" Not that she was complaining, but being stuck hovering on the edge of another orgasm was almost painful. She held perfectly still, waiting for him to answer, trembling against the urge to move.

Chapter
Eleven

*D*raven hovered in the bathroom doorway, watching Ryder claim Morgan, and it was the sexiest fucking thing he's ever seen. It was all he could do not to reach into his pants and stroke himself while he watched.

He knew he should turn away, give them their privacy, but it was like he was compelled to watch, partly because of a tiny thread of worry that Ryder might lose control.

When she came, he nearly spilled himself in his pants.

He adjusted himself, wincing at the aching pressure, ready to close the door when he heard her strained question. He couldn't stop himself from yanking open the door and hurrying across the bedroom. Ryder's eyes were wide, fear darkening them, and Draven immediately understood the problem.

He lay down at the edge of the bed, a bit sad to see the gorgeous baby doll nightgown still covered the important bits, then leaned forward until his face was next to Morgan's. Pleasure and confusion clouded her deep sky-blue eyes, but a hint of anger turned the color almost violet. "He's never allowed himself to make love to anyone, never allowed his wolf such freedom. What's happening is totally normal. It's called knotting, where his cock swells after his orgasm."

"Fuck..." Ryder brushed his face against Morgan's hair,

embarrassment turning his cheeks red. "I never thought—"

Morgan chuckled, a snort escaping her, and Ryder's mouth snapped shut with an audible click, then his eyes closed as if he was in pain…or pleasure.

"Give it ten minutes or so and the swelling will go down." Though he knew he should keep his trap shut, he couldn't. The need to touch her was almost unbearable. "Or…"

"Or?" Morgan's laughter subsided, her eyes narrowing as if suspecting a trick—*smart girl.*

"Orgasm." He licked his lips, suddenly wondering about the wisdom of his plan. "If you have another orgasm, it will appease his beast, and you'll be released."

Instead of being pissed off at the intrusion, turning into a possessive beast like he had this morning, Ryder glanced at him over Morgan's shoulder and gave him a nod.

Giving him permission to join them.

Only then did Draven second-guess his scheme to get close to Morgan.

Though he was desperate to touch her, he didn't want it to be this way…not as a means to an end. He'd been watching her when she was near, casually touching her, observing her reaction to his siren's touch.

Seducing people was like breathing to his kind.

But beyond a smile or a little flirting, she didn't seem affected by his darker nature. Her reaction was so outside his norm, his siren curse so much a part of him, he didn't know who he was without it. Instead of seducing her, he stood back and struggled to get his bearings.

And falling a little bit more in love with her each day.

He could manipulate people's emotions with nothing more than a touch or a carefully worded suggestion, but she never once pulled away or doubted him.

Not once.

She baffled the living shit out of him, and he would do

anything in his power not to scare her off, anything to protect her from the demons that tormented him.

She only had to be near the guys for the lust surrounding them to explode off the charts—enough to keep his hunger in check. Since she'd claimed him, he'd discovered just being near them could sustain him. Unfortunately, the demon he carried was a ravenous beast, tearing his insides apart, enraged at having her near and not giving in to the temptation to slake his lust. A dark voice whispered it would be so easy to seduce her, and it was all he could do to resist.

He needed her.

Not just for the hunger, not just for the sex.

He needed her to feel whole.

He would not ruin the fragile emotions between them over lust.

He wanted it all—he wanted her love.

And tricking her was not the way to do it.

He would not give in to the dark cravings, even if it killed him.

Morgan watched the playful sparkle in Draven's sea-blue eyes turn turbulent, the darkness from his past drawing him away from her. Not about to lose him, she quickly cupped his face and kissed him, pouring all her love into it.

Everything about him stilled.

She didn't even think he was breathing as she gently traced her tongue along his lips, the need to deepen the kiss like a craving. Fuck, she knew he was a siren, but what she felt for him came purely from within her.

She had the ability to withstand magic, but he'd never once tried to seduce her or use his magic on her when she was unaware.

Not once.

She pulled away and saw his shattered eyes bleeding so many

emotions her heart cracked. She skimmed her fingers across his brow, smoothing out the furrows, wishing she could fix all the fissures in his soul. "I see you. Not your demons, not your past. Just you, the man underneath. The man I adore."

When he flinched, she slipped her fingers into his hair, holding him tight, able to feel him pulling away from her. "I've kept my distance because I thought you needed time to sort out your feelings, but maybe I was wrong. I love you." She rested her forehead against his. "I've always loved you. Siren or man…you are mine."

"By the gods." A shudder went through him, and he searched her eyes, seeking the truth, almost like he was afraid if he blinked she would vanish.

"For a siren, you seem to have forgotten how this orgasm thing works. Touch first." Ryder grabbed Draven's hand, placing it on her bare thigh. "Now kiss her."

Draven gave a tortured groan, his fingers biting into her thigh, then his mouth was on hers. Maybe she should be embarrassed about being mostly naked between the two of them, but she couldn't, not when everything felt so right.

Draven's hands moved up, skimming along the silky material so lightly she shivered, his kiss turning gentle, as if he was savoring every moment. He tugged on the ties closing her nightgown and slowly pulled the bows free. The silken material ghosted along her skin as it fell open, exposing her body to him.

Then she felt Ryder trace his fingers lazily along her hip, slowly pulling up the nightie until his warm palm rested against her flesh. She moaned, still able to feel him fully erect inside her, and she resisted the urge to squirm, the heat building through her again.

Draven kissed his way down her neck, then took the tip of her breast in his mouth, sucking hard, and she fisted his hair, holding him close, needing him to keep her grounded. At the same time, Ryder reached between her legs, touching her intimately. His fingertips were light, more of a tease, but the combination short-circuited the rational part of her brain.

She reached back, raking her fingers along Ryder's thigh and hip hard enough to make him surge into her, and they both groaned. His touch firmed, and pleasure sizzled through her veins. Draven reached for her other breast, his grip strong as he learned her shape. Needing to give him pleasure, she reached between them to cup the length of him through his pants, and he flexed against her, biting down hard on her neck.

And she was helpless to do anything as an orgasm began to tingle along her limbs.

"That's it." Draven whispered to her, pulling back to watch her. "Let me watch you come."

She couldn't stop her hips from rocking against Ryder.

He growled as she tightened around him, his cock hitting her just right to send her over the edge. Her vision darkened, and she floated on a cloud of bliss. Her palm tingled, and she'd swear she could feel the mark stitch itself into her very bones. It burned for a few seconds, then the constant ache nibbling at her flesh went dormant again.

A murmur of male voices roused her from deep euphoria. By the time she had enough energy to crack her eyes open, it was to see Ryder give her a gentle smile and slip out the door.

"Where's he going?" she grumbled, too tired to do anything but roll onto her stomach, utterly relaxed for the first time since she could remember.

"Breakfast." Draven grabbed her ankle and gave it a playful tug. "Time for a shower."

"Mmmm." She kicked out at him with her other foot, and he immediately released her and leapt out of the way. "Go away."

Before she could react, he grabbed her ankle and gave a good yank.

"Ach!" Right before she would've face-planted on the floor, he hiked her up and slung her over his shoulder. He marched into the bathroom and nudged open the shower stall, flipped on the water, then shoved her inside. Water hit her in the face, and she sputtered, pushing back her wet hair to glare at him. "What the actual fuck?!"

It was his smug smile that sent her over the edge.

Something must have showed on her face, because his smile fell, and he hastily took a step back. But not fast enough. She lunged forward, grabbed his shirt and yanked.

He landed in the shower next to her with an oomph, water pelting down on the back of his head and pouring down his face, then spilling down his shirt, plastering it against him in a way she suddenly found fascinating.

"You're asking for trouble, babe." He slicked his hair back with a crooked smile. "Are you sure you can handle it?"

Though he wore a teasing smile, a serious undertone haunted his voice, and her playful mood evaporated. No matter what she said or did, he'd never be convinced she wasn't influenced by his siren abilities. It would continue to fester, and the darkness in him would grow.

"Let's do this." She rolled her shoulders, then lifted her arms like a prize-fighter and beckoned him with a "bring it" gesture. "Hit me with your best shot, siren. Let's prove once and for all that I love you of my own free will."

He only blinked at her, his mouth opening and closing in a kind of a silent stutter as if choking on his words, before he finally managed to speak.

"You don't know what you're asking," he whispered, his voice so hoarse she barely heard him over the shower.

"Maybe." She lifted her chin and narrowed her eyes at him. "But you'll always wonder, always doubt. I want you to be happy. If we need to do this to make that happen, then hit me with your best shot."

When he blinked at her owlishly, she dropped her arms and decided to force his hand.

"Water is your element, yes?" She wished she wasn't naked,

feeling a little bit at a disadvantage, then shrugged it off. She'd do whatever it took to make him finally see—and believe—the truth. She stepped farther under the stream of water, temptingly close to him, but stopped short of touching. "Show me."

He grabbed her arms, switching places with her until she was under the spray, warm water cascading down her body. His fingers lingered against her skin, giving her one last caress before he stepped back. Her skin tingled, and she was conscious of him studying her, the mating mark demanding she claim him. While the heat remained in his eyes, it was banked.

"You're sure?" The catch in his voice, like his whole future rested on her answer, pulverized her heart.

She didn't even hesitate. "Yes."

With one last, searching look, he yanked his drenched shirt over his head, tossing it outside the shower stall, where it hit the floor with a loud splotch. Then his smooth, muscular chest was on full display, and she licked her lips, almost able to imagine how he would taste.

Even as she watched, his skin darkened to a light blue tinge. It shimmered slightly under the water, as if catching rays of sunlight. His black hair was darker, wilder. If possible, his blue eyes became even more vivid, as if they glowed from within from pure lust.

The need to touch him burned through her. She even lifted her foot to follow through with the compulsion before she caught herself. She shook her head to help clear away the lust—fat lot of good that did—and gave him a tight smile. "See? No problem."

Instead of answering, he lifted his hand, and pointed a finger at her. Her brows furrowed in confusion, and she squinted as she studied him...and that's when she felt it. Little droplets of water began a slow slide across her skin, warming and cooling at his command until she felt his touch everywhere.

When the water cupped her breasts, she bit back a groan, and she'd swear to the gods that it was him. Beads of water no longer hit the floor but remained suspended in air before wrapping around her. Every touch, every caress a seduction.

A whisper of fingers trailed down her back.

If she dared to close her eyes, she'd swear that he was right behind her, his fingers massaging her scalp.

Water twisted together to become a stream, the touch of hot and cold started from her fingertips and worked up to her neck until every inch of her skin was sensitized. When he began again at her toes and guided the stream of water up her legs, brushing along her ankles, caressing the backs of her knees, even tracing along the insides of her thighs, it was all she could do to lock her legs to keep them from buckling.

Then he was touching her between her legs, a gentle stroke that sucked all the air out of her lungs. She let out a tortured groan, and almost gave in to the temptation to close her eyes and just enjoy the attention.

She gritted her teeth, and it took all her concentration to push away the sensations. The magic sizzled in the air between them, the water sliding off her and splashing to the floor as she broke the spell he wove around her.

She nearly cried out at the loss. She might even have whimpered, but she managed to stay on her feet and not fling herself at him like a hussy. "Are you satisfied?"

Because she sure as hell wasn't!

The loss of him left her feeling achy and alone, and she realized it was the same thing he probably felt after his encounters with others while he fed. She didn't like knowing he was so alone and isolated from the world. Sure, he had the guys, but that wasn't enough.

He gave a slow nod, still a little uncertain, and she wanted to smack herself for not thinking of it sooner. She smiled, and something in her expression made him back up a step.

"Do you trust me?" She held out her hand, palm up, and waited.

He looked nervous, but it was the small spark of hope in his eyes that made her breath catch.

"Always." Then he placed his hand in hers.

He didn't pull her closer, just stared at her and waited.

Morgan prayed she knew what the hell she was doing. She reached out with her other hand and placed her palm over the mating mark on his hip, connecting them. The pair of koi fish almost felt like they were moving for a second, as if eager for her touch. She closed her eyes and let herself fall into the darkness. Then she took all her love, how he made her laugh, how she felt when he called her babe, every scrap of emotion like a warm ball of light and tossed it at him.

He stiffened, his breath caught, and she opened her eyes to see that his were closed. His eyes were moving, as if he was searching through every emotion, every feeling.

It felt like an eternity later when he finally opened his eyes again.

The blue in them blazed so bright her breath stuttered in her lungs. Then he cupped her face, pressing her back against the cool tile behind her, his body surrounding hers. "You love me."

"Like I've been telling you since forever." Morgan rolled her eyes. But any playfulness vanished a second later, and she grabbed his wrists. "I've *never* had any doubts. Not once."

"You love me." His voice was hoarse, his eyes tracing her face almost reverently, his hands shaking slightly, and she slipped her arms around him.

The awe on his face made the back of her throat ache. "I love you."

The words barely left her mouth before he was kissing her. His lips were gentle and slow as he explored her, almost as if he'd never kissed a girl before her. For a siren rumored to have had his way with nearly every girl in the Academy, she found his bashfulness around her endearing.

He made her feel like she was the only one who ever mattered to him.

He pulled away, his chest heaving, then wrapped his arms around her and swung her around in the shower with a whoop of pure joy. The water seemed to freeze midair, tiny diamonds sparkling around them.

She wrapped her legs around his hips, his pure joy contagious. He watched her face as he leaned closer, then he was kissing her like his survival depended on it. She expected him to take her hard and fast, but he worshipped every inch of her body with his lips and hands, using the water to bring her right to the edge, but refusing to send her over.

When he moved to kneel before her, she knelt with him. "No more waiting."

She reached for his pants, struggling with his belt for a second before freeing his erection, and she marveled at the silken, heated feel of him. He leaned his forehead against her shoulder, his groan guttural. Instead of waiting for him to struggle out of his drenched jeans, she climbed up him and wrapped her arms and legs around him.

He cradled her gently, and she watched in awe as the shower stall filled with water. In seconds, they were weightless, cocooned in their own private world, only their heads and shoulders remaining above the surface. The water wrapped around her in a giant caress, cupping her breasts, licking at her ankles and behind her knees, and nibbling along her back and neck.

"Draven…" Her plea was hoarse and needy.

"I'm here." He cupped her face, staring at her intently as he gently pushed his way into her. He stilled only when he was seated fully inside her, leaving her feeling full and achy. "I'm not going anywhere."

Then he began to move. The water held them suspended, whispering kisses along her skin. When it reached between their bodies, she couldn't hold back any longer and screamed his name. Draven's roar was drowned out as the water dropped away from them and the shower began to drain almost as quickly as it filled, leaving her clutching him.

He gently lifted her in his arms, the water drying off them in seconds.

They didn't get far when the koi fish etched on her hip began to burn like it was searing onto her very bones. But instead of fading away, it was like a puzzle piece clicked into place and the rest of the mating marks flared to painful life, her bones feeling like they were being infused with molten steel.

Draven grunted, then landed on his knees cradling her in his arms, as if to shield her, and she knew he was feeling the same pain. Her vision darkened, her body too distracted by the pain to remember how to function, the marks feeling so heavy she couldn't move.

Then like a rubber band snapping, the pressure that had threatened to shatter her body as easily as glass simply vanished. After a heartbeat of silence, the rest of the guys were in her head as the mating connections were blown wide open.

Emotions and thoughts flooded her, each of the guys projecting so loudly her head throbbed. Grabbing her skull, she gave a sharp whistle, and another, and another, until they fell silent. They were still there, but the force of them was muted. Without even having to see them, she knew the guys were charging up the stairs. And a few seconds later the door burst open, and she found herself snatched away from Draven.

Ryder was the first to reach her, yanking a blanket off the bed to wrap her up in the warmth of his arms. He sat on the bed, pulling her onto his lap like he had no intention of letting her go again. Ever.

"What just happened?" She blinked up at all of them, her skin still sensitive under the mating marks. The etchings looked the same, but they felt different…deeper.

Permanent.

Kincade knelt at her feet, his face softening as he looked up at her, and it scared the bejesus out of her. "What's wrong?"

Ascher grabbed her hand and gave a squeeze, while Atlas and Draven gathered closer.

It was Kincade who spoke. "Nothing's wrong. The mating marks are there to bind us together. It helps the group work as a more cohesive team, the compulsion in them binding the warriors to the witch to keep her protected. But sometimes, when there is a strong emotion like love among them, the connection deepens. It's so damn rare that it only happens once in a hundred pairings."

"And it usually takes decades, if it happens at all." Atlas tucked a strand of hair behind her ear, allowing himself a second to caress her neck before he pulled away. The action shocked her, especially since the dark part of him was muted during the day, the reserved elf never allowing himself to show emotions of any kind. "It allows us to communicate with each other. You'll have to learn how to control the volume and how to turn it off and on if you ever want peace or even a modicum of privacy ever again."

"It also gives the whole team the ability to fight as one unit," Ryder murmured. "We'll know where everyone is at any given time." His pleasure was echoed by a small rumble from his beast.

"You can even hear and see through another team member's eyes with enough practice." Draven grabbed a shirt and pulled it over his head. There was a contentedness to him now, a calm that had always been missing. "I think the only thing missing was for you to complete the connection among us."

Her mouth dropped open, and she glared at each of them. "Why the hell didn't anyone tell me?"

The guys exchanged a glance, and Ryder pursed his lips, answering for everyone. "We thought you knew."

She huffed out an annoyed breath, clutching the blanket covering her nakedness. "Is that why you've been avoiding me the past few months? Because you were waiting for me to start the process? I ran around practically naked in front of you morons to get your attention."

"We wanted to give you a choice." Kincade growled at her,

annoyance making his eyes a wintery green. "We wanted to give you time to adjust to your new position."

"Next time just use your words. It was like you all took a vow of fucking chastity." She pushed away from the guys, stomping away from them to rummage around in her bag. "The mating marks were getting pretty painful with their demand to be completed."

"What do you mean?"

When she turned, Atlas stood in her way, demanding an answer.

"Exactly like it sounds." She clutched her clothes to her chest, suddenly uncertain in the face of his harsh expression. "The marks were driving me insane back at the Academy. The need to be close to you morons was verging on being painful, but ever since we arrived, it's gotten worse."

The guys each looked at each other, as if silently discussing the issue, and it was all she could do not to kick their individual asses, and she growled between her clenched teeth, "Words, people."

"How do you feel now?" Ryder edged in front of her, blocking out the rest of the room.

Instead of answering right away, Morgan cocked her head and took stock. The markings were silent, no longer aching. Going on instinct, she pressed her fingers against the dew-covered metallic spiderweb that spread across her lower palm and up the wrist of her left hand, connecting her to Ryder.

The almost-embossed-metal strands thrummed under her touch.

Seconds later, Ryder's emotions poured into her brain.

Pure, unadulterated terror.

She reached for him, afraid the fear would swallow him whole, and he smashed her against his chest.

"The marks only hurt when a threat is near," he rasped. "Something out there means you harm."

Chapter
Twelve

"*I*'m not sure why this is such a big deal." The guys had barely allowed her time alone to dress. She slipped into the bathroom, but they refused to let her even close the door. Now everyone was gathered around the breakfast table, all eyes on her, and she was starting to feel cornered.

"It's not like I haven't been in danger a hundred times before."

Ryder was making pancakes, while Atlas created a mixture of nuts, wildflowers and mushrooms and a small cup of dandelion tea. She was fascinated that all the guys seemed to know how to cook. For some reason, she found it incredibly sexy.

As she shoveled another forkful of food in her mouth, she studied the others as unobtrusively as possible. They were chatting with each other, passing around the food, none of them the least bit jealous.

Like they were family.

Just as they put the last of the food on the table, a bottom cupboard on the other side of the kitchen opened silently. The guys didn't seem to notice when the leprechaun calmly strutted out.

Only when he gave a tuneless whistle did the guys whirl.

They tensed but didn't pull their weapons.

Séamus climbed up into the seat at the opposite side of the

table from Morgan.

Atlas was the first to move, setting a small tray in front of the leprechaun.

The small man licked his lips greedily, then proceeded to shovel food in his mouth faster than her eyes could track. Less than a minute later, he sucked on his fingers, gave a pleased sigh, and patted his belly before picking up his drink and downing it in one gulp.

After a large belch, he relaxed back in his chair, and still none of the guys around the table moved.

"What can you tell me about the wendigo and how we can defeat them?" Morgan prompted him.

"They are soulless beasts called from hell. They—"

"Called by who?" Atlas interrupted.

"By the very people trapped within the wards." Séamus looked at him like he was an idiot. "Wendigo are soul-bound by the ones who called them. By day, they are human, but at night, the creatures rule."

"The neighbors." Morgan said their name like a curse and shoved away from the table to pace. "I knew there was something wrong with them. Who the fuck are they?"

Kincade shoved away his plate. "My best guess is they are what's left of the original coven."

"What do you mean?" Morgan paused mid-step to stare at him.

"The witches must have called—"

"Yeah, you don't have to tell me." She waved a hand. "Evil witches…blah, blah, blah. What I meant is *why* are they still here?"

"The witches must have lost control, and the neighbors are what's left of the coven."

"Remember, they be soul bound. They're infected and no longer human." Séamus looked at his empty plate a little mournfully, then pushed it away. "They're bound to hell now, which means they've been infected by pure evil."

"Which means they can't leave with the wards intact." Morgan sighed, then rubbed a hand down her face. "The same wards that I strengthened when we first arrived. When darkness fell, the wendigo emerged, saw the wards and became enraged and attacked."

Morgan glanced at Ascher, remorse slashing her insides to ribbons. "You were injured because of me."

Ascher snorted, then calmly rolled up his sleeve to show her he was completely healed. Not even a hint of a scar remained. "They attacked because they're evil creatures from hell. And the huge numbers of missing people are proof they would've come after us eventually."

"And they'll come for ye tonight." Séamus pushed away from the table and hopped to the ground. "They're starving. Wendigo have an insatiable hunger that can never be satisfied. Eating the flesh of their prey while still alive and juicy, staves off the need, but it only holds off their cannibalistic nature for a few hours at most. They'll even crack open bones to suck out the marrow."

The leprechaun's expression was a little ghoulish, like he relished the telling. Despite having seen him eat his nuts and flowers with such relish, Morgan's instincts screamed beware. "How do you know?"

"A lot of people have gone missing. They can't hide all those bones. But fewer and fewer people venture into these woods. The animals are all gone. The wendigo are starving, going feral, eating each other. Ye're like a buffet to them. While they might crave humans, they'll hunt yer kind. They hunger for the supernatural, because yer energy and magic sate them longer. It's the only thing that will satisfy their hunger, even if only for a while. They won't be able to resist ye." Séamus gave a casual shrug and headed toward the cupboard. "There's a warren of caves and caverns a few miles from here where they toss their bones. The grounds are riddled with them."

When he grabbed the open door, he turned back toward her.

"Good luck on yer hunt. I really hope ye survive. Be wary of the neighbors. They were tainted long before they were turned." He tapped his nose, like he could smell the bad souls even at a distance.

"You don't want to join us?" She was a little surprised, having assumed he'd want to protect his treasure.

"I've been here long enough to ken I'm no match ta them. I've tracked them to the caves, but I'm no good in a fight against the beasties. Be careful." Then he turned and entered the cupboard, vanishing from one second to the next.

"It's best that he left." Atlas opened the cupboard to verify that he was gone, then turned to face her. "You can't trust him."

Her brows furrowed. "We have a deal."

"Leprechauns are considered Irish fairies…derived from the Tuatha De Danann. They're known tricksters." Atlas flipped his knife, the blade appearing as if he'd pulled it from out of nowhere.

"Aren't you a Tuatha De Danann?" Morgan couldn't resist pointing out.

"Exactly." He spoke with a perfectly straight face. "That's why I know. Leprechauns are like the coins that they so value. While one side might be lucky, there's always a balance in everything. The other side is cursed."

"Explain." If Séamus was a threat, she needed to know. She would not put her men in danger. She'd come too far to lose him.

"If you catch a leprechaun, you are granted three wishes—luck."

"And if you fail?" She wasn't sure if she wanted to know the answer. If she'd learned one thing over the last few months, it was that nothing was as it appeared. Usually the most innocent-looking were the most vicious.

"Their demons are more real than most." Atlas's green eyes darkened, his beauty almost alien when he stared at her so directly. "Their darker nature must be fed as well."

"But he kept his word by showing up today and giving us the

information he promised." She didn't understand why he'd do that if he wanted them gone.

Atlas closed his eyes briefly, as if he was praying for patience. "Once a Tuatha De Danann gives their word, they never go back on it."

"And I promised him he'd be safe if he helped us." Morgan began clearing off the table, no longer hungry. "None of us have any interest in his treasure, so this is a non-issue."

She dumped the dishes in the sink, then ran the water and added soap. "We need to focus on the bigger picture…we need a plan for how to deal with the wendigo."

Ryder nudged her aside and sank his hands in the warm, soapy suds, impervious to the scalding water. Before she could reach for the towel to dry, Draven snatched it away with a smirk, then playfully fluttered the towel in her direction to shoo her away.

Ascher was the one who stood and pulled out her chair again, waiting patiently for her to sit. Only after he pushed her in did he speak. "I think Séamus is correct. We killed two of those beasts, but not without taking a lot of damage. But when we searched for the bodies, they were already gone."

"You think they just got up and walked away?" Kincade looked skeptical.

"Impossible." But Morgan heard the doubt in her own voice. "We practically turned one of them inside out. There was no way that anyone could've found, much less picked up all the pieces in just a few minutes."

"The leprechaun did mention that they are soul-bound," Atlas mused. "To kill the creature, we will have to kill the host as well, or they'll continue to return. Death isn't permanent for them."

"Are there any books in the library that might help?" She glanced at the guys as she pushed back her chair. Though she'd hate to put more people in danger, the last thing she wanted to do was risk the lives of her men by fighting an army of indestructible creatures conjured from hell. They needed backup. "Did we get communications up?"

"The cell towers in the area don't reach this far." Draven diligently dried a pan before placing back on the stove. "I took a look at the communications, but everything was torn out. Whatever magic kept it working wore off a long time ago."

"And I don't know enough about magic yet to get it up and running." Morgan grimaced, hating the feeling that she was letting the guys down. "Will the truck make it back into town?"

Kincade was already shaking his head. "Not without some serious work. The vehicle might make it to town, but I doubt it'll make it back."

Morgan nodded, the tasks that needed to be done piling up in her mind. "Someone needs to fix the truck. I want to check out the library. If the witches are the ones who summoned the wendigo, maybe they left some information behind on how to stop them. I also want to strengthen the wards again."

"I want to check out this cave system." Kincade rose to his feet, stretching his arms over his head, but she wasn't fooled by his relaxed attitude.

He wanted to hunt.

"We need a plan first. We have no way of knowing if those creatures actually live in those caves, or if they crawl out of hell every night. What if they sleep in them during the day? Or if the neighbors have the caves watched and notice us trespassing?" She walked toward the door, planting herself in front of it. "We have surprise on our side right now, but we need to assume they're watching us."

Kincade sighed, the fight going out of him. "You're right. We'll work in pairs. You and Ascher will stay in the house. Search the library and fix the wards."

"I'll search the grounds in my wolf form." Ryder turned away from the sink, drying his hands on a towel.

"Since I don't know anything about vehicles, I'll go with you." Atlas sheathed his weapon and pushed away from the wall where he'd settled during the discussion.

"Which leaves me and Kincade to fix the van," Draven grumbled, casting her a pleading look as he lifted his hands. "I don't do grit and grime. You know I work better with water, right?"

Morgan shivered, intimate flashes of their time in the shower heating her body, and she snorted at the twinkle in his eyes. "Dork."

Ascher sat in the study, absently turning pages of the latest book in his lap, but the words kept swimming in and out of focus. He leaned his head back, rubbing his tired eyes, the pounding headache he woke with intensifying, like something was trying to crawl out of his skull.

The only thing that seemed to make the sensation bearable was Morgan.

Unable to resist the temptation of being close to her, his beast crept forward—until a crippling pain blasted through his insides. Fire erupted along his veins, like his hellhound was burning away his flesh, and he gave himself over to the need to shift. He slid off the chair, dropping to the floor on all fours, before his legs gave way and sent him sprawling.

As if his pain called her, Morgan burst into the room, her hair flying behind her. Magic leaked from her, raw power seeping out from her aura, as if she forgot to turn it off when she gave the wards another boost. She dropped to her knees behind him, cradling the great beast's head in her lap, running soothing fingers along the top of his head.

"What the hell just happened?" Her face was scrunched up adorably in her concern, and he licked her hand to show her he was all right.

But he wasn't sure.

The change usually only took seconds, just a flash of heat he usually welcomed.

"It's that bite." She reached for his leg, running her hands over his foreleg, and he leaned into her, her touch easing the ache that seemed to have settled into his bones and wanted to rip him apart.

And he very much feared what she said was true.

Something from the bite had infected him.

His beast was impervious to diseases and sickness.

But he'd healed.

Besides sore muscles and a headache, he'd been fine.

So what had he missed? He searched his beast form for any sign of infection or injury and found nothing. And he very much feared whatever was wrong with him was only going to get worse.

If he told Morgan, or if she even suspected he was hurt, she'd order him to leave the coven, and he couldn't allow that. The witches needed her to take down the wards. No way in hell would Morgan do it willingly.

And there was no fucking way he would allow them to sacrifice her.

He would leave over his dead body.

Unfortunately, he very much feared it might come to that.

Chapter Thirteen

$\mathcal{M}$organ shook her head with an exasperated sigh when Ascher staunchly refused to turn back into human form. The bastard could understand her perfectly well but remained in his hellhound form to avoid talking to her. When she tried to connect with him using the mating marks, the only thing she could understand was that he believed he could protect her better this way.

Stubborn beast.

The search of the library was a bust.

Whatever information the witches uncovered, they took it with them when they left.

Giving up, she headed toward the kitchen to begin dinner, wanting to surprise the guys. Since she didn't know how to even boil water, she put together sandwiches, then shoved them into the basket on the counter.

As she headed out the door, Ascher on her heels, a snort escaped her at the ridiculous picture they must present. "I'm fucking little red riding hood."

A sense of déjà vu struck her as she exited the house, and she scanned the tree line, searching for who was watching them. It almost felt like a game. She pushed out her senses, searching for any threat, but found nothing.

Again.

It was beginning to piss her off.

Either something was watching them…or she was losing her mind.

Shaking off her frustration, she sauntered toward the vehicle, noting Draven and Kincade were still laboring away under it, only their legs visible. Ryder was once more in human form, his black T-shirt stretched tight across his back when he moved, making her forget what she was doing until Ascher nudged her. Atlas was leaning against a nearby tree, flipping his blade, his expression distant.

"What did you find?" She passed out the sandwiches while the rest of the guys gathered around.

"The truck is basically fucked." Kincade had grease smeared across his forehead, while sweat made his white shirt cling to him in a very distracting way. "It will run, but not far, and definitely not fast."

Draven crawled out from under the truck, not a speck of dirt or dust on him.

"Did you take a nap under there instead of help?" Amusement tinged her voice.

"Of course not." Draven rolled his eyes dramatically. "I commune with nature, and it stays off me. The only time I get dirty is when it suites me."

She snorted at his sexy smirk. "Idiot."

She tossed him a sandwich, not trusting him enough to get closer, not with that twinkle in his eye. She finished passing out the food, then turned toward Atlas. "What did you find?"

"Nothing good." He stared at the sandwich like it was an alien creature he'd never seen before, then carefully tucked away his knife and accepted the food.

"Sorry." She couldn't stop the heat that flooded her cheeks. "I'm not much of a cook."

He looked at her from under his brows, then slowly

unwrapped the sandwich. "Then it will be my pleasure to teach you."

He took a big bite, staring at her the whole time, and for some reason, her mind flashed to the night they spent together. She cleared her throat, wishing she could clear her mind of dirty thoughts as quickly. "Uhhh…"

Ryder took pity on her. "The forest is devoid of animals, leaving only a few rodents and small birds at most. It's like the area is tainted with the ghosts of the dead, keeping the other animals away from the predators that roam it at night."

"We found the edges of the caves." Later afternoon sun sparkled through the trees, making Atlas almost appeared to glow. "The place reeked of death."

"So Séamus was right."

Atlas wrinkled his nose at her comment, the only reaction he showed to express his dislike of the leprechaun. "My guess is they take those they don't immediately eat there and keep them locked up till they're needed."

Bile soured the back of her throat at the thought of being kidnapped and kept in a cave, watching while creatures from their worst nightmares ate people, and knowing it was her turn next. "Is there any sign of the wendigo?"

"None." Ryder eyed the basket, and she smiled and handed him the remaining sandwiches. "Their tracks are all over the forest. They're not even bothering to hide them. Some areas are so heavily traveled, I can't sort them out."

She could tell it bothered him that he'd failed.

"It was the stench." Atlas looked a little green at the memory. "One sniff and it burned through our senses, killing them. Whatever tracks remained couldn't be picked up past the putrid rot."

Morgan swallowed heavily, nose wrinkled, vividly recalling the smell from last night, as if one of the creatures was standing in front of her.

"Why wait for supper?" Morgan turned toward Kincade. "Why not go over there now and confront them?"

"Or just eliminate them?" Draven absently flipped his blade, his expression hard. "Why give them a chance to come after her?"

"And if they aren't the problem?" Kincade crossed his arms and propped himself against their battered vehicle. "What if they want our help to eliminate their ties to the wendigo? What if they have a plan?"

"Do we want to take the chance that you're wrong? That they might come after her?" Ryder blew out an annoyed breath, a snarling undertone in his voice.

Morgan rolled her eyes. Her overprotective mates were at it again. "I hate to say it, but Kincade is correct. We can't make this call based on my safety. If there's even a chance the coven members who are left might have a way to kill the wendigo permanently—we can't pass up the opportunity."

"I don't like it." Draven looked off into the distance, as if he was already thinking of ways to eliminate their neighbors.

Kincade agreed one thousand percent with Draven. He didn't want Morgan anywhere near those creatures, while in human form or not. Something about this hunt didn't sit right with him.

It wasn't just that she was in danger...they were going to be gunning for her.

While he knew she could protect herself, every instinct said not to leave her side.

He just wished he fucking knew how to protect her.

Her stubbornness and her will to fight for what she believed in were what he loved most about her, but the shards of glass churning in his stomach warned this time was different.

He trusted Morgan with his life, enjoyed letting her take the lead with the team because she was that fucking brilliant, but he feared one misstep and they would lose her.

Which was completely unacceptable.

He didn't give a fuck if the neighbors were innocent or guilty. The only thing that kept him from going over there and eliminating the threat was they might know how to kill off the creatures permanently. Wendigo were whispered about in myths and legends, unstoppable beasts he wasn't sure they could defeat, not if the fuckers could rise from the dead.

Defeat wasn't an option.

Morgan was too important to them to even allow her to be injured.

A muscle jumped in his jaw as he watched Morgan flirt with the guys. This was supposed to be a vacation to make her fall a little bit more in love with them. A chance for them to woo and romance her.

Not fucking hunt beasts from hell.

He ran his fingers through his hair, wishing he could snatch her up and run, but it wasn't an option. He hated to admit it, but if they wanted to get to the truth about the wendigo infestation, they needed Morgan in the fight.

No matter what, he'd do whatever it took to make sure she survived, consequences be damned.

Supper was approaching fast, and Morgan suffered a spate of nerves. Every instinct screamed to nuke the place, but she was afraid it was much too late for that. They couldn't take the chance that the creatures wouldn't be destroyed.

She paced down the hall, then stopped in front of the last door and knocked. Atlas opened it a moment later, and her tongue stuck to the roof of her mouth.

He was wearing tight leather pants, a belt holding them low on his hips.

And that was it.

His hair was already starting to turn silver as the sun lowered on the horizon. It was loose, the silken strands hanging straight down his back, leaving his chest on full display for her to gawk at like a love-struck teenager…or, if she was honest with herself, like any woman with a heartbeat, because he was a freaking piece of artwork, sculpted by the gods to tempt anyone with a heartbeat.

But it was his bare toes that did her in.

They made him look less like the asshole who wanted to kick her ass when they first met and more like the man she had fallen completely in love with.

When he leaned against the doorframe and cleared his throat, her head shot up to see him looking down at her with an amused half smile. "Have you come for a visit?"

And damn if his lyrical voice didn't make her immediately think of sex.

Every inch of her tingled, anxious to feel his fingers trail over her skin, and it was all she could do to close her mouth and blink away the veil of lust that had fallen over her.

"Erm, uh…" It was only when her hands tightened on the shirt she'd brought with her did she remember why she came to see him.

The shirt.

Of course.

Not sex, she reminded herself.

"Here." She thrust out her hand, the silken material sliding through her fingers. "I wanted to return this to you."

Instead of taking it, Atlas crossed his arms, watching her as if amused by her reaction to seeing him half naked. "You should wear it tonight. You might need it."

"What do you mean?" It took more effort than it should have to lift her attention to his face and keep it there.

"If something were to go wrong, the shirt would act like armor." He lifted his chin at her in a small nod. "Wear it."

"All the more reason for you to have it back." She didn't like the idea of him going into battle unprotected.

Atlas slowly straightened, then stepped closer until he filled the doorway gazing down at her, the dark umber in his green eyes luring her closer. He lifted her chin, his thumb rubbing along her bottom lip, distracting her enough that she nearly forgot what they were talking about until he spoke again. "I have a feeling it's not me they're after."

He dropped his hand, stepped back and shut the door right in her face, cutting off any further conversation. Morgan stared at the closed door in shock for a second longer, raising her fist to pound on it. Then she lowered her hand and spun on her heel, knowing no matter what she said, she'd never be able to get him to change his mind.

She went to her room, hesitated a second, then took off her shirt and slipped the faerie material over her head. It slithered down her body before it cinched tight. A splash of red appeared on the white material, spreading to cover the entire shirt, the fabric thickened until she looked like she was wearing a red leather bustier. Underneath was a billowing, long-sleeve red shirt that tightened around her wrists like cuffs.

She turned to look in the mirror, feeling a little awkward, not used to wearing anything but black.

And was shocked to see herself looking sexy and kick-ass at the same time.

The door opened, and she turned to see Draven enter. He stopped dead when he saw her, his jaw dropping. Ryder entered next, caught sight of her and slammed into Draven, sending the smaller man stumbling into the room.

Then both men proceeded to stare.

"Too much?" She glanced down a little doubtfully, running her hands along the smooth leather.

"No!" Draven reached for her, as if to stop her from changing, then he cleared his throat and shook his head. "You look stunning."

"Perfect," Ryder rumbled, his voice barely above a growl, the sound making her shiver, as if he was the big bad wolf ready to devour her.

"I can't wait to see Kincade's reaction." Draven gave her a blinding smile and opened the door for her. As she moved out into the hall, both men followed, completely forgetting that they were going to change.

She was conscious of them trailing her down the hall. Without looking, she called over her shoulder. "Stop staring at my ass."

She could practically feel Ryder blush.

"Babe, that's like asking a guy to stop breathing," Draven purred. "With an ass like yours, not looking would be a crime."

Morgan snorted, charmed despite herself, and she couldn't resist adding an extra sway to her hips just to torture him. Draven's muffled groan and curse were reward enough.

Atlas waited by the door, appreciation darkening his eyes as she walked down the steps toward him, but he didn't say anything as he opened the door with a sweeping bow. Kincade and Ascher were waiting at the bottom of the steps, quietly talking over what to expect at supper.

She didn't like Ascher's pallor, her amusement over the guys' reactions to her outfit fading.

"I thought you were feeling better." She charged down the steps, stopping just short of the ground so she could glare down at him. Knowing he wouldn't tell her shit, she touched the obsidian marks twirling up her hands and down her arms.

The sensation of falling into a dark pit seized her. Her insides felt like they were on fire, while her skin was coated in a thin layer of ice. Then his hellhound appeared, launching himself at her and pushing her out of the connection.

Morgan staggered and would've tripped on the steps if Ryder hadn't been there to catch her. He grabbed her shoulders, holding her steady as she struggled against the disorientation.

"What the fuck is happening?"

Ascher grimaced, looking anywhere but at her. "If I have to guess, they marked me. It's their failsafe to make sure we do what they want."

"Marked you?" Morgan stormed toward him, stabbing her finger against his chest, allowing her anger to take over because she was afraid to let the fear out or it would swallow her whole. "What the hell does that mean?"

Ascher brushed the backs of his fingers against the side of her face, as if for the last time. "It means if we don't find a cure to the wendigo virus, I'm very much afraid I will never be leaving this place."

Chapter
Fourteen

*R*yder brought up the rear as everyone tromped through the woods toward the neighbors' house. The closer they got, the stronger the stench became, until he couldn't smell anything else.

They could've driven, but none of them wanted to be caught in a vehicle that could break down at any moment, especially if they needed to make a fast getaway.

While he listened to the others bicker about the merits of attacking first, he worried that it was much too late. By marking Ascher, they'd set the perfect trap for Morgan.

What they didn't realize was they sealed their own fate as well.

Morgan would never let them live for harming what she considered hers.

As they broke through the tree line, the house came into view. It was run down, a little shabby, the plants overgrown and not nearly as grand as the coven. Two guards were posted outside, one in plain view, the other hidden, but not nearly well enough to escape Ryder's notice.

There was something savage, almost feral about the way they watched the team approach.

Not like they were enemies.

Not a threat, either.

More like the team members were prey, and the guards were

starving.

The scruff on the back of his neck stood on end, and his wolf dug his claws into the ground and hunkered down to wait for the perfect time to spring. Claws burst from his fingertips, and he quickly curled his fingers into fists to hide them.

As they approached the front porch, he wanted to shift and stand guard in front of Morgan, anything so he wouldn't be separated from her by more than a few inches. The closer they got to the building, the more the feeling grew, almost like a premonition...that if he didn't remain alert, she'd slip through his fingers and be lost to them forever.

Morgan struggled to breathe the foul air, swallowing against the urge to gag. As they approached the long-forgotten house, the door creaked open, and the woman they met earlier greeted them with a bright smile while the overpowering smell of her sour perfume wafted out like a slap in the face.

"I'm so glad you could make it!" Leanne smiled brightly, then stood to the side and beckoned them forward. "Welcome!"

Magic tingled against her skin as she approached, and now she was close enough, Morgan could tell it was a powerful spell. If the woman ever had magic, she didn't have any now. Instead of an entryway, the house opened up to a modest-sized kitchen. Pots were on the stove, dishes were in the sink, but a wrongness hung in the air.

There was no clutter, no mess, or even any trash in the garbage. The appliances were running, but there was an emptiness to the house. Though food was supposed to be cooking, she couldn't actually smell any.

Once they were trapped within the confines of the house, the smell worsened, the taste of rot lingering on the back of her tongue.

"The dining room is this way." Leanne trailed Morgan inside then headed down a hall, indicated a room on the right, smiling over her shoulder at them as she led the way. "We've been looking forward to seeing you all day. I hope you're hungry."

There was something about her smile, a sharpness to her teeth that put Morgan on edge. The guys didn't say anything as they followed, but as she entered the dining room, she halted when she saw five males standing idle, almost like they were lying in wait. Their eyes were so vacant, it raised the hair on the back of her neck.

"Please, have a seat." Leanne went to the sideboard. "Let me get us some drinks."

Morgan entered the room reluctantly, making sure to stay on the side of the table opposite the minions. Her guys lined up on either side of her until they looked like two sides ready to rumble like movies of old. The table was set for dinner, the dishes laid out, the silverware at the ready.

Everything looked perfect.

So why did it all feel like an act, like the room was used for some other purpose?

Her necklace warmed in warning, and she quickly grabbed it in her hand before the witch noticed. The liquid metal slithered along her fingers, not like water, but thicker, similar to mercury. Then the magic left it in a rush, leaving the metal cool to the touch.

She traced the lines of the necklace with her fingertips and didn't need to look to recognize the symbol was the eye of spirit—a circle with a triangle in the center and an eye in the middle of that. The etchings along the outer edges were a protection spell against spirits, an incantation that allowed the wearer to see into the world beyond.

Dust motes danced in the air, seeming to gather in the corner, and a cloudy shape floated across the room to stop in front of her. The apparition sharpened, and the image of a young woman appeared. She reached up, touching Morgan's face, the single word escaping her lips only a whisper of air. "Remember."

The room flickered, lights dimmed, and an older image superimposed over the room, like Morgan was looking through a window into the past. Instead of the neatly placed dishware, the table was dirty and stained, the surface scarred, the chairs broken. The windows were shattered, dead leaves and branches scattered about as though animals had made nests all over the place. The wallpaper hung down in sheets, revealing mold slowly creeping across the walls.

Another flash blinked into view.

The room was cleaner…somewhat. But the main thing that caught her attention was the person strapped to the table, his mouth stuffed with a cloth to muffle his screams. Witches circled the table, chanting in a language that was hauntingly familiar. Candles flickered, as if disturbed by an invisible wind.

The guy on the table locked eyes with her, as if he could see her, and he was silently screaming for help. When Morgan glanced around the room in the vision, she saw Leanne holding up an ancient leather book, her green eyes shimmering feverishly, tainted magic swirling in the room like a swarm of hungry bugs. The air tasted like sour milk, and magic prickled painfully against her skin, like maggots were trying to burrow into her flesh to consume her magic.

A dark shadow seemed to coalesce around the man, taking the form of a wendigo. As the shadows thickened, the shape solidified, and the stench of death saturating the air turned sour. The shadowy figure yanked his arm back, then slammed his fingers straight into the guy's chest.

The man grunted, gasping in pain. When the creature pulled back, a juicy, sucking sound echoed throughout the room. Resting in his hand was the man's still-beating heart. Splotches of blood splattered across the table as the creature gave a mighty howl and consumed the heart in three ravenous bites.

"Please, won't you have a seat?"

Morgan blinked away the vision or whatever the fuck she saw and watched Leanne passing out drinks, setting them along the table as if she hadn't used the surface to sacrifice someone's soul.

Morgan glanced around the room, but found no sign of the ghost, the spirit no doubt having used the last of her energy to send the warning before retreating back to the underworld.

Making no move to take her seat, Morgan stared at Leanne with new eyes. "Why are we here?"

"So you know." With a moue of distaste, Leanne set down the tray of drinks with a clatter. The smiling, friendly neighbor image vanished, revealing a hardened bitch who would go to any extremes for more power. "Pity. I was hoping we could have a talk and you would be reasonable."

The five guys in the room shifted, blocking the exits and windows, but made no move to attack. They were expressionless, their movements like automatons, Leanne's stranglehold over them absolute. There was a weird energy around them, the opposite of animal magnetism, and her skin crawled, trying to get away from the wrongness that oozed from them.

"Be reasonable?" It was all Morgan could do not to call on her blades and kill them all. The guys must have picked up on her rage and spread out behind her. "What happened to the last crew who came to investigate the coven?"

"They never made it past the first night." Leanne shook her head, the pity in her words not matching the malicious gleam in her eyes. "We were unable to warn them in time."

Which Morgan assumed meant they were either turned or eaten.

"And how did you say you came to live here?" Morgan didn't believe the woman's bullshit for a second. "The Academy wasn't aware of anyone living on the property."

"We came through the portal and were permitted to stay and help protect the property to earn our keep."

It sounded plausible, but Morgan didn't believe it.

And she was done playing games, conscious of the sun sinking lower and lower in the sky as each minute ticked past. "You were a part of the original coven, but somehow they're dead and you're still alive. What happened?"

"You know." Leanne gave a sigh, wrinkled her nose, and picked up a drink from the table, swirling the liquid in the cup. She seemed so unconcerned that they knew the truth the tiny hairs on the back of Morgan's neck lifted.

"You wanted power—"

"I wanted a way to protect the coven, but the stubborn fools refused to listen." Leanne slammed her glass down, liquor sloshing over the edge to splash on her hand, which she shook off with an irritated flick of her wrist.

"You wanted to be the leader of your own coven," Morgan countered. "You wanted to prove you were better."

"People were dying!" Leanne snarled. "The spell was supposed to prevent that. Make us stronger. Make us unstoppable. Not turn us into stark raving monsters."

"Except the monsters were uncontrollable, and even more people have died as a result of your meddling." Morgan couldn't understand why people had to mess with something they didn't understand. She knew from experience it only led to more trouble.

"A side effect of the spell." Leanne waved her hand, like the details were unimportant. "We can fix it." Her minions turned their eerie eyes on Morgan, but there was nothing but murder and mayhem staring back at her. Leanne appeared both hopeful and determined to do whatever it took to get what she wanted. "We just need someone with enough magic to repress the beasts' ravenous urgings and allow us more control. Someone like you."

The last two remaining guys entered the room, stood by doors, and Morgan's protective instincts kicked into gear.

They weren't asking for help.

They were looking for a sacrifice.

"Been there, done that." Morgan shook her head. "I won't do it again."

The woman laughed, her smile confident. "You will if you want to save your mate."

The words were like a blow to the gut, and she whirled, her eyes locking on Ascher, her gaze dropping to where the wendigo had taken a bite out of his arm. Then fear turned to rage, and the air around her began to stir as her magic rose with her emotions.

"What did you do?"

"Those bitten by a wendigo turn into one. By tonight he will no longer be yours. Unless you do exactly what I want, he will become mine." Leanne sauntered over to the sideboard and poured herself another drink, a smirk playing around her mouth. "If you want to save him, you'll need our help."

"What gave you the idea that I'd be strong enough to help you?" Morgan inched closer to the guys, not trusting Leanne's minions.

Kincade looked cool and calm, ready to explode into action at the slightest provocation. Draven and Atlas were studying their opponents as if trying to decide the easiest way to dismember them, not letting the conversation distract them. Ryder bulked up, his eyes shimmering as he battled his wolf, while Ascher looked shaken…and resigned.

Be damned if she would just hand him over.

Leanne laughed, the sound full of giddy pleasure, and she lifted her drink in salute. "I could tell by the way you reset the wards without a full coven." The woman inhaled deeply, almost like she was trying to catch an intoxicating scent. "You reek of magic, so much that I can almost taste it on you."

She licked her lips, her eyes flashing yellow as avarice distorted her face, and Morgan realized the woman was more wendigo than human no matter what face she wore.

Morgan very much feared they would need more than their fighting skills to win this one. Leanne asked her to break the spell, but Morgan didn't think it was to rid themselves of the wendigo infection. They wanted out. To stop them, Morgan needed to take a look at the spell they used. "I want to see the book."

Leanne lifted her eyebrows, a picture of innocence. "What book?"

"If you really want my help, I'll need the book." She would not be denied. If she wanted any hope of saving Ascher, she needed that information. Every book, every page regarding the wendigo had been stripped from the coven.

Leanne narrowed her eyes, obviously not wanting to share her secrets. "Fine."

She stomped out the door.

As soon as Leanne left the room, the woman's control over her minions wavered. The rest of her pack crowded closer to Morgan, licking their lips like they couldn't stop themselves, making her feel like a prime slab of rare beef.

"Out in the hall. Now." The metal cuffs she wore melted down her fingers until blades formed in her hands, and the rest of the guys quickly followed her lead by pulling their weapons.

The minions stalked them every step of the way to the kitchen, their eyes gleaming yellow, their nails lengthening into claws as their control disintegrated.

"Here you go." Leanne strolled into the kitchen, completely unconcerned by the threat.

Draven intercepted her, grabbing the book so Morgan was free to fight.

"Don't damage it." Leanne warned as she stepped back. She crossed her arms, a smirk curling her lips as she eyed Ascher possessively. "And you might want to hurry back to the coven. When the change comes over your little mate, he'll try to kill you and your men."

"Why did they let us go?" Morgan didn't trust it, and neither did the guys, if the way they kept glancing behind them was any indication. None of them wasted any time, and hauled ass back to the coven, running full out. The sun was only a memory in the sky, the light dying faster than they could move.

"We're not going to make it," Ryder charged through the group, grabbed her and threw her over his shoulder. He kicked up his speed, leaving the others behind.

"What the hell!" Morgan snapped, then heaved a sigh of exasperation. "We have plenty of time."

But she knew no amount of talking would convince Ryder otherwise. Instead of fighting a battle she couldn't win, she relaxed in his grip. They arrived back at the coven just as the last of the light faded from the sky. Ryder was breathing deeply, but not really winded, more anxious, as if expecting an attack at any second.

He took his time lowering her to the ground, letting her body slide down his front, and she smiled when a little rumble of pleasure escaped his chest. Shaking her head to clear it of her inappropriate thoughts, she took a step away, already missing his fresh forest scent.

When he tried to herd her inside the coven, she refused to budge. "Not without the others."

With a low, bass growl, he seemed to grow as he towered over her, and she patted his chest, almost charmed by his caveman antics. The sound stopped the instant her hand touched him, and he seemed to deflate. "For me?"

Damn him.

"How about a compromise?" She walked up the steps of the coven and opened the door, then stood on the threshold with her arms crossed. "If trouble comes, I'm just a step away."

He grunted, obviously not believing her.

Smart man.

No way in hell would she leave them to fight without her.

It didn't take more than two minutes for the other guys to

appear. They were out of breath, slightly rumpled, but unharmed, and her insides relaxed at seeing them safe and whole. As the rest of the guys jogged up the stairs, Ascher remained on the bottom step, gazing up at her with such intense sadness that her heart ached and fear exploded through her.

She took an involuntary step toward him, very much afraid he would bolt if she got any closer. "Ascher?"

He shook his head, taking a step back. "I won't risk you."

When he moved to go, she charged down the steps after him. "If you don't come inside, I'll just have to stay out here with you."

She was nothing if not stubborn, and he knew it.

She could feel Kincade and Atlas staring at her, debating whether to drag her inside with them, and she glared at them over her shoulder. "Don't even think it."

Only when they remained where they were did she turn back to Ascher. "Can your hellhound burn out the infection?"

Ascher ran his hand over his head, glancing away from her. "No. It's magical."

Which meant she was the key.

She could fix him, but how?

"Does anyone else feel like this was a test?" Draven dropped the book at his feet, the thump seeming to vibrate up her legs, calling to her.

"And we failed when we refused to do what she wanted," Kincade agreed.

Atlas studied the tree line, then glanced up at the rising moon. "They'll be coming for us."

As if he'd summoned them, howls erupted through the night.

Before anyone could move, shadows burst out of the trees, the shapes nothing more than a blur. One second Ascher was standing in front of her—the next, one of the shadows plowed into him and he was gone.

"Ascher!" Without hesitation, Morgan grabbed her blades and charged after him.

Chapter Fifteen

*B*efore Morgan could get to Ascher, another creature charged into the clearing. The beast was massive, towing over her. He was gaunt to the point of emaciation. His skin a chalky gray, barely stretched over bone, his fur patchy, as if he had mange, the strands matted and tangled.

His eyes were deeply set in his sockets, his lips tattered and bloody as if he chewed on them to appease an insatiable hunger. The odor of decay and rot clung to him, embedded in his fur and billowing out with each breath, strong enough to knock her back a step.

Seeing her seemed to make him hesitate, but not for long. With a roar, he lunged at her, and she dropped to the ground, the claws aimed for her throat slicing through air, mere inches short of taking off her head.

She kicked out, only for him to leap over her body in a single bound. Then Kincade was there, ramming into the beast in his stone form like the creature was nothing more than roadkill to be plowed over. When two more wendigo bolted into the yard, she had no more time to think.

All the guys were engaged in the fight. Draven and Atlas worked as a team, their movements in tandem as they sliced and dismembered their opponents...only it didn't kill them. No matter how battered or how many pieces had been hacked off, the beasts peeled themselves off the ground and kept coming.

Ascher fought like a demon possessed, holding his own against the creature. But instead of trying to tear him apart, the wendigo seemed to recognize Ascher as one of them, keeping him occupied—just biding time, waiting for the wendigo in him to rise.

Only Ascher was having none of it.

Smoke rose from the ground where he stood, the stench of burnt fur clogging the air. His clothes were singed as his hellhound fought back with everything in him. For every blow he took, he returned it twice as strong.

She counted six creatures.

Since she doubted Leanne would bother to get her hands dirty, it meant one creature was still missing. Morgan stood in the front of the yard, turning in a slow circle.

It was only then she realized the wendigo were targeting the men.

The initial attack on Ascher had been to draw her out, while the attack on her was to lure the rest of the men into the fight. They either wanted to bite her men and force her hand or take them out completely and leave her vulnerable.

Not gonna happen.

She almost missed the slight shift in the shadows to her right. A wendigo crept low to the ground, clinging to the darkness, the creature only a few yards from Ryder's unprotected back and inching closer. Morgan ran toward it and leapt through the air, landing between it and Ryder, taking the blow meant for him. Claws tore through her side, and she brought up her arm in time to block the fangs aimed to rip out her throat.

She braced for pain, only to have her shirt turn into chainmail. Instead of eviscerating her, the claws nicked her flesh. His mouth crushed her forearm, the fangs burrowing into her flesh instead of ripping her arm off completely.

Pain streaked through her, and she gritted her teeth, cursing her own stupidity for allowing herself to be bitten. The guys would get themselves killed trying to cure her—or release hell on earth to save her—and both options were unacceptable.

Taking advantage of the wendigo's closeness, she pulled her blade and swiped at the beast...only for him to stumble away, hacking like he was trying to cough up a wicked hairball. Wisps of black smoke and tiny dust particles exploded out of him, and he dropped to his knees. As she glanced at the others, she realized she and her men would never survive until dawn, not without becoming infected...or worse.

Draven had dropped to one knee under a particularly vicious attack when a shape burst out of the trees. It streaked forward and tackled the wendigo, taking him down in a jumble of arms and legs...and wings?

"Loki?"

Then she felt like slapping her forehead—of course!

He was the silent stalker she'd sensed the past few days.

Loki's hide hardened, but instead of a stone statue she expected, his movements became fluid as he systematically ripped his target to shreds.

Using the distraction, Morgan dropped to her knees, and began to etch a symbol in the earth using her blade. The glyph was foreign and intricate. With each swipe, she pushed magic into the knife, leaving behind a tiny spark of magical residue with every stroke. The presence of the void surrounded her, getting stronger with each line she scratched in the soil, her determination to protect the ones she loved burning bright.

When she finished the last stroke, she brought the blade up and swiped the edge across her palm until blood flowed. She slammed her hand hard against the ground, and pure power surged out of her until the ground began to shake. Magic wormed its way under the surface, cutting through pure rock as easily as swimming underwater.

As soon as the magic hit the wards surrounding the property, magic shot up in the air in a stream of blazing lights. A clap of thunder like a sonic boom echoed in the clearing, and a giant wave crested over the trees, slamming into the clearing from all sides. The magic sloshed around the front yard, easily passing clear through objects…until it hit the first wendigo.

It was like the creature was incinerated, the inside of him exploding outward in a shower of dust and smoke that swirled away and vanished into the darkness. Screams of pain and rage echoed in the clearing as the other creatures quickly suffered the same fate.

With a victorious howl, Loki charged into the night after the wisps. "Loki, wait!"

But he was already gone, unable to resist the bloodlust, the need to hunt the enemy a driving force. She took a step to follow him when Kincade snapped at her, "Morgan. Don't."

She turned toward them and froze as the wall of power shot toward them. Kincade and the others didn't even flinch, completely confident that her magic would do them no harm.

A stab of worry slashed through her.

The magic was coming too fast.

It was going to slam into her men like a tsunami and drown them under the weight of it.

She lifted her arm to pull it back, only to have the magic nip at her fingers in reprimand.

Asking for her trust.

If she wanted to get rid of every trace of the wendigo, she needed to let it run its course.

Holding her breath, she reluctantly dropped her arm, her heart in her throat.

The wave streaked through them one at a time. The magic clung to them like a giant caress, sparking against their skin and healing any injuries. When it released them, they staggered, but remained unharmed.

The magic hit Ascher harder than the others, almost as if it was trying to crawl inside him and pry something out. A gurgle of pain seemed to strangle him, and he dropped to his knees before the magic reluctantly released its hold.

He gazed over at her, and he answered her unspoken question with a small shake of his head.

He was still infected.

The magic splashed against the house, climbing up the walls before soaking into the building. The shabbiness faded, the greenery bloomed. The windows mended themselves, and the glass panes sparkled even in the darkness.

As the magical glow faded, the whole building shimmered for a second.

Then the door creaked open, and warm light spilled out, as if to welcome them inside.

A shadow crossed the doorway, and Séamus stepped into the opening, beckoning to them. "Them creatures will be back soon. Ye best hurry unless ye wanna go up against 'em again."

Before she could even get to her feet, Kincade and Ryder each grabbed one of her arms and helped her rise…then tightened their hold when her legs wobbled, and she almost face-planted. "Why do I feel so…drunk?"

"Ye be drunk on power." Séamus chuckled as he backed away to let them enter. "It can happen when ye use too much magic at once."

Kincade and Ryder hauled her forward, entering just a step behind her. Draven grabbed the book on the top steps before following. Ascher hesitated at the door, looking off into the trees like he was thinking of leaving.

Not fucking happening.

She reached out, grabbed the back of his shirt, and yanked him in over the threshold. Ascher stumbled into her, quickly catching her around the waist when she tripped over her own feet, and she found herself plastered up against his chest.

"You didn't change." She pressed her forehead against his

chest, hating the way her insides shook at the thought of losing him.

His grip tightened on her hips, then he gently grabbed her shoulders and pushed her away. "Not yet."

Sorrow swamped her, dragging her under until it felt like something precious was slipping through her fingers.

Séamus slammed the door, dusting off his hands like he'd taken care of the wendigo all on his own, and she jumped at the loud bang. "Ye just watch out. The hangover is gonna be a bitch."

Chuckling like he'd told the best joke in the world, Séamus turned on his heel and waddled out of the room, no doubt to raid the kitchen for more of the snacks Atlas made for him.

Now that he mentioned it, her head felt like someone was slamming an icepick into her eyes. She pinched the bridge of her nose, hoping to relieve the pressure. "Why?"

"You're not used to using the pure magic of the void. You stressed yourself." Atlas placed his fingers against her temple, gently rubbing in tiny circles to relieve the pressure.

In the silence, there was a slight scratching at the door, and everyone in the room paused, glanced at each other and pulled their weapons.

"Help…"

The plea was so weak she wouldn't have heard it if not for her enhanced hearing. When she would've stepped toward the door, Atlas blocked her way, and she glared up at him.

"What are you doing?" She poked his side until he grunted and glanced down at her. "Move."

"No." His expression was ruthless, leaving her no doubt he'd knock her out and tie her up if that's what it took to keep her safe.

Poking at him had jarred her injuries, cracking open the wound until fresh blood oozed out.

Ryder inhaled deeply, streaking to her side and grabbing her hand. He gently rolled up her sleeve, revealing the deep gouges raked down her forearm. "You were bitten."

The guys completely forgot about the door as they spun toward her. She didn't even see them move before she was surrounded. Draven dropped the book with a thump, and reached for the hem of her shirt, lifting the material to reveal four claw marks etched along her hip. The slashes were slight, leaving only a light bead of blood behind.

"Fuck!" Ascher looked devastated, like he'd done the deed himself and infected her.

A muscle jumped in Kincade's jaw, and he snatched up the book. "We'll find a solution in here. I—"

A menacing howl echoed in the distance. Kincade flinched and set the book aside, whirling to face her. The rest of the guys froze, all of them staring at her with such worry she could barely swallow past the lump in her throat. Wanting to put them at ease, she rolled her eyes playfully. "I have no urge to howl at the moon. Relax."

"Please…"

She'd almost forgotten the desperate plea. Using the guys' distraction against them, she was at the door before they could protest, and wrenched it open. Curled on the stoop was a naked man. When the door opened, he swallowed hard and reached out to her. "I can help you."

Morgan instantly recognized him as the man who was tied to the table in her vision in Leanne's dining room. Without thought, she grabbed his hand and pulled him inside.

Before she could slam the door, Loki burst into the coven in all his naughty, winged glory. He dropped a severed arm at her feet with a meaty thump, beaming like it was a prize, while the congealed blood splattered across the floor. His butt wiggled, his tail lashing, waiting for praise.

Atlas quickly slammed the door shut, but Morgan couldn't tear her eyes away from the bloody arm, the torn tendons and muscles twitching like they were was still receiving commands. Pure rot bubbled up from the blotchy skin, the flesh turning into a putrid liquid while they watched, patches of fur floating on the surface. A squelching sound bubbled up from the arm as it melted down to black sludge.

"That's disgusting." Morgan tore her eyes away and didn't hesitate to throw her arms around Loki. "You big doofus! I thought I told you to stay back at the Academy." She pulled back to admonish him but couldn't stay mad when his tongue rolled out and slapped her upside the face with a sloppy kiss.

Instead of fear, the gardog looked like he'd just had the time of his life.

When none of the guys seemed surprised, she glared at them. "How long have you known?"

"After you left for town with Ascher, he showed up here," Draven admitted, not looking at her. "I found him stalking me when I went to check the buildings."

"I found him scratching at the back door, begging for scraps." Atlas appeared unrepentant for keeping the secret from her.

Kincade rubbed the back of his neck, his green eyes guilty. "The Academy called me an hour after we left. I figured he'd show up here sooner rather than later."

She glared at Ascher and Ryder, only to see they weren't the least bit surprised. "You, too?" She frowned at all of them, completely exasperated. "Why would he hide this from me?"

"Because he wants to protect you," Kincade answered, like it explained everything.

Morgan grabbed Loki's massive head, searching for injuries or bites, sighing with relief when she found nothing. She shook her finger at him. "Bad dog. No more hiding from me, understand?"

He whimpered and hunkered down like she'd threatened to beat him. Unable to resist his big puppy-dog eyes, she sighed again and leaned over to kiss his nose. "Thank you for coming to our rescue."

He gave her another lick, then scrambled away, chasing his tail until he spotted the strange man huddled by the door. He approached slowly, then sneezed and grumbled low in his throat as he backed away. He hunkered down next to her, curling his tail around her ankle, threatening to trip her when she stood.

Loki wasn't wrong.

The man stank to high heaven, his skin a sallow yellow, his eyes sunken deep. Dirt seemed to cling to him, blood crusted around his fingers and mouth, and Morgan leaned weakly against the door. "My blood cured you."

She whirled and took a step toward Ascher when a bitter chuckle stopped her short.

The man clutched his ribs as he pushed himself upright. "Nothing can cure me, not after being marked by hell, but you have time. Your bond is protecting you for now. As long as you resist Leanne's call, resist the urge to eat human flesh, there's hope."

He coughed, a wet, squishy sound, and blood bubbled up and spilled out of his mouth. Since he'd entered, his skin had reddened, as if he'd been out in the sun for too long. He was panting, sweat pouring down his face. When she took a step toward him, he shook his head. "Before the night is over, hell will claim me. There's nothing left to save, not after the things I did."

A series of yips and growls came from outside until it sounded like the house was surrounded. The guys spread out and peered through the windows.

"They're issuing a challenge. They want you to answer their call and join them. Despite the racket, you're safe as long as you remain in the coven." The man coughed again, but instead of blood, tiny globs of dark tar and wisps of smoke seeped from his mouth and nose. When he stopped and leaned his back against the wall, his lips were blackened. His fingers were stained as well, the tips charred and cracked, like he'd stuck them into a flame.

"What's happening?" When she moved to help him, Ascher grabbed her arm and held her back.

The man laughed, only to have it end in another cough, which made him look even sicker. The charred marks were past his wrists now, his nose and mouth black and cracking. "Ask your hellhound. He knows."

Morgan glanced at Ascher, but he only had eyes for the man on the floor. "He sold his soul to hell. They've come to claim it."

A tremor went through the man. He threw back his head as pain racked him, his jaw clenched as smoke began to rise from his skin.

"Come out, come out, wherever you are," Leanne called in a singsong voice, the words garbled by fangs. Claws clicked on the glass, then a horrible screech echoed around the room as Leanne dragged her claws over the windows. "You can't hide forever! You'll answer the call eventually. They all do."

And the outside world fell silent, which made everything worse.

At least when they made noise she knew where the creatures were lurking.

Morgan knelt next to the man, careful not to touch him. "Maybe you couldn't save them, but you might be able to help me save my men. Will you tell me what you know?"

The man coughed again, heat blasting from him like a furnace. He leaned weakly against the wall, searching her face, before he nodded weakly. "It's too late to save the others. They've given themselves over to the cravings completely. Their souls are now rotten to the core. They *like* the killing. They crave the taste of human flesh. It's like an addiction."

He looked away from her as if ashamed, his voice hoarse. "I've tried killing myself, but it never works. My soul is bound to the wendigo. Whenever night falls, I wake, alive and healed to live another day in hell. The cravings are painful, an insatiable hunger that's impossible to resist. I tried, by the gods, I tried—and failed."

His eyes were red-rimmed and anguished when he glanced at her. "Your blood broke the hold that kept me bound to that foul creature. Leanne won't be happy with the news. She enjoys her power too much." His chest rattled with each breath, like his insides were liquefying.

"I have no way to thank you for freeing me...other than by telling you what I know. Leanne believes the answers are in that book, but she can no longer access the book. You must hurry—you don't have much time to save your man. If the cravings become too much, you'll have to lock him up. It's the only thing that'll stop him from turning into one of them completely. Leanne had planned to kill him and take you, but that changed when he was bitten. Leanne loves the idea of having your mate. She knows you care for him, and she's betting you'll give her whatever she wants for the chance to save him, but it's all lies."

He ran a shaky hand down his face, grimacing as pain racked him, and he wheezed, "By now they know you've been bitten, too, and they'll be coming for you sooner rather than later. Be careful."

"Why?" Atlas stepped forward, towering over them, looking ready to beat the answer out of the guy if need be, not caring if he would get burned in the process. She reached back, pressing her hand against his boot, not wanting to risk him getting infected as well.

To her relief, he halted immediately and gently brushed his fingers against her hair as if he couldn't be near her and not touch her in some way.

"The bite affects witches differently than us creatures. It will consume your magic first. Only when it's sucked you dry will the curse run its course and take your soul." When he smiled bitterly at her, she saw his teeth were chipped and cracked. "They need your magic to break the wards. If they have no use for you..."

They would have no use for her men.

They were marked for death.

"How long?" She tightened her lips against the urge to curse the unfairness of this fucked-up situation.

"It burned through the witches in less than a week, some

succumbing faster than others." Laughter shook his shoulders, and he licked his cracked lips. "Leanne made sure she was the last, even going so far as to steal the magic from the others to try to fix things, but I think she knew by then it was too late. She refused to let anyone challenge her for leadership…she made sure of it."

"If we kill Leanne, will it save the rest?" Kincade crouched next to her, his question more of a demand.

The man snorted, then coughed again, smoke drifting out of his mouth this time. "We're not werewolves. Doesn't work that way. Be safe. Kill that bitch."

Before she had a chance to ask more questions, he grabbed his throat as if he couldn't catch his breath. Smoke rose from his body, and she watched in horror as his ribs began to crumble and cave into his chest. Flames licked at his flesh as if ignited from within, the skin charring and filling the room with a rancid smell as it spread.

Ascher's arm wrapped around her waist from behind and yanked her backwards…just in time to watch the body erupt in flames. The fire was pulled inward, the skin bubbling up, the flesh melting away. The stench of burnt flesh saturated her senses until the smell made her want to scrape her tongue clean, then shower for at least a decade.

Even when only bones remained, she'd swear she saw him move—only to have the bones collapse a second later into a pile of dust that burst upon impact and flew up into the air. Tiny cinders swirled around them briefly before they winked out and vanished into nothing.

All that remained of the poor man was a charred stain where his body had been.

Chapter
Sixteen

"*F*uck me." Draven dragged his fingers through his hair, unwilling to even consider the thought of Morgan being taken away from him in such a horrible, painful way. He wanted to charge outside and rip into the wendigo threatening them, wanted to hunt down that bitch Leanne and erase her from existence.

Only none of that would save Morgan.

Powerlessness threatened to choke him.

This was supposed to be a vacation, a trip to show Morgan that they worshipped the very air she breathed. Time to show her there was more to life than hunting and the Academy.

Show her they were family if she wanted it.

This was not supposed to be the end of them...because if anything happened to her, they'd have nothing left. They'd become hollow husks of their former selves, stuck biding their time until they died.

Fear and rage reverberated in the air, the rest of the guys barely holding their shit together. But when he looked at them for answers, he saw the same helplessness staring back at him.

No fucking way!

He wouldn't allow this to happen now she'd finally claimed them.

"What would happen if she went back to the Primordial

World?"

"I doubt it would stop the infection," Kincade gripped fistfuls of his hair while he paced.

"Agreed." Atlas was staring at the charred remains, turmoil making his eyes pure umber. "It's the last place she'd want to be trapped without magic. The whole kingdom is still in unrest. Even with all of us, now that she's been acknowledged as the heir to the throne, people will come after her."

"We call the Academy." Ryder pulled out his phone, cursing when it showed they had no service, almost crushing the device in his fury.

"We can't risk bringing more people inside the wards. That's exactly what Leanne wants." Morgan turned away from the charred outline, her resolve firming. "I won't do it. The bite isn't affecting me yet. If it comes down to it, I'll drag the infected into the void and close it behind us."

Draven thought he was going to be sick. No fucking way was she leaving him behind. He loved everything about her, but he refused to let her stubbornness get her killed.

Everyone began arguing at once, but it was Ascher's quiet words that shut them all up. "And if you turn and open up the portal? Your army would have access to all the worlds."

Morgan's lips tightened—she didn't have any answers.

"So that gives us a few days to figure out how to save the world," Draven muttered. For him there was no alternative.

The forgotten book at his feet caught his attention, the ancient bindings worn and tattered. He bent and scooped it up, the power thrumming from it giving him hope.

Time was ticking down too fast.

The answers had to be in here.

Any other option was unacceptable.

"We use this." Draven lifted the book and held it out toward Morgan, silently urging her to agree with him.

He wouldn't accept any other answer.

Morgan stared at the book that held her future, almost afraid to take it. She wasn't afraid of what would happen to her, but she *was* terrified of what would happen to the guys if she failed.

She walked over to Draven, the musty scent of old books reminded her of hours spent in MacGregor's library, and she gingerly accepted the book.

As soon as she touched the leather, a wisp of magic snaked around both her and Draven, triggering a spell. The magic felt familiar, and she realized it came from the ghost who appeared to her at supper, the witch who'd used the last of her magic to lock the book.

The world around her faded, replaced by a forest.

The smell of greenery smashed into her, a hint of dark earth and damp leaves. It only lasted for a second before being replaced by the now-familiar stink of rot, the slightest hint of it on the breeze enough to overpower everything else. The scene was so vivid, she could feel the underbrush snatch at her, the rough ground beneath her boots, even the touch of the full moon against her skin.

"What the hell?!" Draven was standing next to her, taking in the scene, quickly grabbing for his blades.

"Wait." Morgan reached over, clamping her fingers around his wrist. "Watch."

They both turned at the sound of rustling of leaves, and a younger version of Leanne burst out of the undergrowth, running like her life depended on it, screams of terror and pain chased after her.

A quick glance in that direction showed a group of hunters being torn apart by a wendigo, the coppery scent of blood and death blooming in the night air.

Leanne's team.

A few of the hunters raced after Leanne, and one of them grabbed her arm. The man was big, clearly the leader if his battle scars were any indication. "You need to open the portal. We need to send it back."

Leanne was shaking her head, struggling to pull away from him. "No, we must head back to the coven and alert the others. They'll know what to do, how to stop—"

The big man got into her face, spit flying as he yelled, shaking her hard enough to rattle her teeth. "Do it or we're all dead!"

Leanne struggled for another second before giving him a look of pure hatred and doing as he demanded. Just as the portal ripped open, the wendigo tore through the trees, the massive creature taking a bite out of the closest hunter.

It only took seconds for the creature to slaughter the poor guy, the remaining hunters doing their best to force the wendigo closer to the portal. When Leanne would've run, the old hunter grabbed her, then dragged them in front of the portal to stand like bait.

Leanne struggled and cursed, but the old man stood firm as the creature bore down on them. Seconds before it would've plowed through them, the old hunter shoved Leanne out of the way. The creature hesitated, swiping at her leg, taking a nasty bite before the hunter charged into the fray. When the wendigo lunged for the old man, they fell through the portal, and it sealed behind them.

The scene around them blurred as time sped past.

They watched in horror as some of the hunters peeled themselves off the ground and headed back to the coven, having no clue what they were taking back with them.

It wasn't until a few days later that everything went to shit.

Leanne figured it out first, but instead of telling the others, she watched while the creatures slaughtered the remaining hunters.

It was over in seconds.

The witches survived for a while trapped inside the coven, but Leanne knew time was short. She was turning. Instead of looking for a way to eliminate the wendigo, she decided to try and save her own ass and searched for a way to harness the beast's power. No need for hunters if they had their own unstoppable army. "If we can control them, no more witches have to die. We can have complete control over everything. No more hunters. No more Academy. No more rules to follow."

Unfortunately, nothing they did worked.

Leanne was the last to turn, her cunning and devious nature marking her as the strongest—an alpha able to control the others. She tricked the witches into going outside during the day, and her men immediately captured them.

Leanne kept the witches alive long enough to force them to use their magic to fulfill her dream of creating an unstoppable army. Only nothing worked, their magic gradually fading, and Leanne handed the remaining witches over to the wendigo to be slaughtered, smiling as blood and gore splashed everywhere.

"Morgan!" Ryder grabbed her shoulders, knocking the book out of her hands and dragging her back to the present.

Draven blinked across from her, his face pale. "What the hell just happened?"

Morgan leaned against Ryder, grateful for his strong arms around her. "Honestly? I think one of the witches cast a spell to lock the book before she died so Leanne couldn't have access to it. I saw her shade at the house when she showed me the truth about Leanne. I think she was warning us."

"This happened before?" Kincade came to a stop in front of her and glared. "When were you going to tell us?"

Morgan resisted the urge to kick his legs out from under him. "I don't know—do you think it best we talked while we were being attacked and they were trying to eat our faces off? Or before when we were running for our lives? Or would it have been better to interrupt the dying man who was trying to help us with his last breath?"

Her chest was heaving in frustration by the time she finished, and she snatched her arm away from Ryder to glare at the others in the room. "Does anyone else have a comment?"

A tiny smile played along Atlas's mouth, who was clearly amused by her outburst, but it quickly disappeared. "Thanks to your visit to the underworld, you're more susceptible to seeing the remnants of the dead than the rest of us. When you touched the book, you must have triggered the spell. Since Draven was touching it at the same time, he went along for the ride. What did you learn?"

"Something came through the portals." Draven came to stand next to her, slipping his hand into hers, giving her a reassuring squeeze, and the smell of gooey, delicious chocolate goodness with a bite of sea salt that was uniquely him filled her lungs, the tension slowly ebbed away. "The former team encountered it on their patrol, but they didn't understand what they found. Though they managed to send the creature back through the portal, the majority of them were slaughtered."

Flashbacks of the battle skipped before her eyes, the brutality making her shiver. "They didn't know they were infected until they began to change."

"And by then it was much too late." Ascher wiped his palm over his chin.

"Oh, it gets worse." Morgan pulled away from Draven, crossing her arms. "I think Leanne opened the portal on purpose. She knew what was happening the whole time and didn't warn the others. She wanted to save the wendigo—"

"—more like herself," Draven scowled at her, but Morgan kept going.

"—and use them like guard dogs to hunt creatures that come through the portals."

Kincade heaved a sigh, nudging the book with his boot. "Maybe that was her original intent, but not anymore. Now, she's just trying to save her ass. They're starving without food, slowly eating each other."

"She thinks she has control, and she wants Morgan to bring

down the wards to set them free." Ryder didn't look happy about it either, the scowl on his face enough to make a grown man cower in fear.

"They've been surviving on scraps, starving and munching on whoever entered their territory." Ascher glanced at the window, searching for the creatures out in the darkness, as if seeing his future. "They've killed so many that people around town think this place is haunted."

"They were waiting for the wards to fall until you strengthened them." Atlas bent and picked up the book. "They were close to escaping—and they're not going to let you ruin everything. You're their ticket out of here." Atlas handed her the book, looking down at her from under his lashes. "That is unless we can find a way to stop them."

"Why do you think they came after us tonight? Why not give Morgan time to discover a way out?" Draven couldn't keep still, pacing back and forth, never straying beyond touching distance from her.

"Because she can't risk you leaving," Ascher murmured, his blue eyes locked on hers. "Most witches don't have a problem cutting off their mates. If it was her, she would've run at the first sign of trouble. She sent them after us to bite you and ensure you can't leave until you've fixed the problem."

"Or she thinks she'll be able to control Morgan while the infection spreads." Kincade was grim as he looked over their group. "After your display of power, I wouldn't be surprised if Leanne will try to extract your magic by any means possible."

Morgan made a face at the idea of being a sacrificial lamb. Been there, done that. She grabbed the book from Atlas. "Yeah, I think I'll pass."

Kincade glanced at the door, then nudged Morgan toward the library. "Go, do what you have to do. The guys and I will take shifts, patrol the house and keep an eye out for Leanne and her pack of killer beasts."

Morgan reached out and clutched at his shirt when he would've moved away. "Do not engage, you hear me?" She gave him an extra shake for good measure. "Because I don't think I could handle it if anything happened to you guys."

Kincade crushed her to his chest, kissing the top of her head, then set her aside. "We'll keep you safe for as long as you need."

She swallowed hard as he walked away, fully aware that he didn't actually promise her anything. Atlas gave her arm a squeeze, a silent promise to keep an eye on Kincade, before he followed the gargoyle. Ryder engulfed her in a giant hug, sweeping her off her feet, not letting her go until her spine cracked.

"Be safe." Morgan rested her head against his chest, calming at the reassuring beat of his heart under her ear. "Don't do anything foolish."

Ryder slowly lowered her, then bent and kissed the daylights out of her. His tongue swept into her mouth, as if desperate for the taste. When he released her a second later, she stumbled on unsteady legs as he walked away.

Draven cupped the back of her neck, drawing her closer, resting his forehead against hers. "You can do this. If you need anything, I'll be right here."

When he would've pulled away, she brushed her lips against his, trying to reassure him that everything would be all right.

Ascher cupped her elbow, pulling her away and steering her toward the library.

"You're staying with me?" She was pathetically grateful for the company.

He didn't answer her for a moment, seating her on the couch before sinking down to sit at her feet. He took the book from her and set it on the table. "Being near you keeps the cravings at bay." He leaned against her leg, wrapping his fingers around her ankle a little possessively, then gave a sigh. "Your touch keeps her voice from getting into my head."

Morgan rested her hand on his shoulder and squeezed. "What

can I do?"

He glanced at her from over his shoulder. "Don't let me hurt you or the others."

She swallowed the lump in her throat. Though everything inside her protested doing as he requested, she nodded. It was the least she could do.

She picked up the book, setting it on her lap, and took a deep breath.

All she needed to do to save them was find a way to break the spell without setting the wendigo loose in the world.

No pressure.

Chapter Seventeen

$\mathcal{M}$agic snapped and sizzled along her skin when she touched the book, as if it was tasting her. Morgan held still and waited. Only when the book gave a weird hum did she dare to flip open the cover...and cursed to see nothing but blank pages.

"What the actual fuck?!" She flipped through the tattered pages, the empty sheets mocking her. While some books were just books, magical tomes were something else. It was a failsafe, a way to protect themselves against discovery from both humans and other witches who would use the book against them if the seal was broken without permission.

The only way to bypass the protection was if the owner of the book granted permission. Only then would the pages reveal their secrets. Some books held so much magic they actually decided who could access their pages.

"What's wrong?" Ascher leaned over and immediately saw her dilemma. He flipped the cover shut, taking a look at the etchings on the front. "It's a grimoire, a witch's personal diary of spells and magic. It's old, more than a few centuries, passed down through the witches' bloodlines."

"I can feel the power in it." Morgan shook her head with a huff, turning the book over and over, hoping to find some clue how to crack the code.

Only to find nothing but scarred leather.

She slammed her hand against the cover, spreading her fingers as anxiety nearly stole her breath. If she didn't find something to help her mates, she was afraid none of them would come out of this alive.

And that was not acceptable.

The book warmed under her palm, and she yanked her hand back as fire licked at her fingers. It wasn't like a warning, more like a lock, asking for verification.

"What's wrong?" Ascher looked ready to shoot to his feet to defend her, and she patted his shoulder.

"Wait." She allowed her own magic to stir, the tips of her fingers resembling different galaxies whirling to life. The magic splashed against the cover, and she gasped when the rusty, battered cover shimmered and rippled until it resembled a small, leather-bound book in excellent condition. The cover was a deep blue with familiar golden symbols etched into the cover, the tattered pages now pristine.

"I think it's another book that escaped the destruction of Library of Alexandria." She ran her fingers over the raised surface with awe. "But how would they get it or even be able to open it?"

Ascher pursed his lips, his eyes narrowing. "Or maybe the original book is what they saw. Maybe your touch is what made it reveal its true form. It could be how the books were smuggled out of the library before they were destroyed."

"And it could be why they were unable to find what they wanted." She rested her hand over the top of the book, suddenly nervous to open it. What if it didn't have any of the answers they needed?

"Or maybe they didn't have enough magic to access it." As if sensing her worries, he laid his hand over the top of hers, and leaned against her thigh. "You can do this."

Part of her eased at his warm coal scent. Taking a deep breath for courage, she nodded and cracked open the book, concentrating on what she needed most…a way out of this mess.

Ascher watched Morgan struggle to read the book, her face darkening with every hour that passed. Only when the morning sun peeked through the windows did he finally lean over and gently close the cover.

"Hey, I was reading that," she protested, her eyes red, her face tired.

"You either found the answer and didn't like it or there are no answers and you refuse to accept it." He carefully set the book on the table and turned toward her. "Which is it?"

When she looked away, her lips pursed mutinously, he let out the breath that had been caught in his chest ever since he'd been bitten. He didn't so much care that he would die, but he'd do whatever it took to make sure she survived.

Ascher stood, then pulled her up into his arms, waiting until she looked up at him. "Tell me."

He thought she'd protest or pull away from him. Instead, she gave a defeated sigh and rested her head against his chest and clung to him. Her reaction worried him more than anything else, like she'd already accepted defeat.

He ran his hand up her back, cupping the nape of her neck, his chest hollowing as he realized this might be one of the last times he'd ever be able to hold her.

"What are your symptoms?" Morgan tipped her head back, gazing at him with those beautiful blue eyes of hers that stole his heart the first time he saw her.

He could deny her nothing. "Shakes. Sweats. I can hear Leanne at times, urging me to go to her, although that compulsion is muted when you're near. When darkness fell last night, I felt a little feral, struggling to control the need to hunt. With the sun, the worst of the effects are gone, leaving me slightly nauseous but more like myself."

"And if I hadn't been with you last night?"

There was a tremor in her voice that made his chest ache, but he answered her honestly. "If I didn't have you in my life as my mate—if I didn't have something to fight for—I very much fear I would've given in to my hellhound and burned myself out. I refuse to be a slave to anyone again." He cupped her face, making her look him in the eye. "I only have one master. I live for her, and I'll die for her."

When her eyes watered, he slammed his mouth down on hers, and the hunger he'd been battling all night vanished.

The only thing that would satisfy him was her.

Steam rose from his skin, his beast scorching hot, making his lust burn even brighter. Her intoxicating scent of summer wildflowers reminded him of home, and he grabbed her hips, lifting her up until she wrapped her legs around his waist. He fitted her close, his erection throbbing at her nearness, the ache to be in her one more time nearly bringing him to his knees.

Not willing to put her at risk just to appease his lust and take the chance that he'd harm her, he eased back on the kiss, groaning low in his chest when she tightened her legs around him in protest.

"Ah-hem." Someone cleared their throat behind them.

Ascher tightened his hold around Morgan when she nearly launched herself out of his arms. He refused to let her go. Not just yet. Ascher turned to see Draven leaning against the doorway, calmly watching them. Exhaustion lined the siren's face as he studied Morgan, assuring himself that she was safe.

Only when he seemed satisfied did he straighten and give them a knowing smirk. "Breakfast is served."

Morgan groaned in frustration, allowing her head to drop

forward, and she pressed it against Ascher's shoulder, not nearly ready to let him go. He gave her a last, single, chaste kiss on the back of her neck, the heat of him enough to make her shiver, and she reluctantly loosened her legs and allowed him to lower her to the floor.

A few hours ago Ryder snuck into the room and built a fire, spending most of the time sneaking glances at her. Draven had brought food, setting it on the table, then putzed around the room, putting away books for as long as possible before he left.

Atlas and Kincade stopped by at intervals, periodically checking the room, confirming the locks on the windows were secure each time—like the thin, fragile sheet of glass was what kept the creatures at bay and not the wards. She didn't call them on it, understanding their need to be near.

And every time they glanced at her, she ended up more frustrated when she came up with nothing.

Loki snuck in next, cleaning up the food on the table with one gulp before taking his place in front of the fire with a heavy sigh. When Séamus strode into the room a few minutes later, the two of them stared at each other in curiosity.

She'd swear a spark of mischief gleamed in their eyes and nearly groaned. "Ascher?"

She was praying she was wrong.

"May the gods save us!" He closed his eyes as if pained. "There's two of them!"

Morgan couldn't help but groan, positive she could already feel them plotting. Ascher gave her a lopsided smile, and the tension in the room broke, the growing ball of lead in her stomach as time ticked down easing up enough that she could swallow without feeling the need to throw up.

For the next hour, she dozed on and off, the heat of him making her sleepy, and she realized Ascher did it on purpose. She didn't wake up until just as dawn broke, sending a glow like live coals across the sky. She stretched, careful not to dislodge Ascher from where he leaned against her. She lightly brushed his hair away from his forehead, an ache building in her chest like a bubble ready to burst.

Blowing out a breath, determined to find an answer, she picked up the book and tried again.

Despite staring at that damn thing all night, she was no closer to answers than she was when she started. The damned thing was written in fucking riddles she had no way to unravel.

With the dawn, no clear answered jumped out at her. She glared at the book. When she would've tossed the blasted thing across the room, Ascher grabbed her hand and threaded their fingers together. She swallowed hard, struggling with the knowledge that she might have just spent her last night with him.

Wait a minute...

She bolted upright, a vague idea sprouting in the back of her mind.

"That's my girl." Ascher bumped shoulders with hers as he pulled her out the door. "Don't give up on me yet."

Morgan instantly felt like an ass and tightened her fingers around his. "Never. I'll never give up looking for a way to keep you safe."

It was a vow.

Even if he turned, she would never give up on him.

As they neared the kitchen, she heard the guys arguing, and she hung back as the topic of their discussion reached her ears.

Her.

Chapter Eighteen

"*L*eanne has no intention of letting Morgan live." Kincade could barely contain his rage, his body having a hard time staying human at the thought of the danger they'd put Morgan in by taking her on this stupid fucking vacation.

If they'd stayed at the Academy, none of this would've happened. He couldn't help but blame himself for everything.

He stopped pacing and planted his fists on his hips. "Morgan is too strong. Leanne won't be able to abide the idea of losing her alpha status to anyone else."

"Agreed." Atlas spoke from the stove, keeping busy, but Kincade knew the elf...he was seconds away from losing his shit. Loki lay panting at his feet, easily snatching up whatever Atlas *accidently* dropped.

"We're trained hunters, but it's only a matter of time before we'll need supplies," Draven pointed out as he set the table. Kincade worried about him the most. Darkness haunted the siren's eyes, the deadly assassin keeping all his anger bundled up. When he finally lost control, Kincade hoped no one was caught in the blast, more than a little afraid that Draven would destroy himself with his need to keep Morgan safe.

"You're assuming they won't try breaching the walls before then." Ryder prowled around the table, filling the cups, struggling to hold his human shape. Kincade watched claws slice free of the wolf's fingertips, noticed the careful way he spoke, trying not to reveal a mouthful of fangs. "It's a good bet they won't wait us out. They're too impatient, their beasts too volatile to control."

Kincade agreed.

Besides, it went against his training to wait for an attack.

They needed to make a plan of their own.

Heat prickled along his back, the tension inside him easing, and he turned toward the door, already knowing what he would find. "Morgan."

She stood in the open doorway, tired and rumpled, and so fucking beautiful his breath caught. When he was able to confirm with his own two eyes that she was alive and unharmed, the knots eased out of his shoulders.

He curbed the impulse to go to her and gather her in his arms. Instead, he used the mating marks to brush lightly against the bonds to gauge her state of mind, not caring if he was violating her privacy.

He had to know she was okay without the others seeing how concerned he was about her condition. Her worry and exhaustion flooded his mind, nearly crushing him under the weight, but none of it was about herself.

All her concern was for them.

Though he wasn't surprised, the knowledge nearly gutted him.

"What did you find?" All their hopes rested with her. If she turned, he wouldn't have the heart to kill her. He would stay at the coven for the remainder of his life, searching for a way to make things right.

Ascher answered with a small shake of his head, and Kincade's gut felt like he'd swallowed glass. "So does anyone have suggestions for how to proceed?"

It took everything in him not to order Morgan back to the Academy, but he knew he wouldn't be able to budge her. He didn't care that she was infected—as long as she was alive to survive another day for them to find a cure was fine by him. They could keep her contained, locked away, but he swallowed his suggestion before he even voiced it.

She would never leave any of them behind.

She would never leave when a danger threatened the rest of the world.

And no matter how much he wanted to bundle her up and run away with her, she was too stubborn to let him get away with it.

Though it frustrated the hell out of him, heaven help him, it was one of the things he loved most about her.

Morgan trudged into the room and slumped into her seat. Loki trotted to her side, then plopped down next to her, and she gratefully rested her feet on his warm body. She placed her elbows on the table and dropped her head in her hands, not looking forward to the upcoming conversation…and their disappointment at her failure to find a cure. "The book was full of riddles. If there's a cure in there, I wasn't able to find it. And while I have a plan, I don't think anyone's going to like it."

Peering around the room, she saw the guys had stopped what they were doing to watch her expectantly, and she wished she could give them the answers they wanted. The plan was harebrained at best.

She leaned back in her seat and slowly rolled up her sleeve.

The gouges in her arms remained raw, not healed like Ascher's. The wounds oozed a black tar that burned when it hit the air. The pain was so minimal she barely noticed it, but she had a feeling it wouldn't stay that way. Once it began to burn more and more of her magic, she feared it would consume her.

"The wounds on my stomach healed like normal." Meaning they were gone in hours.

The guys gathered around her. When Atlas reached out to

touch the injury, she yanked her arm away. "I think my magic is fighting the infection."

"You're a witch. It affects you differently. This could be how the infection burns off your magic. Then once it's gone, the infection will spread—and it *will* eventually kill you," Kincade countered, his scowl of worry etching deep lines on his face. "What did the book say?"

Morgan scowled back at him but knew he wouldn't let it go without answers. She tipped back her head and closed her eyes, the words imprinted on her brain since she'd read them so many times, and she repeated them back at the guys.

"Touched by the gods and forged in fire
Purified by the flames of hellfire's light
Only one can carry the burden of night."

Three fucking sentences.

That was it.

The room fell silent, everyone looking grim, and she threw up her hands in frustration. "It's obviously talking about me, but nothing else makes any fucking sense and we don't have the time to figure it out."

Ryder sat next to hear, resting his forearms on the table and leaning closer, his arm less than an inch away from touching her, like he couldn't help himself. "What's your idea?"

Now that someone had asked, doubts about the wisdom of her plan preyed on her mind. If Kincade was correct about her magic being affected, if her guess was wrong, she could get them all killed. She licked her lips, glancing at the guys, wishing she could send them away, but knowing they'd never leave without her.

"My blood." She rubbed her forehead, trying to ease the ache building in her skull. "When the wendigo bit me, he turned human again."

"And then burst into flames." Draven shrugged when everyone turned to glare at him, and he shoved a piece of toast in his mouth. "What?" he demanded, spraying crumbs. "It's true."

When he said it like that...her throat closed. "Forget it. It's not worth the risk."

"I think she might be on to something." Atlas turned away from the stove and put the food on the table before glancing at her. "That man was bound to hell. Ascher has yet to give in to the cravings. It could work."

"It's too risky." Morgan untangled her feet from Loki and shoved her chair back, refusing to even listen. "What if something goes wrong?"

She couldn't live with knowing she was to blame for his death.

"Don't you think I should get a say?" Ascher took the other seat next to her, stopping her retreat dead, his intense blue eyes so full of love she could barely breathe from the heartache.

"And if I'm wrong?" Her voice broke. By the gods, she couldn't risk losing him.

"I'm dead either way." Ascher pushed the plate away from him, leaning over so she couldn't escape his gaze. "At least this way you're giving me a chance. If there's even the slightest opportunity for me to remain at your side for even a second longer, I'm going to take it."

Her stomach tumbled, and she was suddenly glad that she hadn't eaten anything. She reached over and squeezed his arm. "You're sure?"

He twisted, grabbing ahold of her hand and placing it against his chest, right over his heart. "Absolutely."

Morgan nodded, her resolve firming. She stood, then plopped her ass in his lap and looped her arm around his shoulder. "Then bite me."

He blinked away the dazed look in his eyes at her nearness and shook his head. "No bite. A cut. I can—"

"No." Morgan placed a hand over his mouth to silence his protest. "It has to be a bite. I don't want to chance fucking this up. If we only have one shot, we do it my way."

Ascher searched her face before nodding grudgingly.

She turned and glanced at the others around the room. "This goes for everyone else, too." She narrowed her eyes when Kincade opened his mouth to protest. "If this works…" she shook her head to rid herself of any shred of doubt, "…no one leaves this house or fights without a taste of my blood."

Ryder cleared his throat, struggling to meet her eyes, his attention landing on her lips instead. "My bite… my wolf…" He looked to the others for help.

"He's worried about what his bite might do to you," Atlas translated bluntly.

"I was told a witch can't be changed." She glanced at each of them, trying to resist leaning into the comfort of Ascher's arms and failing.

"Technically, yes." Ryder boldly met her gaze, his brown eyes blazing. "But nothing works as it should when you're around. What if I'm wrong? I would never live with—"

"Well, I could." She reached across the table and grabbed his arm before he could pull away. "I'm not afraid of being turned. I—"

"You say that now, but even the smallest chance is too much of a risk." He jerked away from her, standing so fast his chair toppled to the ground with a clatter as he began to prowl about the room, shaking his head and muttering to himself.

"You didn't let me finish." Morgan leaned back against Ascher, feeling his arms come around to hold her. "I don't care if I'm turned or not. I don't run with the wolves at the Academy because I need the exercise. I run because I love being with you in either form. I run with them because there's something pure about them, something so elemental that it's beautiful. Whether you're human or wolf, I love you just the way you are."

Ryder stopped moving, fisting his hands on his hips, his shoulders heaving as he struggled to contain himself. "I…you…but…"

"If I'm turned, you should know that it in no way means I'll obey you, though." Morgan winked at him when his head whipped up to stare at her, his mouth hanging open. "Just wanted to let you know, alpha or not, I'm going to be a pain in your ass."

A smile transformed his face slowly, the shadows in his eyes lightening until laughter burst out of him.

The dread building in her chest eased, her love a glow that forced out any doubts. As his laughter trailed off, she lost her smile. "If you can take the risk of ingesting my blood, I'll take the risk of turning. Fair trade?"

He only hesitated for a second longer, then gave a jerky nod. "Deal."

His husky voice sent goose bumps racing across her skin. His wolf peered out through his eyes, promising his devotion no matter what happened, and the back of her throat ached when she thought of the assholes who made him feel worthless for being a shifter.

"Are you sure you want to do this?" Kincade took the seat she'd just vacated, while Ryder righted his chair and resumed his spot. "If your blood is the cure, then how did you become infected?"

"I'm not sure if I'm the cure at all. Right now, I'm banking that the infection is consuming my magic and hasn't spread through the rest of my body yet." She glanced at the guys, humbled by the absolute trust shining back. "It's a gamble, but I'm afraid if we fight them as we are now, we won't stand a chance."

Kincade studied her for a heartbeat longer, then nodded. "I'm not ready to live without you. I'll follow you anywhere, even if it's straight to hell."

Each of the guys nodded, all of them in complete agreement.

Not one hesitation.

Tears burned the back of her throat, leaving her unable to speak, and she glanced down as emotions threatened to drown her. That they would give up everything for her...she lifted her head, forcing herself to look at each of them. "I thank the gods every day that you guys came into my life. Before you, I wasn't truly living. I never knew love had the power to give me a future I never dreamed possible…a future where I can be happy."

She blew out a shaky breath, not used to having her heart stripped bare. But she knew no matter what happened, they were the glue that kept her together. She cleared her throat and glanced up at Ascher. "Ready?"

Ascher glanced at the others, and Morgan cringed. "We can go into another room."

Ascher's arms tightened around her when she moved to stand. "No. If something should go wrong…I want them here for you."

He meant in case he turned…or worse…died. The lump was back in her throat, and she released a shaky breath. "Nothing is going to go wrong."

She wouldn't let it.

Her determination solidified—if anything bad happened, she'd go to hell and drag Ascher's ass back. Simple as that.

He was a damn hellhound. He'd know how to stay safe until she came for him.

She tipped her head back and shook the hair way from her face, leaving her throat bare. "How do you want to do this?"

Ascher leaned forward, stealing a chaste kiss that sent her heart skipping and left his breathing ragged. Then he leaned down, nibbled along her neck, before he whispered in her ear, "I'll be quick."

Before she had a chance to say anything, he tugged her shirt to the side and sank his fangs into her shoulder. Morgan jolted at the pain, heat from the bite spreading through her veins, and she couldn't stifle her moan as the pain turned to pleasure. She reached up and cradled his head, her fingers sinking into his hair, almost groaning again when his fangs retreated, already missing his touch.

He reached up, bracketing her face with his hands, resting his forehead against hers, his eyes full of love and wonder as they waited.

It didn't take long.

A grimace contorted his features. Hands found a way around her waist, and she was wrenched backwards. She kicked and squirmed to be set free, but the hold only tightened, cutting off her air, a silent threat to behave or be removed.

She recognized Atlas's touch.

Only he would be that ruthless, never willing to take a chance with her safety, taking the risk that she would hate him for it if anything bad happened.

She stopped struggling when she saw Kincade and Ryder catch Ascher as he dropped to the floor. They held him carefully while he thrashed, his roar of pain echoing in the kitchen.

When smoke began to rise from his body, everything inside her shattered.

"No-no-no-no-no-no." She threw back an elbow, slamming it into Atlas's gut, then flung her head back, cracking her skull against his nose.

His grip loosened a fraction, and she tore herself free, dropping to the floor and skidding the few feet that separated her and Ascher. Very gently, she brushed back his hair and cradled his head in her lap, not even feeling the touch of flames licking at her fingers. His clothing began to slide off in tatters, cinders burning holes in the fabric. Little wisps of ash and cinders floated in the air, swirling around them like tiny, angry demons.

The smell of singed flesh coated her mouth as the guys burned, none of them releasing Ascher despite the pain. Draven dashed for the sink, turned on the water, and used his control over the element to douse the guys.

Steam filled the kitchen until it felt like they'd all been dragged to hell with Ascher.

"Fight, damn you!" As if he heard her plea, his brilliant blue eyes cracked open. Smoke began to rise from him as he fought back. She barely felt the heat as she cradled him. Then he rolled to his side and she held him while he vomited up great globs of black, stringy tar. Steam rose from the gunk, and Ascher hacked and coughed until she was afraid he would puke up his insides.

The dark substance smelled of rot and decay as it slowly pooled across the floor, so putrid she had to cover her nose to keep from retching.

When Ascher dropped back to the floor, his arms too shaky to hold him, she curled herself around him, nearly shaking as hard as him. "I've got you. You're going to be all right."

Only when he lifted his hand and patted her head did she give a choked laugh, the anxiety melting away to giddiness. "It worked!"

Very gently, Ascher leaned down and kissed the crown of her head. "And I think I might have figured out some of your riddle—I'm your flames of hellfire. With your blood, I was able to burn out the infection."

He reached forward to touch the black tar, and she quickly grabbed his wrist, not wanting him anywhere near that crap, not again. But instead of touching it, a tiny spark leapt from his fingers and landed in the black mass. It went up like gunpowder, the air whooshed and crackled around them as the tar was consumed by the flames, the heat nearly incinerated her eyebrows even from a foot away.

The flame was intense but lasted only a few seconds.

But the stench of rot billowed around them, nearly knocking her on her ass. "Now I understand why the wendigo smells so wretched."

She waved her hand in front of her face, trying not to cough. The spot where the tar had been looked like it had eaten into the floor. As the last spark faded, Ascher fell back against her with a groan. She quickly untangled herself, concern making her stomach churn, and she patted down his body, frantically searching for any injuries.

The bite on his arm was back, split open. It looked raw and

painful, but clean.

No sign of infection at all.

She probed the wound, giving a watery chuckle when he grumbled and waved his hand as if shooing away a pest.

"Who's next?" She glanced back up at the others, wincing when she saw blood crusted around Atlas's nose and mouth, the back of her skull throbbing in sympathy. "Sorry."

He swiped away the trickle of blood and released a heavy sigh. He reached up and wrenched his nose back into place with a grunt. "I guess I should consider myself lucky that you left my balls intact."

Morgan did her best to quash her smile as she blinked up at him. "I like your balls. I would never hurt them, not when you just started to remember how to use them."

The rest of the guys covered their laughter with loud coughing, and she'd swear Atlas's lips twitched, if only for a second.

"I'll go next." Kincade rolled his shoulders, like he was preparing himself to face an epic battle and took a seat. "Draven and Ryder can help Ascher clean up and find him a new set of clothes."

As they hauled the hellhound to his feet, his arms draped over both their shoulders, he gave her a small smile. "If we continue this way, I'll be running around naked by the end of the week."

"Come on, lover boy." Draven smacked Ascher's chest, then grunted as they dragged the hellhound out the door. "And when did your ass get to be so heavy? Maybe lay off the cakes."

She smiled as she heard them squabble all the way up the stairs, then Kincade leaned forward and snagged her hand, threading their fingers together as he dragged her closer. "You can still change your mind."

Morgan ran her fingers along his temple, using her fingernails to scratch his scalp until he leaned into her touch. "Let's do this."

The rest of the guys bit her without incident, each taking just a sip of her blood. None of them had a violent reaction like Ascher, but if the way their cocks rubbed against her while she sat in their laps was any indication, they enjoyed the taste of her.

Her body ached to take advantage of the situation, and she cursed that Leanne was still free, the bitch pissing her off even more for keeping her from her men.

Besides being horny as fuck, the bites didn't affect her at all.

When it was Loki's turn, the guys ended up chasing the damn beast throughout the house, and she'd swear the gardog was snickering at their antics. When they finally had him pinned, he refused to bite her.

Grabbing a knife from the small of Draven's back, she quickly ran the blade across her palm. All the play went out of Loki, a whimper catching in the back of his throat. When she reached out to caress his face, he anxiously licked her hand as if to erase the small cut.

Ryder had been the last to bite her. He'd remained within touching distance ever since, watching her like a hawk, as if expecting her to shift at any moment. Morgan knew exactly what he felt.

As the others gathered, she paced the room, barely breathing, watching the others like they were a bomb waiting to go off.

Kincade finally walked over and gathered her close. "I'm not sick. If anything, I feel stronger and better than ever."

The rest of the guys nodded their agreement.

All except Ryder.

He stared at her with his heart in his eyes.

Not wanting him to suffer the doubts alone, she grabbed his hand to get his attention and pulled him close. His eyes were wide and panicked as he searched her face until she patted his chest. "I feel perfectly fine. How long does it normally take to know if I'll turn?"

A blush swept up his cheeks, and he dropped his eyes, mumbling, "The next full moon."

Morgan squashed her smile. "So, tomorrow night."

He nodded, his breath hiccupping in his chest. "Did you change your mind?"

"Never. Wolf or not, I will never leave your side." She stretched up on her toes and brushed her lips against his. She gave him a bright smile, waiting for the tension to ease out of him, then turned to face the others. "So what's the plan for taking the bitch down?"

Chapter Nineteen

"*T*hey're stronger during the night." Atlas had changed his clothes before he returned to the kitchen, all signs of damage to his nose completely gone. "They also outnumber us."

"We'll need to take them by surprise. Hit them during the day." Kincade nodded his agreement. "If we split—"

"We stay together," Morgan interrupted. "It's just too dangerous, and more so if they catch us by surprise." She refused to leave them vulnerable, especially since she didn't know if her blood booster would do diddly-squat.

If they were bitten, she somehow doubted they'd be able to withstand the touch of hellfire the same as Ascher.

"We stay together," Draven didn't hesitate to agree, pursing his lips as he studied her. "You were able to help Ascher, so why aren't you able to push the infection out of yourself, too?"

Morgan carefully picked at the wound at her arm, scratching the itchy flesh that wasn't covered in the black, tar-like substance. "I could try—"

"No," Kincade grabbed her arm and squeezed her fingers. "What if you end up burning out the magic faster? We can't risk having it speed up you turning."

Burning out the infection… Morgan rolled her shoulders, feeling the phoenix flutter along her back as a new idea took root.

"The flames from the phoenix might be strong enough to kill the infection."

But she doubted it.

She glanced at everyone, only to see them adamantly shake their heads.

"Not worth the risk." Ascher looked a bit pale at the suggestion. "I won't let the infection take you. If we can't find another solution, I'll use the hellfire to kill it. No need to take the change until all other options have been explored."

Instead of being afraid, Morgan was relieved to have him in control of that part. While she loved the phoenix, the bird was young and inexperienced. The creature battled dragons and won, but she wasn't sure how it would be able to battle something as tiny as the infection in her system. Not to mention the phoenix was magic itself. She couldn't risk the exposure spreading to the bird.

Morgan resisted asking Ascher to try, at least for now, not until Leanne was dead and in the ground. Something about that damn passage she found in the book nagged at her.

She was afraid she might actually need to figure out what the fuck it meant before the evening was over, if she wanted to have a chance of saving them.

Pushing away her worries, she stood and glanced out the window, not liking the silence that had fallen. "Let's head out. Maybe we can catch them unawares."

"Ascher and Ryder will shift." Kincade got to his feet, all business as he directed the guys. "Ascher, stick close to Morgan. No matter what happens, keep her alive."

Ascher and Ryder immediately stood and stripped. Despite the seriousness of the situation, she was unable to tear her eyes away from the gorgeousness of both men. Their muscles were so well defined, her breath caught at their raw power. She remembered their touch like a phantom caress, and she swallowed hard, vowing to do whatever was in her power to make sure they all survived.

The dusting of hair that covered Ryder's chest and trailed down his abs urged her fingers to follow the path. His sandy brown hair was shaggy, reaching well past his shoulders, and she ached to sink her fingers in the strands.

Magic splashed into the room as his wolf surfaced. Ryder didn't turn away or hide from her gaze as his eyes began to glow, a combination of wolf and human staring boldly at her, showing her what to expect if there were any consequences to his bite.

Not intimidated at all, she stared boldly back at him.

A tiny smile crinkled the corners of his eyes at her challenge, his amber eyes hypnotizing, as if his beast loved her spunk. If she concentrated, she could pick up his wild, earthy, fresh green scent.

Wisps of charcoal smoke rose from Ascher's naked body, drawing her eyes. The smoke quickly obscured his nudity, his bones cracking and snapping as he shifted. The edges of the smoke drifted away to show a familiar solid black hound of mammoth proportions.

As she studied him, she could swear she saw hints of red in his rough, fur-like hide, like rivulets of lava flowing along his chest. The smell of warm coal, a mixture of charcoal and fire, tinged the air, inviting her closer to his warmth, urging her to burn with him.

He padded toward her, his body huge, small wisps of smoke rising from where his paws touched the wooden floor, giving away his amusement at catching her gawking.

A movement to her right drew her attention in time to see Ryder, even more massive than Ascher, prance toward her. His fur was a sandy brown with white undertones, but his brown eyes were what always startled her the most—human intelligence and wolf cunning stared boldly back at her.

He came to her side as if the others didn't exist, leaning against her leg briefly, as if telling her to stay safe, and she tangled her fingers in his fur, scratching him between his shoulder blades. Ascher came to a stop on her other side, the heat radiating from him urging her to lean against him. The mating marks covering his shoulder shimmered, the black lines highlighted by a dusky red that resembled live coals.

The other guys were too busy checking their weapons to pay attention to the magic. Draven collected the guys' clothes and shoved them into a backpack, quickly slipping it over his shoulders. When the guys headed toward the entryway, the hounds followed on her heels.

As she passed the flash-charred stain on the floor, a shiver snaked down her spine, like she'd just stepped through the ghost of her future.

When they headed outside, Loki was hard on her heels, and she stopped to kneel next to him. "I need you to stay here and guard the house."

The gardog immediately shook his head, letting loose a massive sneeze that sent slobber flying. Instead of letting him scramble away, she grabbed the scruff of his neck and hugged him close. "Wait until nightfall. If we're not back, you need to get back to the Academy and warn them."

Loki backed up and yanked himself away from her grip, then promptly sat with his back toward her and stuck his nose in the air. Morgan caught his tail and gave it a gentle tug. "Will you do it for us? For me?"

He glanced at her over his shoulder, his face drooping as he moped, and she gave him a quick hug, kissing the top of his head. "Thank you."

He heaved a sigh, then seemed to melt into a puddle of sad dog on the floor. Though part of her felt bad for abandoning him, she couldn't bear for anything to happen to him. If she was in danger, she didn't doubt for a second that he'd die to save her. While he was big and brave, he was just a puppy yet.

Hers to protect.

And if things didn't go as planned, it was vital for someone to warn the Academy.

Draven slipped his arm around her shoulder and steered her

toward the door. She only allowed herself to lean against him for a second, before she got her shit together and pulled away.

As they exited the building, she half expected to find some sort of ambush waiting for them.

Only to see no sign of anything in the woods at all.

"Ye're all fools," Séamus muttered, appearing out of thin air, watching them from the doorway. He was wringing his hands, fretting, a forlorn Loki sprawled at his side. "Ye're all goin'ta get yerselves killed."

Then, without another word, he slammed the door in their faces.

She snorted, a little tickled by his snarly attitude.

"Stay close." Kincade took the lead, and the rest of the guys spread out in a circle around her.

She rolled her eyes but didn't protest. It wouldn't make any difference since they wouldn't listen to her anyway. Since it made them feel better, she'd learn to live with their quirks.

Kincade waited until he had everyone's attention. "We'll clear the property around the house first, remove any traps in case we need to make a speedy retreat."

The guys were every inch the assassins, willing to go to war and risk everything—to save her.

She rubbed her chest, her heart aching with the weight of her love for them.

No matter what happened, she regretted nothing.

She must've been broadcasting her emotions through the connection, because every one of the guys paused, then opened their thoughts until she was flooded with love and determination to come out of this alive and build a future together.

What they didn't realize was that they'd already given her more than she ever expected by simply loving her.

With one last touch, the guys fell silent, their footsteps barely even stirring the grass, much less making a noise as they threaded through the trees. They were systematic in their search, moving as a team, like they'd done a thousand times before.

A glimmer in the tree line caught her attention, and she changed direction, Ascher staying glued to her side. The trees opened up to reveal the rutted driveway…and the truck abandoned in the middle of it.

The rest of the guys emerged from the trees, each from a different direction, so silent it was eerie. The truck was old and battered, the driver's side door flung open. As she approached, the scent of blood hit her first.

Atlas and Draven guarded her back, while Kincade approached the truck from the other side. A second later, he dropped back. "Clear."

Morgan didn't hesitate to approach, recognizing the stench of death that she associated with the wendigo. "Whoever came, they took him."

She noted the amount of blood, not enough for a death blow, more like the person's head was slammed against the steering wheel. "Whoever they took, they're still alive."

Draven opened the passenger's side door, riffling through the glove box. Napkins and papers fluttered out, but nothing of importance. Ascher pushed forward, his nose in the air. He sneezed, then stilled. He leaned heavily against her, sending her a clear image of the guy behind the counter at the grocery store, and she instantly understood. "That old man…he came to check on us."

And he was now paying the price for it.

A heartbeat passed, then she tipped back her head and screamed her fury to the sky, "Fuuuuck!"

In spite of everything the wendigo had done to them, it was this small act that triggered her rage. Her blood heated, and her magic stirred in response to her anger—and she nearly dropped to her knees when the injury on her arm sizzled. She cradled her arm away from her body as black tar oozed out of the gouges. It dripped to the ground, and she watched as it sucked the life out of the plants a foot in every direction.

The grass withered, turning brown before flaking apart to dust. The black dirt became parched and brittle, every drop of moisture and minerals gone.

"Morgan." Atlas reached her first, curling his fingers into fists to keep from touching her when she flinched away from him. Recognizing the problem, he acted quickly, stopping the others from getting close. "Calm. You know it's a trap. If they wanted him dead, there would've been a lot more blood and gore."

She breathed through the pain, Atlas's lyrical voice doing more to calm her than his words. "I know, but if we don't save him before the night falls, they'll literally eat him alive. We have to stop them."

Draven gave her a vicious smile as he twirled and spun his blade. "We will, love."

When no one argued with her, she relaxed. "We need to set a trap of our own." She glanced at Ascher and Ryder, her voice going hard. "Please tell me you can track them."

Ascher's smile was all teeth, his fangs gleaming, while Ryder immediately set his nose to the ground. Before they traveled more than a few yards, Kincade grabbed Ryder's scruff. "We need a plan first." He rubbed his jaw, his light green eyes turning frosty. "They should be vulnerable during the day. We'll infiltrate and take their house first. I don't want to head off to the caves only to find ourselves surrounded."

Though Morgan wanted to protest that they were wasting time, she kept her mouth shut…because he was correct. If they wanted to have any chance of surviving tonight, they had to play this smart.

Heat wrapped around her throat as her necklace tightened and twisted, and she reached up to clutch a small circular pendant. The symbols were foreign, like two glyphs overlapping the other.

And she had no fucking idea what they meant.

When her fingers ran over the small etchings, a swell of

protectiveness surged through her, and she knew she needed to find the source in order to find answers.

The guys noted her subtle movements—they always noticed everything about her—and spotted the change to the necklace. It wasn't the magic they sensed, but her reaction to the necklace, especially since it saved their necks more than once.

The trek through the trees seemed to take forever, but only a few minutes had passed when the small manor house came into view. The guys spread out, keeping everyone in sight while they monitored the house.

But the place had an air of abandonment about it. The house looked in even worse condition than the day before, if possible, the walls ready to collapse from a strong wind. Shutters were gone, the shingles missing, the stairs warped and rotted. A darkness peered back at them through the windows, warning any who dared enter that they might never leave.

"Anyone else picking up anything?" Draven glared at the building as if trying to see through the walls.

"Nothing." Atlas didn't wait, breaking cover and boldly striding toward the front porch. Morgan didn't hesitate to follow, sticking to him like his shadow.

No way was she going to be ordered to stay behind.

Kincade cursed, but didn't try to stop them, and the rest of the group quickly followed them inside. The place looked ransacked, chairs tipped over, walls torn apart, the floors ripped up.

"No wonder they kept us in the kitchen and dining room when we visited." The rest of the place was a landfill of bones and broken furniture.

"It's been cleared out." Draven stormed back into the kitchen where they'd gathered, dropping his now-empty pack he carried. Ascher and Ryder followed him in their human forms, pulling on their shirts.

"They've been gone since yesterday." Ryder didn't bother looking up as he buttoned his shirt. "My guess is they never returned from stalking us last night."

"They knew we would come after them." Kincade kicked away a pile of garbage at his feet, and a bottle spun across the floor...only to disappear clear through the far wall.

Morgan heard the glass roll and thunk down steps, one after another, and she hurried across the room. When she would've reached for the wall, Draven grabbed her arm and pulled it back down to her side.

"Let us go in first, in case it's booby-trapped." He gave her fingers a little squeeze, then reached for the doorway.

And ran smack into the wall with an oomph.

"Wait," Morgan bit back her snort and tugged on his arm. "Do it again but close your eyes."

He frowned, clearly puzzled, but didn't hesitate to do as asked.

This time, when he took a step forward, he disappeared clear through the wall. She quickly reached for where he'd vanished, only to have crumbling drywall meet her fingers. She pressed her hand against the wall, anxious now that he was out of sight. "Draven?"

"Bring lights," his muffled order floated back to her, and she rested her forehead against the wall, anxiety easing its claws from her guts. Taking a deep breath, she lifted her head and dropped her arms, turning to face the others.

Before she could even ask for flashlights, Ascher lifted a hand and a small flame burst into life. Not to be outdone, Atlas lifted his hand, a small globe of light floating in the air above his palm.

Morgan rolled her eyes, then closed them and stepped forward, half expecting to face-plant into the wall. The temperature dropped ten degrees when she stepped through the partition. Only when Draven grabbed her arm to steady her did she open her eyes, barely able to see him just a few inches from her face.

It didn't take long for the others to join them on the tiny landing.

The stairs were dark and dank, moisture having long since

rotted the stud walls, the rough wooden steps crumbling. When she tried to take a step down the stairs, Kincade lifted a hand and went first. And she let them, more amused by his fanatical concern for her safety at this point than annoyed. The rest of the guys quickly followed.

"Take care." Ryder reached back and calmly plucked her up in his arms, cradling her to his chest as they descended into the abyss. Mold and dust swirled around them as they entered the basement, the floor nothing more than black dirt. The walls were just piles of large rocks with cracked cement holding them in place. The ancient shelving in the center of the room had long since collapsed, leaving the rest of the room bare.

Kincade shared a look with the guys, and they each went to a different section of the wall without being asked and began searching. If the stairs were hidden, there was a reason. Ryder carefully deposited her near the steps and joined the others. Feeling very much in the way, Morgan walked toward the center of the room where the shelving had collapsed, then bent when it appeared the wood had been torn apart instead of buckling from age.

"Hey guys..." She began throwing the wood aside, moving faster when it looked like a trap door beneath. "I think I found something."

Kincade reached her first and nudged her aside. It didn't take more than a few minutes for the wood to be cleared away to reveal a large, rectangular trap door set into the middle of the floor. A heavy, rusted metal ring beckoned her forward. When she stooped to get a closer look, the whole surface began to glow with different symbols.

"A spell." Atlas crouched next to her, running his hand above the door as if he could feel the magic, then he glanced up at her. "Do you think you can break it?"

"Do we want to break it?" Ascher remained close by her side, ready to snatch her away from danger. "This could just be a distraction. It's already past noon, and if we're not in a safe place by the time night falls, we'll be no match for the wendigo. And I have a feeling they're not going to allow us the luxury of hiding in the coven for another night."

"I think they're hiding something. Maybe answers." Draven didn't glance at any of them as he studied the trapdoor. "Can we really afford not to know?"

The answer was...they couldn't.

"Do it." Kincade reached down to touch her shoulder. "But if anything feels off, stop immediately."

Morgan studied the spell, noting that there seemed to be more than one, each layered on top of one another in a random pattern. The tricky things with spells was when you weren't the one who cast them, they often had nasty repercussions when you messed with them.

While she was usually able to break spells that were cast on her, the cost was often very unpleasant. The only way to really break a spell was to have more power than it did. The stronger the spell, the harder it would be to break, and this one would be a doozy.

It was going to fucking hurt.

She clenched and unclenched her fingers, shaking out her hands, and braced herself for the pain. Not giving herself time to think about it, she slammed her palm down on the door.

And sucked in a startled breath when it felt like she'd just shoved her whole arm in an aquarium teeming with starving piranha. Magic crackled along her hand, the tips of her fingers turning black. Her skin cracked as the magic tried to peel the flesh off her bones.

What she didn't anticipate was the way the injury on her other arm reacted to the magic.

The bite felt like it was trying to consume her, devouring the magic almost as fast as she called it forth. In retaliation, the heat from the spells sank deeper, invading her bones until she'd swear that fire ants had burrowed into her body, leaving her flesh and bones a honeycomb of holes and passageways. Sweat beaded on her forehead when the first binding on the door cracked, and she nearly whimpered when she realized there was another spell left.

They guys yelled at her to let go, helpless to do anything. To pull her away could cause the spell to rebound and kill her.

Morgan ignored their pleas.

She could do this.

She had to—too much was at stake for her to fail.

She could no longer feel her hand, her arm twitched and tingled in agony, like thousands of needles had been slammed through it, while her shoulder muscles felt like they were being pulled apart like taffy.

Then the pain sank deeper, like she'd been injected with something that slowly rotted her veins from the inside out. Unable to hold back her scream, she fell back on her ass, but she refused to let go, refused to give up.

She was close.

Just when she was sure she was about to pass out, the last spell finally shattered.

Magic fizzled and crackled angrily, then spidered across the surface of the door like a line of gunpowder had been lit. She yanked her hand away from the lick of flames, leaving a layer of skin behind.

She quickly twisted away and lost the few bites she'd managed to eat at breakfast. Ryder's strong arms slipped around her waist, while Draven knelt next to her and carefully held her hair back.

Only when she was able to catch her breath again did she lean against Ryder, letting him support her weight. Draven gently cradled her mangled hand, his face devastated. "They set a trap to kill—"

"No trap." Morgan grimaced when he probed a delicate spot on her fingers. "But the spells were meant to kill anyone who tampered with them. It's just the nature of spells. It shouldn't have been such a big deal to break them, but I forgot to take into account how greedy the infection is for magic."

She curled her fingers away from Draven, wincing when her burned skin cracked and began to flake, the wounds weeping fresh blood. She struggled to stand, wobbling precariously when she headed back toward the trap door. "It's done. I'm already healing. And like you said, we're on a tight timeline."

When Ryder cupped her elbow to help keep her upright, she was grateful for the support. None of the guys looked happy with her, but they didn't protest.

What was done was done.

Kincade reached for the bull ring handle, pausing for Atlas to get into position while the others moved in front of her, like the last line of defense. She wanted to roll her eyes at their antics, but she couldn't help but be grateful when she felt like a stiff breeze could blow her over.

Kincade lifted the hundred-pound door like it weighed nothing, the metal screeching as if it hadn't been opened in decades. Stale air and the stench of rot and decay wafted out, and she shuffled closer to Ryder, burying her nose in his shirt while she peered around his massive shoulders.

Only to see a large pit.

When everyone shuffled closer, she followed and peered down to see a single man seated at the bottom. What little remained of his clothes was dirty and torn, not an inch of skin clean, his hair nothing more than a rat's nest.

When he tipped back his head, their eyes locked, his a brilliant yellow. She swallowed hard. "They summoned you from hell, but they didn't have the power to return you. When they forced you through the portal, Leanne sent you here, didn't she?"

"What are you saying?" Kincade's voice was harsh as he grabbed her arm and pulled her away until she was facing him, but she didn't have to say anything. The knowledge had turned his eyes an icy green. "Tell me he's not the original wendigo who started this whole fucking mess."

Unfortunately, she couldn't.

Chapter Twenty

"Technically, I believe Leanne is the one who caused everything by summoning him." Morgan slipped out of his hold, unable to keep herself from peering back down into the pit to stare at the man who hadn't moved since they opened the gate. "Why isn't he trying to kill us?"

"Because he's trapped." Ascher ran his hand over the bottom of the door they pulled open, revealing a number of symbols etched into the surface. "These are special seals to keep evil at bay. The same seals that keep the doors to hell closed."

Familiar symbols.

The same fucking symbols as were on her necklace.

Morgan leaned over the pit, noticing the same seal was carved into the walls and repeated all the way to the bottom of the tunnel in a spiral pattern. The man looked normal except for his eyes. He was slumped against the floor, like he no longer had the will to move.

"You should listen to him." The man spoke with a throaty rasp, like his voice had been ruined from screaming for too long. "By the time daylight falls, I'll become the monster once more and no one will be safe."

"So we can trap them," Morgan leaned closer to study the symbol, only to have Ascher shake his head.

"It will only stop the wendigo." He nodded his head down into the hole. "He can climb out in his human form. Only the magic on the door was keeping him trapped."

Ryder was instantly at her side, a snarl on his face, ready to leap down into the hole to rip the man apart.

"Don't." Morgan grabbed his arm. "It won't help anything. He'll only come back after night has fallen."

"I say we leave him here for now." Draven didn't bother glancing at the man in the hole. "We're wasting daylight when we need to find where Leanne and her pack have hidden, not to mention find a way to destroy them."

"The only way to get rid of them is to send them back to hell." Ascher looked grim at the prospect.

"Why is that a problem? It's obvious they can be sent through portals." She glanced at the guys, not liking the look they were exchanging between them. They were trying to protect her, but she feared it was much too late for that. "I'm strong enough to open a portal."

She flexed her fingers, biting back a grimace at the slow healing, the damage more severe than she expected. Feeling was returning in painful waves, the flesh knitting together, the skin looking new and waxy. "It would hurt like a bitch, but if that's the only way to destroy them, we—"

"Being strong enough isn't the problem." The deep, raspy voice rose from the pit, and she leaned forward to see the guy pull himself slowly to his feet. "What will escape while the portal is open and you're distracted is."

"He's right." Ascher didn't look happy about agreeing with the man. "While most people don't have the power to do it, the practice was banned centuries ago for that reason. Any witch who tries will have their powers stripped and all knowledge of the paranormal world wiped from their minds."

"Morgan…" Something about Atlas's tone had her whirling toward him. But Atlas wasn't looking at her, he was staring down at the stranger with an unfamiliar expression on his face…awe. "I know those markings."

Morgan followed his gaze to see a series of swirling lines and dots along the man's temple and down the side of his face. It wasn't tribal. The tattoo looked more like braille. "What do they mean?"

"He's an old fae warrior, one of the mythical six elves who stopped the civil war more than a thousand years ago. They were said to have been granted great power from the ancient gods, so they could keep the Primordial Realm safe. They're premiere hunters who can take down armies." Atlas absently touched his temple like he was tracing the tattoo. "Each one was given a special tattoo, a badge of honor for surviving the great battle."

"He's an elf?" Morgan peered through the darkness, trying to see beneath the snarled and matted hair and layers of dirt. Instead of silver or white hair, his was pitch black, his face pale, his ears barely coming to a point. "He doesn't look like a typical elf."

"Because he's not. The six were chosen for their pure hearts. Once the great wars ended, they faded back into the myth and legend. Some say once their jobs were done, their magic faded, while others said the gods killed them and took back their power. It wasn't long after they vanished that the Council of Races was established to govern the realms."

"And you think they were cast into the underworld?" Morgan waited for the man to respond to their chatter, but he remained stubbornly mute.

"It would make sense." Atlas's eyes hardened, the umber in them expanding. "Maybe they were infected, then banished, but it wouldn't be the first time the Council of Races decided to get rid of a threat to their power by taking matters in their own hands."

"The longer a living person stays in the underworld, the more twisted they become," Ascher murmured.

Morgan remembered her mad dash through the underworld, how it tried to consume her. She had no doubt being stuck there any length of time would warp anyone, especially if the vengeful occupants found them.

"Why did Leanne summon you?" Morgan crouched next to the gaping pit. Ryder placed a hand on her shoulder to steady her—or stop her from jumping down—and she squeezed his hand reassuringly.

The elf stared at her with those yellow eyes of his for so long it felt like he was seeing into her very soul. She used the time to study him as well...his lips were cracked, his face sallow, like he hadn't been fed since they trapped him.

Morgan suspected that Atlas might be more correct than he thought...this guy hadn't been bitten. He was drowning in power, an unstoppable alpha. He didn't look evil, but Morgan knew some of the prettiest things were often the deadliest.

"She wanted an undefeatable creature." His bitter chuckle held no humor. "They got more than they expected. Wendigo can't be controlled by magic."

Excitement tingled along her veins. "How can they be controlled?"

"Morgan..." Kincade waited until she looked up at him, his eyes alive with emotions, easily guessing her plan. "No, you can't."

"I'm already infected." She refused to look at the rest of the guys, their disapproval and denial reaching her through their connection more strongly than any shout. "If I can order them back to hell, they'd have to obey."

"No." Draven threw his knife across the room so hard it sank into a stone wall. "It's not worth the risk."

Morgan stood and strode over to him, stopping so close that he had no choice but look at her. The heartbreak on his face made her ache. "We're assassins. You and I both know the risks...and the sacrifices that must be made. We put others first. We protect others."

"And it's my job to protect you." He leaned down and pressed his forehead against hers, his hands coming up to cup the back of her neck, his grip desperate. "Don't ask me to give up more. I can't lose you."

Feeling like her heart was shattering, she pulled away from the storm brewing in Draven's eyes and stared down at the guy in the pit. "Will it work?"

The guy pursed his lips, his hands on his hips as he gazed up at her. "Only one being can control the creatures of hell...a goddess."

"Or someone touched by the gods?" The first line of the riddle came back to her. She touched the spot right below her collarbone, where the shape of a crescent moon was etched into her flesh. The moon was created by one long swirling line, twisted into an intricate design, with specks of the solar system spinning through it.

The symbol of Nyx...one of the oldest and most dangerous primordial gods...the first goddess and mother of all gods.

If any goddess had the power to defeat Leanne and her men, it was Nyx.

Now, if only she knew how to access and use that power.

"Legends speak of a goddess...by taking the darkness inside her, she could save the damned." The guy in the pit murmured almost distractedly, interest sparking in his yellow eyes.

"What happened to her?" Kincade looked torn about asking, ignoring Draven's murderous glare.

The guy in the pit tipped his head back, his face grim. "She died."

Kincade's flesh rippled like his beast was trying to explode out of him. Draven swore in a language she didn't recognize. Ryder's eyes were a brilliant whisky color, ready to do whatever it took to protect her...even if it meant protecting her from herself.

Only Ascher and Atlas looked like they weren't seconds away from cracking.

"It's a risk." She held up her hands when the guys roared in protest. "But the riddle says it can be done. Ascher is proof of that. My blood mixed with hellfire has to be the key."

"It won't work." The guy in the pit broke the tension between them.

"What do you mean?" At her question, everyone gathered around to stare down at him.

"You're bitten." His nostrils flared, sniffing the air as if he could smell the infection. The pity in his eyes made them dull. "By nightfall, you'll be lost."

"No." Morgan shook her head, pure stubbornness leaking through. "We saved Ascher. The magic in my blood drew out the infection, and he was able to burn the rest of it away."

The man whirled, his eyes seeking Ascher. He scanned the hellhound from head to foot, his eyes widening almost comically. "That shouldn't be possible."

Excitement returning, Morgan crouched and gripped the edges of the pit, dirt crumbling under her fingers. "I can do this."

The man turned and gazed up at her, not saying anything for a moment. "The spirit of the wendigo won't let you go so easily." He licked his lips, revealing small fangs, his hands tightening on his hips until his knuckles whitened as he struggled to control himself. "Your magic tastes too good. It will lure them out."

Morgan blanched, quickly glancing at the guys. "Did I just turn you all into fucking walking, talking fast food snacks by giving you my blood?"

"We're already a target," Draven murmured. "The immunity in your blood might be the only thing that can keep us from turning."

"It will only delay the inevitable." The man glanced around his prison, but she could tell he wasn't really seeing it. "You won't be able to take them on your own."

"What can we do to protect her? The one who bit her turned human almost immediately." Kincade came to her side like he needed to be near her, finally listening instead of rejecting their conversation outright. "Hell claimed him within an hour, burning him from the inside out until nothing but ash remained. Will another bite speed up her infection rate?"

The man in the pit came back to himself and looked up at them, his yellow eyes gleaming in the darkness. The light from Atlas's globe caught his tattoo, and it seemed to shimmer with power. "It'll eat through her magic faster," the man answered distractedly. "While your blood might eventually kill the wendigo, too many bites could very well prove lethal."

"So, no biting." She quickly held up her hands when the men began to grumble and snarl. "I promise."

"Your Leanne has built a small army. During the daylight hours, you might have a better chance of winning than you think. Many were once human and don't follow her willingly. But beware…some have gone insane when they understood what they were forced to do to survive."

"We're running out of daylight." Atlas came to her side, his cinnamon scent inviting her to lean against him. "If she does have an army, we won't stand a chance once darkness falls."

"Take me with you." It was a demand, the man lifting his chin arrogantly. "The wendigo have gone to ground...literally. The underground cave system hides miles of tunnels, a labyrinth of passageways infused with their scent. You won't find them before nightfall. Not without my help. She's counting on it."

"This isn't a good idea." Draven turned to retrieve his knife, then came back to glare at the stranger in the pit.

Ryder and Ascher both nodded their agreement.

Kincade remained silent, his expression calculating, and she turned toward Atlas. "Can we trust him? We don't even know his name."

"Before he was turned, I would say absolutely." Atlas peered over her shoulder at Kincade, looking uncertain for the first time.

Morgan reached up, cupping his face until he looked back down at her. "What do your instincts say?"

"If he gives his word, he won't break it." There was no doubt or hesitation.

She touched the pendant absently—it hadn't been a warning but a premonition.

If they wanted to succeed in stopping Leanne and her army, they needed the man in the pit.

"He goes with us." Morgan smiled at Atlas, getting up on her toes to kiss his jaw. Then she glanced down into the pit with narrowed eyes. "But only if you give us your word to help us take down Leanne and her pack. Your word that you'll give us warning when the urge to snack on us becomes too overpowering to control."

"You have it. And you may call me Caedmon." Without waiting for a response, he began climbing out of the pit, his movements fast and effortless, like he'd done it a thousand times.

As they emerged from the house, Morgan gulped the fresh air, not realizing how hemmed in she'd felt inside when each breath tasted like death. Instead of following them, Caedmon stayed on the porch and held out his hand, tears in his eyes when the sunlight touched it.

While the others kept an eye on him, it was Atlas that concerned her the most. He refused to look away from the elf, remaining close to her side. "What's wrong? Did we make a mistake?"

"The name...I remember it spoken about in legends. It means warrior." He fell silent, lost in a past she couldn't see.

When he said no more, she prodded him. "Kind of fits in with the assassins."

He immediately shook his head, his silken hair slipping over his shoulder. "Each of the six elves was granted unimaginable power. While each was dangerous and deadly in their own right, some names instilled such fear that people were afraid to even whisper them lest they catch his attention."

Morgan chuckled, not sure if he was in awe of the guy or afraid of him. "You make him sound like the boogeyman."

"No," Atlas answered distractedly. "He's much worse. He never gives up, never slows down until he finds his target. Nothing can stop him."

Much like the wendigo…

Morgan studied Caedmon more closely, easily understanding how so much time on earth—or in hell—could warp a person. "Is he a danger?"

"Always." Atlas stared down at her, his eyes mostly umber as he settled his hand on his knife. "But he'll keep his word. The trouble is that when he turns, even with all our power, we won't be able to stop him. We could possibly defeat the army, but he's old, a pureblood unlike the others."

Caedmon stepped off from the porch, lifted his face to the sky and sighed heavily before turning to look at her. "We need to go or we won't make it in time."

She watched him scan the area, bend on one knee like a hunter of old while he searched the ground, then point off in the distance. "They're that way."

"How do you know?" She had thought he knew the location from Leanne or that he could sense them or something, and felt stupid for making the assumption.

Instead of answering, he just turned to look at her. Brilliant yellow eyes gleamed back at her, the wendigo close to the surface, and she understood.

He was an apex predator.

He didn't need anything but his instincts and skills.

"Keep up. Stay close." And he was off like a shot.

Even with her enhanced training, it was a struggle to maintain his speed. Their surroundings streaked past them as they ran. Atlas kept pace at her side, making sure he remained between her and Caedmon at all times, as though he thought the fae might try to steal her away.

Then, from one step to the next, the ground beneath her crumbled.

She was going too fast to catch herself, and she dropped through air.

Chapter
Twenty-one

$\mathcal{M}$organ gauged the distance to the ground, then grimaced, one thought flashing through her mind—*oh, shit, this was going to hurt.*

The cave was littered with boulders and stalagmites.

And she was about to land directly on top of one.

She twisted her body to keep from being impaled, and her side smashed into a massive pillar, the rock scraping along her ribs. The hit was so brutal the stone cracked, covering the sound of her ribs snapping. Though she braced for impact, there was nothing she could do to stop her body from landing with a meaty thump, hitting so hard she actually freaking bounced.

The breath was knocked out of her like someone had reached into her chest and tried to rip her lungs out through her bellybutton. She skidded and rolled across the rocky surfaces, peeling off layers of skin until she felt raw.

She tried to halt her momentum, but she was going too fast.

Just when her body began to slow, she felt her legs go over a ledge of some sort.

She teetered on an edge, and felt her weight slowly drag her, inch by inch, the rest of the way over. She turned and twisted, clawing at the ground for purchase, her nails snapping to the quick, sending fire burning down her fingers.

She glanced over her shoulder, looking for a safe place to land, and her eyes widened when she saw the abyss that waited to swallow her whole. The putrid stench of rotten corpses rose on its stagnant breath, and she knew she'd found the gorge where Séamus said they tossed the remnants of their meals.

The metal cuff and rings she wore melted down, the liquid warm against her skin, and she slammed the blades into the ground to keep from being pulled completely over the ledge, the blades stopping her slide only inches from the rim.

Knowing the guys would follow her, she sucked air into her lungs despite the agony. "Don't. Jump. Trap."

The effort left her lightheaded, her ribs screaming, as she slowly hauled her body back onto solid ground. Only then did she release her hold on the blades and collapse onto her back. As she stared up at the stalactites in the ceiling, she saw the tiny opening she'd dropped through and shook her head in total amazement.

It had to be less than two feet across.

She wasn't sure if it was good or bad luck that she'd slipped through it.

As the high-pitched ringing in her ears slowly subsided, she heard the guys yelling down at her. Kincade's concerned face filled the small opening, then his expression hardened into determination when he spotted her.

He linked his fingers together, lifted them over his head and began to hammer at the stone to widen the opening. As dirt and small rocks rained down on her, she dragged herself away from the destruction zone, wincing when a nasty cough caught in her chest from the dust whirling in the air. Bones ground together, and she knew more than one rib had been broken.

"Stop. Please."

The pounding immediately halted, and everyone's faces appeared around the hole to stare down at her, each only satisfied that she was all right after a thorough examination. Not wanting to worry them, not sure how much time she had before her presence would be discovered, she pushed herself up off the floor.

She wobbled pathetically, tripping over air as she struggled to get her balance.

"There's a large ridge down here. If you try to jump, you'll only end up going over the edge." She cradled her ribs, feeling the bones shift under her fingers and grimaced. "It was only a fluke that I didn't go over."

Even before she finished, a shadow dropped from the ceiling, and she watched with her breath caught in her throat as it landed in a crouch just inches away from the abyss. To her surprise, it was Caedmon.

He stood slowly, turning to face her, and she had to close her mouth when she realized she was gaping at him like an idiot. "Do you have a death wish?" She huffed in exasperation. "Of course you do."

"One thing has become abundantly clear to me since I was turned...not only can we see clearly in the dark, we're indestructible. The fall wouldn't have killed me." He only gave the abyss a cursory glance, and it was all she could do not to yank him away from the ledge. "I'll take you to Leanne and do my best to protect you."

Sincerity rang from his voice, surprising her, and she nodded slowly.

They could still make this work.

"Kincade—continue on with the plan. Find the entrance of the caves so we can take them by surprise by hitting them from both sides." The guys disappeared, and she heard them arguing. It didn't take more than a minute for Draven to appear in the opening, a brash grin on his face.

"No can do, babe." He slowly lowered himself through the hole, then began to kick his legs back and forth until his body was swinging. "You're the one who made the rules. Remember? No splitting up."

Heart in her throat, she watched him dangle over oblivion.

One wrong move, a simple slip, would either send him into the abyss or impale him on the stalagmites.

"Don't you dare!" But even as she yelled, he let go and she watched his body drop through the air like a fucking missile. He landed hard, his shoulder bouncing off a rock, and she hurried after him, cursing him every step of the way. "I swear to the gods, if we come out of this alive, I am going to make your life miserable."

As she hurried around a large column, she saw Draven slowly pick himself off the ground, swatting away the dirt and dust off his clothes like he'd done nothing more strenuous than walk in the park. She charged toward him, ready to smack him, when his eyes widened in alarm. He swept her up in his arms and spun them, pressing her up against a cave wall just as Ryder zipped past them.

Morgan couldn't bear to watch the others plummet, and tucked her face against Draven's chest. "You guys are going to be the death of me."

It wasn't long before everyone was down, a little bruised and battered, but alive. They gathered around her, and Kincade rested a comforting arm around her shoulder. "We're safe. You can look now."

"You're an idiot!" she growled, lifting her head to glare at him. "I wasn't afraid to watch you fall. I was afraid if I watched, I'd be tempted to kick your ass myself for carelessly risking your lives on something so stupid."

His brows shot up, and he slowly lowered his hand as if she was a rabid dog ready to take it off.

He wouldn't be far wrong.

"What the hell is wrong with you people?" She shoved away from Draven, planting her hands on her hips as she surveyed them. "You could've been seriously hurt or even died."

Kincade grabbed her behind the neck, dragged her forward, and kissed her like he couldn't go another minute without tasting her. His hands and lips demanded everything, and she was helpless to resist, the anger merging into lust, the scent of warm earth and hot stone inviting her to get closer and bask in the heat.

She nearly whimpered when he gentled the kiss and pulled away.

Kincade gave her one last lingering look, the fire in his eyes banked for now, and he turned toward Caedmon. "Do we know where we are in the cave system?" Kincade ran his fingers through his hair as he went back to the man in charge. "How close are we to the wendigo nest?"

Morgan followed the rest of the guys as they gathered where Caedmon stood under the new skylight. Warmth wrapped around her ribs, her left ankle, and right shoulder while her body began to kick up its healing ability, as if it sensed the coming danger and her need to be in top physical shape.

Caedmon lifted his face to sniff the air, cocking his head. When his eyes snapped open, the shards of black in them disappeared until the yellow glowed so brightly his eyes seemed to be made of pure light. Instead of answering, he crouched, then leapt over them in a single bound.

The guys ducked out of the way, quickly tackling her.

But instead of attacking them, Caedmon crashed into a man who just stepped out from behind a column, the two of them slamming onto the floor with a thump. Without hesitation, he reached down and snapped the stranger's neck with a powerful twist that spun the other man's head halfway around.

While she was immune to the violence, there was something unnatural about seeing a man's head on backwards that gave her a pause

Caedmon got to his feet smoothly and grabbed the guy by the ankle, dragged him to the edge of the cliff, and calmly tossed him over the edge. Then he turned and walked back across the room like nothing had happened. "When he turns, it will take time for him to crawl out of that hole. I believe I managed to eliminate the threat before anything was reported back to Leanne, but I can't guarantee he didn't see any of you. They might have discovered our arrival sooner than we expected."

Morgan trailed after Caedmon when he headed toward the exit, only to discover the man had been dragging an old miner's cart of partially eaten corpses.

Or what remained of them.

Most of the remains were hard to identify, but she recognized a femur as being human…and a row of partially consumed human skulls underneath. The flesh was rotten, the color a mottled green and black. Maggots wiggled around in the flesh…or swam in the putrid remains that gathered at the bottom was more like it, and she stopped dead, unable to take another step closer as the nasty smell crawled down her throat.

She was grateful when Ryder slipped his arm around her waist and drew her back against his chest, although she couldn't imagine how he could bear to breathe with his acute sense of smell.

Caedmon didn't even blink as he picked up the ropes to the cart and hauled it toward the edge of the abyss, then booted the rotting remains over the edge before turning around to face them. "To be on the safe side, we should move out as soon as possible."

Instead of being weirded out by his brutal killing, the guys actually appeared comforted. She followed Caedmon, and discovered the exit wasn't hidden so much as tucked behind a giant column of rocks.

Kincade reached over and grabbed her wrist to get her attention. "Let me and Caedmon take the lead." He squeezed her hand, then brought it to his lips and kissed the backs of her fingers. "He knows the cave system, and I can protect myself in my gargoyle form. We'll be the bait. I want you to hang back with the others."

"Very well." Morgan wanted to protest that she should be going first, but she couldn't refute his logic. "Ascher and I will hang back and etch the seals along the walls as we go." She turned to Caedmon. "Work your way around the perimeter of the cave system first before heading toward the nest. I want to leave nothing to chance. When they turn, I want them trapped."

While it would keep the wendigo from escaping, it left her team vulnerable. They'd have to fight in a tight space in unfamiliar territory with a cornered animal that couldn't die.

She just had to pray they were up to the task.

"It will waste daylight," he warned, but nodded his agreement.

It took them more than an hour of precious time to find the exits and place the seals. They had to dodge patrols and guards, but it was done.

The closer they worked toward the nest, the harsher the smells became.

And the sound of yelling.

She easily recognized the old man from the grocery store, his curses echoing down the tunnels. Ignoring the others when they tried to hold her back, she slipped out of their grasping hands and followed the sounds.

And found cages full of people.

At least two dozen of them.

The people were in rough shape. More than half of them had been underground more than a few weeks if their sickly, dirty complexions were any indication. More than a few were malnourished, like they hadn't been fed in days. The toilet was just a gutter running between the cages, a small trickle of water that did little to carry away the waste.

Everyone quieted when they noticed them, pressing closer to the bars of their cages. Morgan immediately went to the first cage, only for Caedmon to hold out his arm to stop her. "If you release them, they'll give away our location. Darkness is closing in fast, and half of them are still human. Instead of helping them, you'll be ringing the dinner bell for the wendigo."

Her arms dropped to her sides, and she felt sick at the thought of leaving them behind.

"Half of them were recently bitten, most likely in preparation for your visit. Those who remain human are just cattle for them to eat. When they turn, they'll be under Leanne's control. Or worse, if you free them now and they run...we can't allow them to leave the caves. If you want to have any hope of saving them, they need to remain here."

"We'll be fine, girly." The old man waved her away when she hesitated, his faded green eyes fierce. "Do what you have to do and kick their asses."

Leaving them went against her every instinct and training, but what he said made perfect sense. Morgan nodded and reluctantly stepped away. "I'll be back. I promise."

Or she would die trying.

"You bitch!" One of the younger prisoners snarled and lunged at the bars, hitting the cage with a clank. He thrust his hand between the metal bars, his hands reaching for her, obviously wanting to beat the crap out of her for denying him. "You can't just leave us here to die."

Before anyone could react, one of the prisoners in the same cage stepped forward and brought down his fist, knocking the kid out cold, and he hit the ground with a heavy thump. "He watched the others being bitten last night, watched the few humans still trapped in the cages with them being ripped apart while they fed."

Morgan felt sick.

They were training them to hunt humans.

Worse, if they'd fed, there was no cure for them.

She stepped forward and grabbed the bars. "Stay alive. If they come for you—fight. One way or another, this ends tonight."

"That's adorable...thinking you can save them." Leanne sauntered into the cavern, a smug smile in place while a dozen of her minions surrounded them. "I'm so glad you could join us. I've been waiting for you. Caedmon—thank you so much for bringing them to me."

**Chapter
Twenty-two**

*C*aedmon stiffened at the accusation, his yellow eyes glowing with hatred as he glared at Leanne.

It would be the perfect trap.

Though he didn't say anything to defend himself, Morgan knew for a fact that he wanted nothing to do with the bitch who'd stuffed him down a hole in the ground and left him to rot. He could've been free if he'd been willing to help build her kingdom. But instead he consigned himself to a different type of hell in that pit.

"Why don't we go somewhere more comfortable, where we can discuss my terms?" Leanne curled her nose up in disgust as she looked at her prisoners, completely oblivious to the fact the stench emanating from her was much worse.

Leanne turned on her heel, not waiting for them to reply.

When Morgan glanced at Kincade, he gave a subtle shake of his head, and she curled her fingers into fists against the urge to reach for her blades. Leanne's men prodded them forward none too gently, nearly sending her sprawling in the muck.

To her surprise, they didn't search them for weapons.

Which made sense, considering the wendigo were indestructible.

They were led through a series of passageways that finally

opened up to a large cavern. The smell was concentrated there, which meant this was where they spent most of their time. Human remains were scattered about the cavern, while urine and feces lay in puddles across the floor.

She couldn't imagine how any human, much less animal, could live that way, but it was like they didn't even notice. Worse, she counted around three dozen of the creatures, much more than expected.

They were royally screwed.

"As you can see, we've outgrown this place." Leanne climbed the steps of the platform at the far end of the cavern, then took a seat on what looked like a large throne. She crossed her legs, then tapped her nails against the armrest, clearly annoyed at being kept waiting. "We need you to take down the wards. With your help, we'll be able to rid this world of the creatures who don't belong without having to risk any more lives."

Morgan blinked at her in complete astonishment. Leanne was completely oblivious to the innocent lives she'd destroyed, not to mention the slaughter she planned to unleash on the world to feed her voracious army. "The wendigo are like a plague. If they're ever unleashed on the world, mankind would be wiped out of existence."

Leanne tsked in annoyance and rolled her eyes, waving Morgan's prediction away as if it was a nuisance. "An exaggeration. Our food supply here has been depleted. An army must feed. Once we're free, we'll take measures to make sure it doesn't happen. The creatures we hunt will more than suffice."

Until they were all gone.

Most supernatural creatures who came to earth were innocent, and only a small percentage actually meant humans any harm.

It also meant if the wendigo were ever set free, everyone at the Academy would be targeted, the school likely the first place they would attack, just to get rid of the threat.

"You and I are the same." Leanne tucked her perfectly

groomed hair behind her ear, her green eyes glittering. "We were trained to give everything to protect those around us. You must see that this is the only way."

Leanne would say or do whatever it took to get Morgan to take down the wards. At one time Leanne might have believed what she was saying, but the woman had become tainted, addicted to the heady power of being unstoppable, and she was determined to do whatever it took to get her way, not caring that she would destroy the world in the process.

"Sorry, but that's not going to happen." Morgan's cuffs and rings warmed and melted down, and she hid her hands behind her back while the blades formed. "You're insane, the infection destroying all capacity for rational thought."

Leanne threw back her head and laughed. "You make it sound like you have a choice."

Then all amusement vanished from Leanne's face. "Darkness is falling. Can you feel the call of it against your skin?" A superior smile twisted her lips. "I don't need your permission. You will obey me. Eventually. Maybe after we feast on one or two of your mates?"

Morgan couldn't help it—she laughed. "Yeah, not happening."

"Kneel before me!" Leanne shot to her feet, pointing to the bottom of the dais.

The comment touched Morgan's mind like the brush of a spider's feet, and she easily swatted it away.

But Leanne was right about one thing. Darkness was about to fall. They had no more than thirty minutes before the shit hit the fan, and if she had a chance to stop it before it all started, she had to take it.

Very slowly, she took a step forward, pretending to fight against the command.

The guys yelled, and a scuffle ensued, and she opened the connection between them, urging them to be ready to move. Rage and worry drifted to her, every one of them disliking the plan, but they obeyed.

Morgan began to bend, but instead of falling to her knees, she leapt the distance between them and brought up her blades. But instead of sinking the weapon into Leanne's chest, a man jumped between them.

The metal entered his shoulder, then her blade seemed to get stuck as it fed, refusing to release its hold as it consumed the magic in him, and they both dropped to the floor. The place around her fell silent as the guy screamed in pain.

Black tar seemed to sweat from his pores while he writhed in agony. Patchy fur sprouted along his arms and face, then receded. His bones cracked as he partially shifted until he appeared stuck between forms.

Only when the liquid stopped bubbling did the knife release her with a hum of pleasure.

Morgan stood and stumbled away.

What remained of the creature, a horrific mishmash of human and wendigo, gave a tortured groan. He turned and began to claw his way toward her, dragging himself down the steps, leaving a streak of thick black tar behind him.

The bones of his arms snapped under his weight. When the body collapsed, it hit the stone with a squelch, black crud splattered everywhere as the flesh continued to break down until all that remained was a large, quivering glob of putrid rot.

Bones gleamed in the mess, and his skull toppled forward with a thunk, snapping away from the spine to bounce down the two remaining steps before rolling to a stop just a foot from her, his macabre smile gleaming up at her.

Triumph filled Morgan, and she gave Leanne a nasty smile. She raised both blades and dropped into a fighter stance, the knives humming slightly with excitement, hungry for more. "You're right. We do have terms to discuss...*your* surrender."

"Kill the men. Take the girl. I want her in chains before sunrise." Leanne shouted her commands, her words thrumming with power, leaving her army with no choice but to obey.

The bitch took the coward's way out, backing away while her men charged forward, disappearing before the first blow was struck. Leanne's men pushed away from the walls where they'd lounged and watched the event unfold, maybe thirty of them in all emerging from the darkness.

A few hesitated as they neared the bones of their fallen comrade…then walked through them, pulled forward by Leanne's command, the bones of their friend snapping under their boots.

Kincade grabbed Morgan's arm, dragging her backwards to join the rest. They didn't wait for the attack but instead plowed their way past the two guards behind them and dashed into the tunnels.

With a roar, Leanne's men charged after them, their feet pounding in the darkness.

Kincade took the lead, his form hardening to stone. As they charged through the tunnels, he smashed into anyone who tried to stop them, either cracking their skulls with his fists or grabbing their arms to swing them against the walls with a sickening thud.

The bodies hit the ground dead, but she knew they wouldn't be dead for long.

By nightfall, they would rise again.

The team was moving fast, the wendigo in their human forms unable to keep up with them, but that wouldn't last either.

Caedmon remained near the rear, ruthlessly dropping any who followed, needing one or two blows at most before they fell dead.

Morgan slashed at one of the guys reaching for Kincade from a side tunnel. The man hissed in pain, his wendigo boldly peering out through his eyes. Instead of attacking again, the man backed away and watched her…as if he knew all he had to do was wait until nightfall to claim her.

Then he disappeared back into the darkness.

The attacks grew further apart until they all but vanished, and a sinking feeling hit the pit of her stomach. "They're waiting for nightfall."

"We're like rats in a maze in here," Draven grumbled, clearly disliking being trapped underground. "We need to get out of the tunnels."

"We can't leave." Morgan dropped back to run next to him, wishing she could touch him. "At least not until after nightfall, or they'll escape the tunnels in their human forms and be free to roam the night. At least we can control the environment down here."

Any time they slowed down, they were discovered within minutes and forced to run again. It was almost like they were being herded or forced to keep moving in order to wear them down.

They needed a plan.

"She's right." Caedmon didn't hesitate to snap the neck of a man who charged out of the darkness behind him, barely slowing his pace before he hauled the body into a side tunnel to cover their trail. "The seals won't stop them until after they've turned."

They passed through so many twists and turns it felt like a deadly version of hide and seek.

Morgan slowed, dropping back to talk to Caedmon. "Take us back to the cavern where we entered."

"Are you sure we can trust him?" Ryder edged between them, forcing her away from the elf, his whisper more of a growl. "He could turn at any time."

"Absolutely." She didn't even hesitate. "I think he's the key to helping us defeat Leanne."

Caedmon seemed startled by her comment, meeting her eyes in the darkness before he gave her a nod and switched directions.

Instead of arguing, Ryder grunted his displeasure, but trusted her judgement. As they wove their way through the rough tunnels, she struggled not to be overwhelmed by the stench. It was like the denizens used the place as a giant toilet, making it impossible for her to detect if anyone was about to come around the next corner.

Time became irrelevant in the darkness. Though she knew it could've only taken five minutes to find the cavern, it seemed to take forever before they were finally back where they started. They killed three more soldiers along the way, but Morgan knew once night fell the wendigo would return, bigger and badder than ever.

As they entered the cavern, the guys spread out to clear the place, the hole in the ceiling, the only source of light, showing it was almost night.

After making sure they were alone, the guys gathered around her, all of them a little battered and bloody. "Can we spread some light? The brighter the better?"

"Your eyesight is perfect." Draven gave her a funny look.

But Caedmon nodded, a small smile making him look dangerously handsome. "And ours is even better. The lights will blind the wendigo and allow us to hide in plain sight."

Understanding dawned, and Atlas began to create globes and scattered them around the cavern. Ascher wasn't too far behind, setting a few fires that seem to burn the very stone as fuel. It didn't take long for the cavern to brighten significantly.

"What's your plan?" Kincade remained by her side, watching the door.

"We'll use the door as a strangle point." She nodded to the opening. "Only a few can enter at a time, so we should be able to take care of most of them there."

"And when they turn?" Ascher glanced at the hole in the ceiling, as if he was thinking about how he could force her to leave.

Morgan pointed over her shoulder. "We'll work in teams. One will kill or maim, and the other will toss them into the abyss. And Leanne will come eventually. She won't be able to resist."

"You have a plan." Draven's expression was shrewd.

Morgan whirled her blades, then allowed them to melt back into her jewelry. "If you can keep her minions off me long enough, I can get to her."

"You can't kill them all, not without them getting you." Atlas wasn't being doubtful, just practical. The odds weren't in their favor.

But talking was over when the first set of minions charged toward them. Caedmon and Atlas lunged forward, their movements graceful and elegant as they easily sliced down their foes. Draven sighed, then nudged Ryder. "I guess we're the cleanup committee."

They shrugged and started dragging the bodies toward the pit before throwing them over the edge. Kincade and Ascher weren't so easily convinced by the plan, staying close to her side. Kincade grabbed her chin, tipping her head back, then sighed heavily. "I recognize that reckless glimmer in your eyes. No matter what happens, you will stay near us. Understood?"

"Of course." No way would she allow anything to happen to them.

Ascher snorted and crossed his arms, not believing her for a second.

Dirt drifted down from the ceiling, and everyone glanced up.

Just in time to see Loki wiggle his big ass through the small opening. He popped out like he'd been launched, and she watched him coast around the cavern before gently coming to a landing in front of her, tucking his wings tightly against his back.

Then he pranced about, proud of himself for finding her.

"Easy, ye great lug!" When Loki turned, she saw Séamus riding him like a horse. "Are you trying to get me killed, ye daft beastie?"

"What are you doing here?" She wasn't sure if she wanted to hug them or strangle them both. Loki made up her mind when he pounced on her and began licking everything within reach, sending Séamus tumbling off his back.

The leprechaun managed to leap off at the last moment before smacking to the ground, landing on his feet next to Kincade. "Ye stupid beast," Séamus huffed under his breath, tugging fretfully at his clothes to straighten them. "He thought ye might need backup, so we managed ta reach that school of yers. About a dozen or so hunters and witches are tromping all over the place topside. We explained the situation, and they be waiting for nightfall to attack."

Morgan could only gape at him.

He could've escaped the house with his treasure while they were distracted by the wendigo, but the sweet fool actually came to rescue her.

The sound of a scuffle came from behind her, and she turned to see three more minions enter. Caedmon and Atlas went into action, both of them taking down their targets almost at the same time. Draven launched three knives in rapid succession, the last man barely making it through the door before he collapsed.

It didn't take long to get rid of the bodies, and Caedmon came to stand at her side. "They're going to be coming in force soon. Their senses are sharpening, so they'll be able to track you through the tunnels."

"How much time?" Kincade didn't bother to pull his weapons, his skin rippling slightly as it hardened to stone again, ready to defend her.

"They'll be here in minutes." Caedmon's mouth tightened. "The higher the moon rises, the less control I have over my beast. If we don't finish them quickly, make sure you send me into the abyss with the others."

Morgan gritted her teeth against the urge to object, but she understood the need to do whatever was necessary to protect those she cared about. She couldn't deny Caedmon the same privilege. Kincade obviously thought the same, giving him a solemn nod.

But she knew that wouldn't stop him from climbing back out.

She could only hope that they'd be gone by then.

She fiddled with her cuff, very much afraid she might not have the skill to defeat him, magical blades or not.

Not if he was the original.

Obviously reading her mind, he focused his whole attention on her. "When I go over that edge, portal everyone out of here immediately. Run and don't come back. The wards will keep me contained for now. Do whatever you need to do to keep everyone out of the coven and the wards strong. Give me time to eradicate the others. Then you must find a way to send me back to hell permanently."

A lump formed in the back of her throat when she realized that he came with them to help...and never expected to leave.

Well, not if she could help it!

Chapter
Twenty-three

*E*veryone took up positions when they heard snarls echoing down the tunnels, the sounds coming from both directions.

"They're here." Ascher stepped close to her side, steam rising from his clothes, his feet searing the stone with every step.

She grabbed his arm, waiting until he looked at her. "When I give the signal, I want you to light this place up. Are you up to it?"

"You have a plan." He gave her a long, measured look, only speaking again when she kept quiet. "You should tell the others."

"They'd only try to stop me." They'd do whatever it took to keep her safe, and she couldn't allow them to interfere. She had a feeling she only had one shot, and she couldn't fuck it up. She touched the injury on her arm and knew they were running out of time. "Trust me."

Then there was no more talking as wendigo flooded the room, barely contained in their human form. Even as she watched, their flesh splotched to the floor with every step, literally rotting off their bodies. Their scalps sloughed off their skulls in clumps, as if something was crawling out of their bodies. Bones snapped while their misshapen bodies stretched and twisted, and the putrid stench of death clouded the cavern.

Instead of waiting, Caedmon charged forward, and his transition happened in a blink of an eye, his beast bursting out of his human shape fully formed. His change wasn't like the others. His body had more bulk, his creature not so deformed, the stench she normally associated with wendigo was missing. The only things she sensed from him were a touch of fire and brimstone. Intelligence gleamed in his eyes instead of the insatiable rage that consumed the others. Then he was gone, charging into battle, systematically tearing into the smaller wendigo.

The others almost seemed like a cheaper version of him.

He crashed into the first wave of wendigo, ripping and tearing into them like a berserker. As if it was a signal, Atlas and Ryder followed his lead and began to shred the nearest wendigo…only for the creatures to relentlessly get up and drag themselves back into the battle.

"Get them into the pit!" Draven charged one, picking it up by sheer brute force, the creature's clawed feet leaving gouges into the stone as the siren hauled the beast toward the edge. The wendigo slashed at his back, tearing into him, but Draven refused to relent.

He dropped and rolled, grabbed the creature's wrists, then flung the beast over his head…and sent it soaring straight into the abyss. The creature gave a bellow of rage, the sound fading as he dropped. It didn't take long for the other guys to follow suit, but the sheer volume of creatures was just too much.

Morgan followed behind Caedmon and Atlas. Every time they demolished one of the wendigo, she used her black blades to make sure they never got back up. Ascher, Ryder, Draven and Kincade worked in teams to send the ones that slipped pass into the abyss.

Loki growled viciously, protecting the guys while they fought. Thankfully, the wendigo's teeth and claws were unable to penetrate his hide. Séamus rode his back, yelling colorful directions, slashing a wicked looking blade at any who got too close. The guys wove in and out of the bright lights, using them like camouflage, able to take many of the wendigo by surprise.

The ground rumbled, and she knew the witches and hunters had breached the tunnels, driving even more of the creatures toward them. Magic saturated the air, and she smiled, taking great pleasure as she slashed the throat of a wendigo trying to rip Atlas's head off.

As more of the wendigo shoved forward, the men were forced to retreat.

There were just too many of them.

From the skylight, a few wispy shapes floated down, and she realized they were ghosts. As they touched the ground, they took human form…except she could see clear through them.

And she released a pent-up breath when she recognized more than a few of them.

The cavalry had arrived.

Their appearance freaked out a few of the wendigo and sent them running, and the ghosts grinned with glee, then systematically stalked the wendigo through the cavern, drifting through stone to grab them.

Once they latched onto the creatures, they would drag them toward the abyss. The beasts were unable to fight back, their blows sinking straight through the ghosts. A few clawed desperately at the ground, trying to escape, but it was no use.

Every once in a while one of the wendigo would make a ghost pause and shimmer, as if it was trying to figure out how to fight back, but more and more ghosts would just pile onto the creatures, using brute force to send the beasts into the abyss.

Ignoring the many nicks and slices littering her body, Morgan did her best to dodge the teeth that snapped at her. Judging from the way they kept surging toward her, she was their intended target.

A series of howls rose from the abyss, made more eerie as it echoed up to them, sounding like an army rising directly from hell. Draven leaned over the edge, then began cursing. "I'd say we have only a few minutes before the first wave makes their way back into the fight."

Ryder hesitated, taking a nasty blow to his shoulder, claws shredding his flesh. With a roar, he ripped out the throat of his opponent, then dragged him to the ledge and launched him into the air like a drunk being evicted from a bar.

Instead of going back to the fight, he stood guard at the ledge with Draven. Ghosts gathered on either side of them as a second line of defense, ten of them in all. Both men began kicking and slicing at any creatures that dared to try to pull themselves out of the pit, while the ghosts would fling themselves over the edge, tearing the wendigo off the cliff and dropping them back into the pit before returning to stand guard at the ledge once more.

While the guys were holding steady, they wouldn't last until sunrise.

They were taking more wounds than their bodies could heal.

They were going to fall.

Denial roared through her, and her magic surged forward, eager for the fight. And she nearly dropped to her knees as pain set her insides on fire, the infection having spread with the fall of darkness.

As she struggled to pull back the magic, the phoenix on her back fluttered to life, but instead of peeling away from her back, it began to pump pure fire into her veins. She braced herself, but the expected pain never came, the fire seeming to push back the infection enough for her to function, but it didn't eliminate it, and she knew the reprieve wouldn't last. Even now the flames were dying. The runes on her back felt heavy, getting hotter and hotter as her magic continued to build.

She looked up just in time to see a wendigo leap over Atlas and head directly toward her.

The magic retreated to a low hum, the burn bearable, and she lifted her blades, blocking a blow that threatened to cave in her skull. Using her kneeling position, she sliced the tendons at the back of his ankles, then slashed the inside of his thighs, aiming for the femoral artery.

Congealed black blood sprayed across the floor, and he gave a bellow of pain, his movements frenzied as he fought to stay on his feet. He slashed at her throat and she twisted, taking the numbing blow to her shoulder, his claws nicking her arm, and her blood poured freely from the wound.

Surging to her feet, she twisted and kicked him in his chest, sending the creature flying back. Though injured, it didn't stop him from crawling toward her, his pitiless black eyes promising only one thing...death.

Without hesitation, she slammed her blade into his skull, watching him collapse. She didn't have time to do much more than straighten before another wendigo surged forward to take his place.

Leanne shoved her way into the room and through the wendigo, her eyes holding a level of intelligence and cunning that was absent in most of her minions. Then her gaze locked on Morgan. "You've ruined everything!"

Every single wendigo in the room flinched and hunkered down at the vicious tone in her voice, terrified to draw her attention. Now that they weren't actively trying to rip off Morgan's face, she got a closer look at the wendigo.

While Leanne's main hunters appeared to be in relatively good shape, the rest of the beasts were more ragged and emaciated, obviously starving. A number of them had more than one bite on their bodies, flesh literally missing from their limbs where they had resorted to cannibalizing themselves.

Female or male, the creatures' genitals were hidden by matted fur, thank the gods. She wasn't sure if she could handle seeing that many cocks swinging in the wind or vaginas flapping.

Leanne was larger than the others, clearly the alpha, and Morgan realized her abilities had nothing to do with the witch herself, but the one who'd bitten her.

"Caedmon passed on his characteristics to you—his ability to think and function as a wendigo." Morgan moved toward the center of the cavern to face Leanne directly. "But the ones you bit weren't so lucky—they became warped and tainted, their minds twisted—taking after you instead of Caedmon."

Evil.

"Lies!" Leanne leaned forward as she yelled, spittle flying. "They're the perfect army ready to do my bidding. Until you interfered." She stalked forward, the wendigo around her scrambling to get out of her way like whipped pups.

Leanne didn't seem any more concerned by personal grooming than the others, not even bothering to wear clothing. Her breasts were more muscular than feminine—any other human characteristics were gone.

"You couldn't cope with being changed, having your magic ripped out of you. It broke something in your mind...which you passed on to the others. Maybe that's why there were so few female wendigo. Let me guess...none of them were witches? Maybe having magic interferes with the conversion. Is that why your army is more beastly? Why they're so unstable?"

"No! The flaw is they were humans! They couldn't handle the transition. You and everyone else will see. When you take down the wards, the world will become a safer place, a better place— because of me. I'll be a hero and people will worship me." She smiled, but her mouth was full of wickedly sharp, twisted teeth...the monster lurking within her now visible for everyone else to see.

And she was completely delusional.

Leanne nodded toward something over Morgan's shoulder, and she whirled to see five wendigo leap out of the pit and surround Ryder and Draven. They didn't attack, but stood still, awaiting orders.

Cocky and sure of herself once more, Leanne strode ever closer to Morgan. "You will drop your blades and step forward or your mates will die."

She could fight.

But they would fail.

They were outnumbered and dawn was too far away.

If they failed, the rescue team would be slaughtered. She couldn't allow that to happen.

Holding out her arms, she dropped the blades and kicked them away…in the direction of Atlas and Kincade.

The guys tensed, both of them ready to move, when she walked toward Leanne. She caught Ascher watching and gave him a subtle nod.

They would soon learn if her idea had merit or if she'd just killed them all.

Pleasure oozed from Leanne, and she strolled among her creatures, trailing her hands over the tops of their heads as if bestowing a favor on them. "You'll see. This is for the best. Once you change, you'll understand."

She came to a stop in front of Morgan, excitement gleaming in her dark eyes, tiny splinters of yellow barely visible in the black orbs. "Now take down the wards."

Chapter
Twenty-four

"*Y*ou started this because you craved power. Only the plan failed and you were bitten." Morgan refused to cower, and lifted her chin as she faced down Leanne. "Instead of defeat, you became more determined than ever to show everyone you're someone important. A force to be dealt with. To be feared. But there is a better way."

A garbled, wheezing chuckle escaped Leanne. "And what way is that? Listening to those old fools at the Academy? Their way doesn't work anymore. The gods are awakening. We need to show them we're stronger this time, or we'll become nothing more than slaves to them once again. What better way can there be?"

The rest of the wendigo they managed to throw into the abyss clawed their way back until the entire army had them surrounded.

"Even as a wendigo, you still crave magic. You literally feed from it." Morgan lifted her hands, showing she wasn't armed. "You've coveted magic your whole life, but you don't see that magic is as much of a curse as it is a blessing—you're only given as much as you can handle."

"You're so innocent." Leanne gave an ugly laugh. "That's what they taught us, what they want us to believe, but it's a lie. Once you're free, I'll show you. We'll be able to control who gets to keep their magic or not."

By killing anyone who opposed her, no doubt.

Leanne leaned closer, the breath of death perfuming the air, her eyes narrowing in warning. "Now bring down the wards. I won't ask again."

"You want magic?" Without giving her a chance to retreat, Morgan closed the distance between them and shoved her hands hard against Leanne's chest. "Have mine."

The moment her hand came into contact with flesh, magic boiled out of her. It snapped and crackled in the air, and the tiny universes embedded into her fingernails began to swirl, the tiny stars flaring bright.

Leanne dropped to her knees, her back arching as the power surged into her, her mouth open in a silent scream, revealing all those wickedly sharp teeth inches from Morgan's face.

The crescent moon symbol carved into Morgan's flesh right below her collarbone, given to her by the goddess Nyx, began to warm like it had been activated. Inside her chest, specks of the solar system spun into life, the space so vast there was no end or beginning.

The magic of the void drifted through her like the cosmic wind, shredding and tearing apart planets and reforming them into something new. That wind howled through her until her skin felt too small for her body. It hit the infection and consumed it without hesitation, like it was a snack.

The bite mark on her arm burned like she'd stuck it into a vat of acid, then black tar began to boil out of her. It felt like tiny claws were tearing into her flesh, shredding muscles and turning her bones into powder, as if anxious to wring every last drop out of her.

As a second wave of magic surged out of her, a scream of pain caught in her throat, and she struggled to fill her lungs with air. Barely conscious of the world around her, Morgan floated in a void of nothingness, no longer able to feel her body.

The magic emptied into Leanne like the blast from a jet engine.

A tiny beam of pure light burst from Leanne's chest, then another, the magic shredding the beast until a shadow of the wendigo was torn away from Leanne and lifted into the air to circle overhead like a cyclone.

Leanne collapsed, gasping for air like she'd forgotten how to breathe, her human form huddled on the ground.

Leaving behind a golden globe of pure magic. It swirled in the air, gathering speed, when rays of light shot into the darkness. As the magic hit the wendigo, more and more shadows were torn away, leaving a massive storm of shadows brewing above them.

Bodies dropped to the ground and didn't move.

As if the cloud of shadows was heavy, it began to lower and circle around them like hungry monsters, desperately seeking a new host.

Wanting freedom.

Morgan lifted her arms, using what little magic she had left to hold the churning mass aloft. But it was a losing battle, her arms shaking as she struggled to keep the shadows from consuming everyone.

The crush of it dropped her to her knees, and she knew she was going to lose control.

"Ascher…" Her voice was raspy, barely above a whisper, and she felt like the life was being drained out of her.

Thankfully, Ascher heard her plea.

Flames erupted from his hands, and he shoved them into the air. The dark cloud erupted in flames until fire swirled above them, ash and sparks raining down on them, the intense heat crackling in the air.

But Ascher didn't stop, continuing to pump more and more hellfire into the storm. Singe marks appeared across his shirt, the holes spreading until it slithered off him in tatters, the fabric catching fire as it drifted to the ground.

Flames licked at her fingers, her skin blackened and cracked. The smell of charred flesh left her dizzy, her arms shook under the strain of holding up the churning mass. She lost control and dropped to the ground. The cloud of fire fizzled, the shadows no longer saturated with black tar.

The ghostly specters circled the room, slinking lower and lower, until they seemed to sense her. Wind howled so loudly she couldn't hear anything but the pounding of her heart. Like a funnel cloud, the shadows shot right toward her, but right before they would've hit her chest, Caedmon tackled her, smashing her to the ground, using his body to cover her completely.

The shadows slammed into him relentlessly, and his yellow eyes glowed with power once more. His jaw was clenched tight, his grip on her brutal. The shadows licked along her skin like a warm caress before being pulled inside him, and he threw back his head, his scream of pain turning into a roar.

That's when she noticed a number of the other shadows seemed to be targeting the people who were bitten by wendigo.

As the wind gradually faded, the silence left behind was deafening. She felt hollow, her magic spent, but not gone.

More like sleeping.

Even the thought of touching magic made her flinch.

She blinked to find Caedmon looking down at her. "What did you do?"

"You saved us." There was awe in his eyes when he gazed at her.

"Come again?" But before he could answer, the guys rushed to her side. Atlas shoved Caedmon away, while Ryder pulled her free and cradled her to his chest. Ascher knelt at her side, patting her down, searching for injuries. Draven and Kincade stood over them, weapons drawn, standing guard.

That didn't stop them from glancing at her every few seconds.

With a gentle kiss on her forehead, Ryder passed her to Ascher, who very gently pulled her to her feet.

"Can you stand?" His voice was raspy, and he trembled as he pulled her into his arms.

Morgan allowed herself a second to rest her head against his chest, fighting a wave of dizziness, all her energy devoted to just staying awake and standing. Then she patted his chest and straightened. "You did it. Thank you."

"Always." He pressed his forehead to hers.

Then Draven slipped his hands around her waist from behind, as if he knew she needed his support. He nipped none too gently where her neck met her shoulder, then chided, "Next time, you let us in on the plan."

Kincade growled, his green eyes cold. "There will be no next time." He gave her a pointed look.

Atlas caught her hand and lifted her arm up for inspection. The injury where the hellhound had bitten her was gone. In its place was a tiny moon that shimmered and glowed blood red when moonlight hit it. He brushed his thumb over it lightly, then glanced at Caedmon, animosity building in his murderous green eyes. "What the fuck happened?"

"Wendigo are creatures of hell." He gave her a soft look, his tone turning gentle. "There is a riddle—"

"Touched by the gods and forged in fire
Purified by the flames of hellfire's light
Only one can carry the burden of night."

Then he glanced at her mates. "It was her. She saved us, but I couldn't let her carry the burden of night. She's done enough."

"What the fuck do you mean?" Draven tightened his hold, ready to take down anyone who tried to take her from him.

Morgan saw the others slowly begin to pick themselves up off the floor. Some touched their arms in awe—they were human once more—while others didn't look happy about it. She noticed less than half of them carried the moon symbol, and she wondered if the others had been proven unworthy of carrying the symbol.

Caedmon stepped into her line of sight, then turned until she could see his back. A giant moon covered him from shoulder to shoulder, the soft glow comforting, the image so detailed, the craggy rocks and shadows were visible. When she reached out to touch it, Atlas grabbed her hand and twined his fingers with hers.

"What does it mean?" She touched the moon on her arm, her finger tracing the outer circle. And why was hers red and everyone else's yellow?

But it was Ryder who answered. "It's a symbol for the *loup garou*. Instead of a taking after wolves when they shift, they'll be a human with wolf characteristics. A werewolf on two legs."

Her mouth dropped open. "Does that—will I—so I…" Her brain just stopped functioning.

"You should be fine." Caedmon came to her rescue.

She blinked up at him, now understanding what he sacrificed for her. "Because you took the curse of the night."

He gave a nod, not seeming bothered by the sacrifice he made…for her.

Ryder tugged her close and crushed her to his chest. He sniffed at her, and his shoulders drooped in relief, his tension draining away. "You were touched, but you're not changed."

Kincade tugged on her arm, studying the symbol of the moon, turning it toward the others. Ryder reluctantly released her into Kincade's care. "What does this mean?"

"She's pack…an honorary member." Caedmon stared at the moon symbol, and the glow brightened, the red almost swirling under his regard, like a cloud traveling across the surface. "An alpha in human form. She's our queen."

Then he knelt at her feet, totally freaking her out. She backed away, nearly tripping over the guys in her haste to escape, only to have them block her exit. "Come again?!"

Caedmon lifted his head at her pterodactyl screech, and she reached down to yank him to his feet, hissing under her breath, "Don't *do* that."

Amusement darkened his eyes at her total freak-out. "For every pack, there is an alpha couple to rule."

"You and me? Hell, I can't even shift," she sputtered, shaking her head in denial, every part of her being wanting to run. "And you're fine with that?"

Because she sure as fuck wasn't fine with it.

"We're not mates, more like alpha queen and her enforcer. For now." He gave her a tiny smile. "It doesn't matter that you can't shift. You were chosen." He gestured toward the moon on her arm, then he nodded toward the twenty or so people huddled together in the cavern. "They're yours to command."

She snorted at the absurdity. "And if I refuse?"

His lips tightened, his eyes hardening. "They'll turn rogue, and you and your men will eventually have to hunt them down."

"But you're an alpha. Can't you—"

"*You* bear the mark. Only *you* are strong enough to hold them together." Then his expression softened, almost like he was stunned that she didn't want the power. "It's the same thing you provide for your mates. Your nearness will ground them, keep their beasts at bay. I'd be honored to take over the day-to-day training. You just need to be an advisor, much like you are at the Academy. Show them how to live in this new world and give them a purpose."

Morgan nodded slowly as plans began to take shape. "They could hunt down people like Leanne and ensure things like this never happen again." Leanne got her army, just not the way she ever expected. "So maybe what happened to them—what happened to you—can be prevented. But only those who volunteer. I won't force anyone to fight."

Caedmon stilled in a way only shifters could—every muscle controlled. Then he bowed to her deeply. "It will be as you wish."

Then, without another word, he spun on his heel and walked away.

She blinked at his abrupt departure and looked helplessly up at her men. "What just happened?"

Kincade gave an amused sigh. "You've made another

conquest."

"And a huge pack who will do anything to protect you," Ryder murmured, a little rumble of pleasure in his chest, the wolf thrilled at the prospect of a whole army to keep her safe.

None of the men appeared concerned about the abrupt change in their lives.

She wanted to protest, but mashed her lips together, unable to reject and condemn the men and women who'd survived so much.

She stood surrounded by her men, her mates, overwhelmed by everything that had happened, beyond ready to call it a night.

Loki was stalking among the other men in the room, his eyes narrowed suspiciously, sneezing occasionally as his tail lashed back and forth, searching for more creatures to hunt. Séamus still rode his back like he'd been doing it all his life, inspecting the humans.

The very naked humans with nothing to disguise their nudity.

Now the fighting was over, it was hard not to notice all the dangling cocks and swaying breasts on display…it was disconcerting to say the least. Draven seemed to notice where her attention was drawn—because of course he would—and chuckled, while Ryder growled at any guy who came near, doing his best to stand in front of her and block her view.

She couldn't help being amused by the both of them.

"Go home," Caedmon ordered her. "You did the impossible and survived. You deserve a night of rest. I'll get everyone here sorted out."

Even before he finished speaking, more than three dozen hunters entered the room, including a dozen or so prisoners she hadn't been able to free—including the old man from the store, armed with a rock and ready to rumble, and a handful of witches—and leading them all was Stanley.

"Where are they? Let me at 'em." The mangy orange cat strutted into the room, his striped fur ruffled and slightly on edge. Some of his whiskers were broken, missing fur revealing old battle scars, but he'd gained weight in the past month, his coat almost shiny.

His yellow, feral eyes locked on her, and his not-so-dainty claws snicked out of his paws. He pointed at her, the wings resting against his back flickering in agitation. "I can't leave you alone for even a second, can I?"

Harper stood behind him, the bossy witch doing her best to smother her smile, obviously happy to have his carping directed at someone other than her. She gave her a nod of acknowledgment, then began directing her people to help the others.

When Stanley saw Morgan standing and whole, the fur on his back smoothed out, and he wound his way through the people, stopping short when he saw Loki gazing at him contemplatively. It was subtle, but the two began to stalk each other through the room. "Don't even think about it, you mangy dog."

Morgan couldn't help but laugh, leaning weakly against Ascher, letting the warmth of him soak into her. She tipped her head up to look at him. "I'm ready to go home."

"You ruined everything!" Leanne charged out of a group of people, two of her original hunters trailing a step behind. None of them were marked. "You took everything from me. Everything. Now you're going to learn what it feels like."

The guys surged forward to protect her, but the men with Leanne blocked them. The whole room surged into motion, magic bloomed in the air, but it was much too late. Leanne hit her squarely in the chest and they both stumbled back.

Then she was falling.

As the darkness of the abyss swallowed her, the light from above faded. She reached for the cliff, scrambling for purchase, but the walls were too far way. She slammed her elbow back, breaking Leanne's hold, but the bitch only smiled.

Then Loki charged over the edge...and a second later, so did Kincade.

"No!" Her heart cracked. At this height, she wasn't sure if she would be able to survive the landing, much less heal—but Kincade wouldn't. Even if he turned to stone, she very much feared the force of it would shatter him into a thousand pieces.

Then wings unfurled from his back.

Even as her mind tried to process what she saw, he dove toward her, arrowing through the air. When he reached for her, she thrust out her arm, feeling his hand clamp around her wrist.

He crushed her to his chest just as his wings snapped open. He grunted at the drag on the wings, their descent slowing…but not fast enough. Loki swooped in close, and Kincade deposited her on the pup's back.

"No! Not fair!" Leanne clawed the air, her shriek of frustration and rage echoing around them. Then she hit with a force that splattered her over the bones of all the people she'd killed, her body impaled in multiple places, the light slowly blinking out of her eyes.

"You did it!" Morgan leaned over Loki's back and patted his shoulder, so proud she could burst. "You can fly!"

Loki pumped his wings hard, just skimming the ground before they began their slow climb. Kincade followed a pace behind, his wings unsteady as he swerved dramatically side from side until she thought he would end up splatting against the wall.

Faces peered down at her from above, men and women arguing, some holding back Ascher and Draven, who were trying to climb down the walls. Seconds later, she and Loki burst over the ledge and shot up into the air, soaring above everyone.

Loki landed with a slight stumble, but quickly regained his footing. She slid off his back, then hugged him close, kissing the top of his head. "You're the best gardog ever!"

The tiny phoenix in the center of his chest blazed brightly at her praise, and he tucked his wings against his back, the edges a deep, burnt red that looked like they were dipped in fire.

Loki barked, and she turned to see Kincade struggling to stay airborne.

His landing wasn't so lucky. He hit hard and fast, face-planting into the ground, where he skidded a few feet before coming to a halt near her feet.

His wings hung awkwardly on his back, his breathing heavy as he pushed himself back on his haunches before he tipped his head back to stare up at her. She dropped to her knees next to him, totally in awe at his miraculous rescue.

She hesitantly ran a finger along the tip of his wing, the leathery hide buttery to the touch. He shivered at the small touch, lust darkening his eyes as if she'd shoved her hands into his pants and stroked him, and she hastily jerked her hand away, a blush warming her cheeks...but she couldn't stop her mind from wandering to the possibilities. "I thought you weren't supposed to get your wings for decades yet."

He grabbed her arm and pulled her onto his lap, crushing her to his chest. Not the least bit put off by his stone form, she clung to him, feeling him shake. "Neither did I."

Heart thumping against her ribs, Morgan reared back and glared at him. "What?!"

Before she had a chance to vent her wrath, they were surrounded, every one of the guys curling around her, needing to be close. She understood the sentiment exactly, clinging to them right back.

It was Atlas who swept her up into his arms. Without a word or glance at anyone else, he headed out of the tunnels, and she looked back to see the rest of the guys following. Her gaze fell onto Kincade, and she watched in complete amazement as he struggled to keep his wings from dragging on the floor.

Then her eyes widened, her mouth dropping open, and she tried to crawl over Atlas's shoulder to get a better look at Kincade. "Wait a freakin' minute—you have a tail!"

Epilogue

Two days later…

The clang of pots and pans jolted Morgan out of a deep sleep. Maniacal laughter and the patter of footsteps had her shooting to her feet, instantly awake. She burst into the hallway, pulling her blades, the guys only a step behind her. They fell into formation and charged down the stairs, heading straight for the kitchen.

When she pushed open the swinging door, she stopped short, only to have the guys plow into her back. Ryder gently nudged her to the side, making room for the others.

And everyone stopped at the threshold next to her.

No one spoke.

The place was a mess. The kitchen looked like it had been ransacked, flour and sugar covering every surface. Pans were scattered everywhere, but that wasn't what caught their attention.

No, that was reserved for the spectacle that was Loki and Stanley. Loki was hogtied, his feet tangled up in a cord with a dozen pans strung together along its length. And every time the gardog twitched, they clattered and clanged.

Worse, Stanley lay beside him, hissing in fury, his wet fur coated with soggy flour like he'd bathed in paste. He licked at his fur, then began hacking like he was going to yak up a hairball.

"He's a menace," Stanley seethed as he struggled to get to his feet, each step suctioned to the floor as he walked. He shook out his fur, sending paste splattering everywhere. "He needs to be dealt with."

Morgan mashed her lips together to smother her smile, while Kincade rubbed his eyebrows and heaved a sigh of exasperation. When she could repress her laughter enough to speak, she shook her finger at them. "I told you not to hunt the leprechaun. You're lucky Séamus didn't do worse."

Neither of them looked the least bit repentant.

Loki likely gave chase for the fun of it, while Stanley looked more determined than ever to catch the leprechaun invading his territory, no doubt seeing Séamus as a giant rodent. It was amusing the first dozen times...hell, who was she kidding? It was funny as hell to see the different ways Séamus outwitted them.

When she turned to head back to bed, she stopped short at the sight of her men. Every one of them were armed, standing around in various stages of undress, their hair rumpled—and sexy as fuck. They took her breath away. Though the worst of their injuries were already healed, they'd cut it awfully close this time, and it worried her.

Atlas looked annoyed, Draven amused, Ascher grumpy, while Ryder was resigned. The wolf swept her up in his arms and began to head back toward her room, the rest of the guys quick to follow.

She looped her arms around Ryder's neck, resting her head against his chest, enjoying the attention. "You're not going to be able to keep me here forever, you know."

"We can try." Draven gave her a naughty wink that heated her face.

As they exited the kitchen, it was to find Caedmon waiting for them, hands behind his back, legs spread in a military stance, immaculately dressed despite the early hour, his straight dark hair brushing his shoulders, every inch of him an imposing elf. She wasn't sure how he did it. He bowed to her, ignoring the others.

"I will see to it that everything is cleaned up before you come down again."

"You don't have to do that." But it was like he didn't hear her, his pace unhurried as he disappeared into the kitchen. Not only was he an elf, rigid in his ways, he was an alpha werewolf on top of it. His time in hell had changed him, broken him down and re-forged him stronger.

And he was content to be her servant.

For now, whispered in her ear, and she didn't flinch away from the possibility as she would have if he was anyone else.

There was something about the broken warrior that survived so much with his honor in-tact that drew her.

And he completely baffled her.

He could have anything he wanted—be anything—and yet he stayed with her.

"You won't be able to change his mind." Atlas gazed at her in amusement. "Tuatha De Danann take their oaths very seriously. You saved his life. He'll be your faithful servant and protector until death claims him. My advice is to enjoy it, and take advantage of everything he's willing to teach you."

She sighed in defeat, having gone round and round with the same conversation with the stubborn fool for the past two days to no avail.

It was like talking to a fucking wall.

Ryder didn't wait for a response, taking the stairs two at a time, not even a little stressed under her additional weight. They all entered her room, where the guys had pushed two king-sized beds together, none of them willing to let her out of their sight.

Most of the witches and hunters had portaled back to the Academy after the rescue, although a couple of hunters stayed to patrol the grounds and clean up the tunnels, while a few witches helped settle the human survivors, wiping their memories to give them peace.

As Ryder gently set her on her feet, she sighed at the hidden oasis they'd created. Despite the horrors of fighting the wendigo, this coven would always have a place in her heart. "I'm going to miss this place when we have to go back."

The guys did that thing where they looked at each other in silent communication. Instead of being annoyed, she was getting used to it, beginning to realize they weren't excluding her—they were gearing up to go to battle or surprise her...usually they were one and the same.

"What if you didn't have to leave?" Ascher murmured, and each of the guys came to stand next to him until they circled her.

"What do you mean?" She had too many responsibilities to just disappear, no matter how often she dreamed of running off with them.

"If we learned anything in the past few months, it's that we work better as a team." Kincade was in leader mode. "The coven is a bit of a fixer-upper, it'll take a lot of work...if you think you're up to it."

Her heart hiccupped in her chest at what he was suggesting, but she could only blink at them, sure she misunderstood.

They would give up the Academy for her.

Give up everything they'd worked their whole lives to achieve.

She could never ask that of them. "I don't understand."

"We can stay here, have our privacy, and portal to the Academy when they need us." Atlas gazed at her with his green and umber eyes, a hint of vulnerability in them she wasn't used to seeing.

"The forest will need a lot of care." Ryder crossed his arms and widened his stance. "Not to mention the *loup garou* see you and Caedmon as their alphas. They'll need your help to keep them from going rogue, and I'd be able to help keep them in check. Train them."

"Not to mention that you'd be able to take advantage of us whenever you want." Draven wiggled his eyebrows suggestively, his smile brash, but she could see the yearning in his eyes.

"You all want this—a place just for us?" Pure joy stirred in her chest. She wanted this so much she was almost afraid to believe it. She tangled her fingers together to keep from reaching for them, hope burning so painfully she could hardly remain still. "You're sure?"

They didn't even bother glancing at each other, everyone responding with a resounding, "Yes."

When she first met them, she wouldn't have dared imagine that they'd make all her dreams come true or that they would've captured her heart so completely. Despite all her faults, they loved her without reservation.

And she was no less devoted to them.

As if to emphasize her emotions, the necklace warmed, melting down and twisting into a little heart with a pair of tiny skeleton keys attached, one word stamped on each—one key to the house and one key to her heart.

"Each of you has stolen a piece of my heart. My home is wherever you are, whether it be here or the Academy." She walked toward them, her heart full as they engulfed her in a mighty hug. A low hum of magic tingled along her veins, as if in approval, before settling into her bones.

She was finally home.

She smiled up at them, feeling hope for the future for the first time. "Whatever comes, we'll face it together."

THE END

~ Academy of Assassins ~

ONLY ONE THING STANDS BETWEEN HUMANS AND
THE DEADLY SUPERNATURAL WORLD…THE ACADEMY
OF ASSASSINS.

Abandoned as a child and unable to remember her past, Morgan was
raised as a hunter, one of an elite group of fighters sworn to protect
humans from the dangerous paranormal creatures who invade our
world…creatures such as herself. Her life changes the day she's
summoned to the Academy of Assassins, a school that trains witches
and hunters to eradicate paranormals who prey on humans. Her first
assignment—find and eliminate the killer who is using the Academy
as their own personal hunting ground.

As Morgan delves deeper into the investigation, she will need to
dodge assassination attempts, avoid the distraction of romantic
entanglements with the devilishly handsome security expert, Kincade,
and his maddeningly overprotective teammates, while keeping the
volatile magic in her blood concealed from those who would use it
for their own purposes. When the danger increases and the school is
threatened, Morgan must unearth her missing memories before
someone finishes the job they started so long ago—killing her and
unleashing a plague that will consume the world.

An Academy of Assassins Novel : Book 1

Meet the Assassins: Morgan, Kincade, Ascher, Ryder, Draven and
Atlas.

~ Coveted ~

Discover what happens when a woman stumbles across a Scottish werewolf imprisoned in a thousand-year old dungeon. Magic and mayhem, not to mention a lot of kick-ass action and some sexy hijinks, of course.

Pack alpha Aiden vows to do whatever necessary to protect his people. When he discovers a plot to harvest blood from his wolves to create the ultimate drug, he's determined to stop them at any cost. And quickly finds himself taken captive. After months in prison, Aiden barely manages to hang onto his sanity. The last thing he expects is a shapely little human to come to his rescue and bring out all his protective instincts.

Shayla is being stalked because of her abilities as a seeker. When offered a job in Scotland, she leaps at the chance to escape. With danger pursuing her at every turn, she must decide if she could give up her magic in order to live a safe, ordinary life. Never in her wildest fantasies did she expect to find a feral-looking man imprisoned in a thousand-year-old dungeon…or be so wildly attracted to him. She didn't need more trouble, but when fate presents the means to help him escape, she doesn't hesitate.

Now they are both being hunted, and Aiden is determined to do everything in his power to protect Shayla…and seduce her into becoming his mate. As the danger intensifies, Aiden begins to suspect that Shayla might be the key to saving not only his people but also the future of his race…if he could keep her alive long enough.

~ BloodSworn ~

Ten years after they bound her powers and banished her, Trina Weyebridge had successfully carved out a new existence in the human world. She put her life as a witch behind her. But, her magic would not be denied, the bindings holding them in check are weakening. Vampires who crave a taste of the powers stored in her blood are hunting her with deadly force and have kidnapped her sister to lure her out. In a desperate bid to free her sister and gain her own freedom, Trina bargains with the all-too-tempting lion shifter who calls out the long forgotten wild side in her...she would be his concubine in return for pack protection. She'd be safe...until they found out the truth.

UNDENIABLE DESIRE. FORBIDDEN LOVE. INESCAPABLE DESTINY.

When Merrick spots a female intruder living on his property, he's intrigued by her daring. Curious to find out more, he follows her and comes to her aid when she falls prey to an attack. After weeks of unnatural silence, his beast awakens at her touch, and he suspects that she might be the only one able to save his race from a disease killing his kind. Not willing to take the chance of losing her, he binds her to him the only way he knows how...by claiming her as his own. All he has to do to save her is uncover the secrets of her past, stop a pack revolt, convince her that she's desperately in love with him in return, and prevent a war.

~ The Demon Within ~

As a punishment for failing his duty as an angel, Ruman finds himself encased in stone in the form of a guardian statue. Every few decades he is given a chance to repent. And fails. Until the totally unsuitable Caly Sawyer accidentally brings him back to life. Nothing is going to prevent him from gaining his freedom, especially some willfully stubborn human determined to kill him.

Caly doesn't trust the mysterious stranger who came out of nowhere and risked his life for hers. As a demon hunter, she knows there is something not quite human about the sexy bastard. Her ability to detect demons is infallible. She should know. She used to be one.

War is brewing between demons and humans. The demon infection that Caly had always considered a curse might just be the key to their survival…if Ruman can keep her alive long enough. Despite the volatile attraction between her and her sexy protector, Caly's determined to do whatever it takes to keep everyone alive. The more Ruman learns about his beautiful charge, the more he questions his duty and loyalty…and dreads the call to return home. If they can't learn to trust each other in time, one of them will die.

~ Electric Storm ~

A WOMAN WITH TOO MANY SECRETS DARES TO RISK
EVERYTHING TO CLAIM THE PACK DESTINED TO BER
HERS.

Everything changed when Raven, a natural born conduit, accidentally
walks in on a slave auction. She only wants a night out with her
friends before her next case as a paranormal liaison with the police.
Instead, she ends up in possession of a shifter and his guardian.
When your touch can kill, living with two touchy-feely shifters is a
disaster waiting to happen.

POWER ALWAYS COMES WITH A PRICE...

To make matters worse, a vicious killer is on the loose. As mutilated
bodies turn up, she can't help fear that her new acquisitions are
keeping secrets from her. The strain of keeping everyone alive, not to
mention catching the killer, pushes her tenuous control of her gift
and her emotions to their limits. If they hope to survive, they must
work together as a pack or risk becoming hunted themselves.

A Raven Investigations Novel : Book 1

~ Druid Surrender ~

A DARK, ENCHANTING TALE OF LOVE AND MAGIC IN
VICTORIAN ENGLAND.

Brighid Legend has been on the run for over a year, hunted by the
people who murdered her mother. Born a Druid with the power to
control the elements, Brighid knows her pursuers will never stop
until she is under their control. To escape detection, she struggles to
hide her powers and finds safety in a small, out-of-the-way village.
But after a series of mysterious accidents, she fears something sinister
has invaded her new home. While she searches for the source of the
trouble, suspicion falls on her, and Brighid flees, only steps ahead of
the villagers seeking vengeance.

Wyatt Graystone, Earl of Castelline, retires when the life-and-death
clandestine investigations he did for the Crown becomes more
tedious than adventurous. Something vital is missing from his life.
The last place he expects to find the missing spark is in a woman he
literally leaps through fire to rescue from being burned at the stake.
But the danger is far from over. To his frustration, the infernal
woman adamantly refuses his assistance, pushing him away at every
turn, when his only desire is to claim her for his own.

But someone has targeted Brighid for a reason. As the threats to her
life intensify, Wyatt is determined to uncover her secrets and do
whatever it takes to ensure she survives. When their pasts come back
to haunt them, they must overcome their worst fears or risk losing
everything. Saving her life is the biggest battle he's ever faced...and
the only one that has ever mattered.

WILL THEIR LOVE BE STRONGE ENOUGH TO SAVE
THEM . . .

A Druid Quest Novel: Book 1

ABOUT THE AUTHOR

Stacey Brutger lives in a small town in Minnesota with her husband and an assortment of animals. When she's not reading, she enjoys creating stories about exotic worlds and grand adventures...then shoving in her characters to see how they'd survive. She enjoys writing anything paranormal from contemporary to historical.

Other books by this author:

A Druid Quest Novel
Druid Surrender (Book 1)
Druid Temptation (Book 2)

An Academy of Assassins Novel
Academy of Assassins (Book 1)
Heart of the Assassins (Book 2)
Claimed by the Assassins (Book 3)
Queen of the Assassins (Book 4)

A Phantom Touched Novel
Tethered to the World (Book 1)

A Raven Investigations Novel
Electric Storm (Book 1)
Electric Moon (Book 2)
Electric Heat (Book 3)
Electric Legend (Book 4)
Electric Night (Book 5)
Electric Curse (Book 6)

A PeaceKeeper Novel
The Demon Within (Book 1)

Paranormal Romance:
BloodSworn
Coveted

Coming Soon:
Shackled to the World (Book2)

Visit Stacey online to find out more at **www.StaceyBrutger.com**
And www.facebook.com/StaceyBrutgerAuthor